HEU-HEU, or THE MONSTER

HEU-HEU, OR THE MONSTER

H. RIDER HAGGARD

Denton & White
2020

Heu-Heu, or The Monster was originally published in 1924.

This version prepared in 2020 by Denton & White.

AUTHOR'S NOTE

The author wishes to state that this tale was written in its present form some time before the discovery in Rhodesia of the fossilized and immeasurably ancient remains of the proto-human person who might well have been one of the Heuheua, the "Hairy Wood-Folk," of which it tells through the mouth of Allan Quatermain.
1923.

CHAPTER I

THE STORM

Now I, the Editor, whose duty it has been as an executor or otherwise, to give to the world so many histories of, or connected with, the adventures of my dear friend, the late Allan Quatermain, or Macumazahn, Watcher-by-Night, as the natives in Africa used to call him, come to one of the most curious of them all. Here I should say at once that he told it to me many years ago at his house called "The Grange," in Yorkshire, where I was staying, but a little while before he departed with Sir Henry Curtis and Captain Good upon his last expedition into the heart of Africa, whence he returned no more.

At the time I made very copious notes of a history that struck me as strange and suggestive, but the fact is that afterwards I lost them and could never trust my memory to reproduce even their substance with the accuracy which I knew my departed friend would have desired.

Only the other day, however, in turning out a box-room, I came upon a hand-bag which I recognized as one that I had used in the far past when I was practising, or trying to practise, at the Bar. With a certain emotion such as overtakes us when, after the lapse of many years, we are confronted by articles connected with the long-dead events of our youth, I took it to a window and with some difficulty opened its rusted catch. In the bag was a small collection of rubbish: papers connected with cases on which once I had worked as "devil" for an eminent and learned friend who afterwards became a judge, a blue pencil with a broken point, and so forth.

I looked through the papers and studied my own marginal notes made on points in causes which I had utterly forgotten, though doubtless these had been important enough to me at the time, and, with a sigh, tore them up and threw them on the floor. Then I reversed the bag to knock out the dust. As I was doing this there slipped from an inner pocket, a very thick notebook with a shiny black cover such as used to be bought for sixpence. I opened that book and the first thing that my eye fell upon was this heading:

"Summary of A. Q.'s Strange Story of the Monster-God, or Fetish, Heu-Heu, which He and the Hottentot Hans Discovered in Central South Africa."

Instantly everything came back to me. I saw myself, a young man in those days, making those shorthand notes late one night in my bedroom at the Grange before the impression of old Allan's story had become dim in my mind, also continuing them on the train upon my journey south on the morrow, and subsequently expanding them in my chambers at Elm Court in the Temple whenever I found time to spare.

I remembered, too, my annoyance when I discovered that this notebook was nowhere to be found, although I was aware that I had put it away in some place that I thought particularly safe. I can still see myself hunting for it in the little study of the house I had in a London suburb at the time, and at last giving up the quest in despair. Then the years went on and many things happened, so that in the end both notes and the story they outlined were forgotten. Now they have appeared again from the dust-heap of the past, reviving many memories, and I set out the tale of this particular chapter of the history of the adventurous life of my beloved friend, Allan Quatermain, who so long ago was gathered to the Shades that await us all.

One night, after a day's shooting, we—that is, old Allan, Sir Henry Curtis, Captain Good, and I—were seated in the smoking room of Quatermain's house, the Grange, in Yorkshire, smoking and talking of many things.

I happened to mention that I had read a paragraph, copied from an American paper, which stated that a huge reptile of an antediluvian kind had been seen by some hunters in a swamp of the Zambesi, and asked Allan if he believed the story. He shook his head and answered in a cautious fashion which suggested to me, I remember, his unwillingness to give his views as to the continued existence of such creatures on the earth, that Africa is a big place and it was possible that in its recesses prehistoric animals or reptiles lingered on.

"I know that this is the case with snakes," he continued hurriedly as though to avoid the larger topic, "for once I came across one as large as the biggest Anaconda that is told of in South America, where occasionally they are said to reach a length of sixty feet or more. Indeed, we killed it—or rather my Hottentot servant, Hans, did—after it had crushed and swallowed one of our party. This snake was worshipped as a king of gods, and might have given rise to the tale of enormous reptiles. Also, to omit other experiences of which I prefer not to speak, I have seen an elephant so much above the ordinary in size that it might have belonged to a prehistoric age. This elephant has been known for centuries and was named Jana.

"Did you kill it?" inquired Good, peering at him through his eyeglasses in his quick, inquisitive way.

Allan coloured beneath his tan and wrinkles, and said, rather sharply for him, who was so gentle and hard to irritate:

"Have you not learned, Good, that you should never ask a hunter, and above all a professional hunter, whether he did or did not kill a particular head of game unless he volunteers the information? However, if you want to know, I did not kill that elephant; it was Hans who killed it and thereby saved my life. I missed it with both barrels at a distance of a few yards!"

"Oh, I say, Quatermain!" ejaculated the irrepressible Good. "Do you mean to tell us that *you* missed a particularly big elephant that was only a few yards off? You must have been in a pretty fright to do that."

"Have I not said that I missed it, Good? For the rest, perhaps you are right, and I was frightened, for as you know, I never set myself up as a person remarkable for courage. In the circumstances of the encounter with this beast, Jana, any one might have been frightened; indeed, even you yourself, Good. Or, if you choose to be charitable, you may conclude that there were other reasons for that disgraceful—yes, disgraceful exhibition of which I cannot bear to think and much less to talk, seeing that in the end it brought about the death of old Hans — whom I loved."

Now Good was about to answer again, for argument was as the breath of his nostrils, but I saw Sir Henry stretch out his long leg and kick him on the shin, after which he was silent.

"To return," said Allan hastily, as one does who desires to escape from an unpleasant subject, "in the course of my life I did once meet, not with a prehistoric reptile, but with a people who worshipped a Monster-god, or fetish, of which perhaps the origin may have been a survival from the ancient world."

He stopped with the air of one who meant to say no more, and I asked eagerly: "What was it, Allan?"

"To answer that would involve a long story, my friend," he replied, "and one that, if I told it, Good, I am sure, would not believe; also, it is getting late and might bore you. Indeed, I could not finish it to-night."

"There are whisky, soda, and tobacco, and whatever Curtis and Good may do, here, fortified by these, I remain between you and the door until you tell me that tale, Allan. You know it is rude to go to bed before your guests, so please get on with it at once," I added, laughing.

The old boy hummed and hawed and looked cross, but as we all sat round him in an irritating silence which seemed to get upon his nerves, he began at last:

Well, if you will have it, many years ago, when by comparison I was a young man, I camped one day well up among the slopes of the Drakensberg. I was going up Pretoria way with a load of trade goods which I hoped to dispose of among the natives beyond, and when I had done so to put in a month or two game-shooting towards the north. As it happened, when we were in an open space of ground between two of the foothills of the Berg, we got caught in a most awful thunderstorm, one of the worst that ever I experienced. If I remember right, it was about mid-January and you, my friend [this was addressed to me], know what Natal thunderstorms can be at that hot time of the year. It seemed to come upon us from two quarters of the sky, the fact being that it was a twin storm of which the component parts were travelling towards each other.

The air grew thick and dense; then came the usual moaning, icy wind followed by something like darkness, although it was early in the afternoon. On the peaks of the mountains around us lightnings were already playing, but as yet I heard no thunder, and there was no rain. In addition to the driver and voorlooper of the wagon I had with me Hans, of whom I was speaking just now, a little wrinkled Hottentot who, from my boyhood, had been the companion of my journeys and adventures. It was he who came with me as my after-rider when as a very young man I accompanied Piet Retief on that fatal embassy to Dingaan, the Zulu king, of whom practically all except Hans and myself were massacred.

He was a curious, witty little fellow of uncertain age and of his sort one of the cleverest men in Africa. I never knew his equal in resource or in following a spoor, but, like all Hottentots, he had his faults; thus, whenever he got the chance, he would drink like a fish and become a useless nuisance. He had his virtues, also, since he was faithful as a dog and—well, he loved me as a dog loves the master that has reared it from a blind puppy. For me he would do anything—lie or steal or commit murder, and think it no wrong, but rather a holy duty. Yes, and any day he was prepared to die for me, as in the end he did.

Allan paused, ostensibly to knock out his pipe, which was unnecessary, as he had only just filled it, but really, I think, to give himself a chance of turning towards the fire in front of which he was standing, and thus to hide his face. Presently he swung round upon his heel in the light, quick fashion that was one of his characteristics, and went on:

I was walking in front of the wagon, keeping a lookout for bad places and stones in what in those days was by courtesy called the road, though in fact it was nothing but a track twisting between the mountains, and just behind, in his usual place—for he always stuck to me like a shadow—was Hans. Presently I heard him cough in a hollow fashion, as was his custom when he wanted to call my attention to anything, and asked over my shoulder:

"What is it, Hans?"

"Nothing, Baas," he answered, "only that there is a big storm coming up. Two storms, Baas, not one, and when they meet they will begin to fight and there will be plenty of spears flying about in the sky, and then both those clouds will weep rain or perhaps hail."

"Yes," I said, "there is, but as I don't see anywhere to shelter, there is nothing to be done."

Hans came up level with me and coughed again, twirling his dirty apology for a hat in his skinny fingers, thereby intimating that he had a suggestion to make.

"Many years ago, Baas," he said, pointing with his chin towards a mass of tumbled stones at the foot of a mountain slope about a mile to our left, "there used to be a big cave yonder, for once when I was a boy I sheltered in it with some Bushmen. It was after the Zulus had cleaned out Natal and there was nothing to eat in the land, so that the people who were left fed upon one another."

"Then how did the Bushmen live, Hans?"

"On slugs and grasshoppers, for the most part, Baas, and buck when they were lucky enough to kill any with their poisoned arrows. Fried caterpillars are not bad, Baas, nor are locusts when you can get nothing else. I remember that I, who was starving, grew fat on them."

"You mean that we had better make for this cave of yours, Hans, if you are sure it's there?"

"Yes, Baas, caves can't run away, and though it is many years ago, I don't forget a place where I have lived for two months."

I looked at those advancing clouds and reflected. They were uncommonly black and evidently there was going to be the devil of a storm. Moreover, the situation was not pleasant for we were crossing a patch of ironstone on which, as I knew from experience, lightning always strikes, and a wagon and a team of oxen have an attraction for electric flashes.

While I was reflecting a party of Kaffirs came up from behind, running for all they were worth, no doubt to seek shelter. They were dressed in their finery—evidently people going to or returning from a wedding-feast, young men and girls, most of them—and as they went by one of them shouted to me, whom evidently he knew, as did most of the natives in those parts, "Hurry, hurry, Macumazahn!" as you know the Zulus called me. "Hurry, this place is beloved of lightnings," and he pointed with his dancing stick first to the advancing tempest and then to the ground where the ironstone cropped up.

That decided me, and running back to the wagon I told the voorlooper to follow Hans, and the driver to flog up the oxen. Then I scrambled in behind and off we went, turning to the left and heading for the place at the foot of the slope where Hans said the cave was. Luckily the ground was fairly flat and open—hard, too; moreover, although he had not been there for so many years, Hans's memory of the spot was perfect. Indeed, as he said, it was one of his characteristics never to forget any place that he had once visited.

Thus, from the driving box to which I had climbed, suddenly I saw him direct the voorlooper to bear sharply to the right and could not imagine why, as the surface there seemed similar to that over which we were travelling. As we passed it, however, I perceived the reason, for here was a ground spring which turned a large patch of an acre or more into a swamp, where certainly we should have been bogged. It was the same with other obstacles that I need not detail.

By now a great stillness pervaded the air and the gloom grew so thick that the front oxen looked shadowy; also it became very cold. The lightning continued to play upon the mountain crests, but still there was no thunder. There was something frightening and unnatural in the aspect of nature; even the cattle felt it, for they strained at the yokes and went off very fast indeed, without the urgings of whips or shouts, as though they too knew they were flying from peril. Doubtless they did, since instinct has its voices which speak to everything that breathes. For my part, my nerves became affected and I hoped earnestly that we should soon reach that cave.

Presently I hoped it still more, for at length those clouds met and from their edges as they kissed each other came an awful burst of fire —perhaps it was a thunderbolt—that rushed down and struck the earth with a loud detonation. At any rate, it caused the ground to shake and me to wish that I were anywhere else, for it fell within fifty yards of the wagon, exactly where we had been a minute or so before. Simultaneously there was a most awful crash of thunder, showing that the tempest now lay immediately overhead.

This was the opening of the ball; the first sudden burst of music. Then the dance began with sheets and forks of flame for dancers and the great sky for the floor upon which they performed.

It is difficult to describe such a hellish tempest because, as you, my friend, who have seen them, will know, they are beyond description. Lightnings, everywhere lightnings; flash upon flash of them of all shapes—one, I remember, looked like a crown of fire encircling the brow of a giant cloud. Moreover, they seemed to leap upwards from the earth as well as downwards from the heaven, to the accompaniment of one continuous roar of thunder.

"Where the deuce is your cave?" I yelled into the ear of Hans, who had climbed on to the driving box beside me.

He shrieked something in answer which I could not catch because of the tumult, and pointed to the base of the mountain slope, now about two hundred yards away.

The oxen *skrecked* and began to gallop, causing the wagon to bump and sway so that I thought it would overset, and the voorlooper to leave hold of the *reim* and run alongside of them for fear lest he should be trodden to death, guiding them as best he could, which was not well. Luckily, however, they ran in the right direction.

On we tore, the driver plying his whip to keep the beasts straight, and as I could see from the motion of his lips, swearing his hardest in Dutch and Zulu, though not a word reached my ears. At length they were brought to a halt by the steep slope of the mountain and proceeded to turn round and tie themselves into a kind of knot after the fashion of frightened oxen that for any reason can no longer pull their load.

We leapt down and began to outspan them, getting the yokes off as quickly as we could—no easy job, I can tell you, both because of the mess in which they were and for the reason that it must be carried out literally under fire, since the flashes were falling all about us. Momentarily I expected that one of them would catch the wagon and make an end of us and our story. Indeed, I was so frightened that I was sorely tempted to leave the oxen to their fate and bolt to the cave, if cave there were—for I could see none.

However, pride came to my aid, for if I ran away, how could I ever expect my Kaffirs to stand again in a difficulty? Be as much afraid as you like, but never show fear before a native; if you do, your influence over him is gone. You are no longer the great White Chief of higher blood and breeding; you are just a common fellow like himself; inferior to himself, indeed, if he chances to be a brave specimen of a people among whom most of the men are brave.

So I pretended to take no heed of the lightnings, even when one struck a thorn tree not more than thirty paces away. I happened to be looking in that direction and saw the thorn in the flare, every bough of it. Next second all I saw was a column of dust; the thorn had gone and one of its splinters hit my hat.

With the others I tugged and kicked at the oxen, getting the thongs off the *yoke-skeis* as best I could, till at length all were loose and galloping away to seek shelter under overhanging rocks or where they could in accordance with their instincts. The last two, the pole oxen—valuable beasts—were particularly difficult to free, as they were trying to follow their brethren and strained at the yokes so much that in the end I had to cut the *rimpis*, as I could not get them out of the notches of the *yoke-skeis*. Then they tore off after the others, but did not get far, poor brutes, for presently I saw both of them—they were running together—go down as though they were shot through the heart. A flash had caught them; one of them never stirred again; the other lay on its back kicking for a few seconds and then grew as still as its yoke-mate.

"And what did you say?" inquired Good in a reflective voice.

"What would you have said, Good?" asked Allan severely, "if you had lost your best two oxen in such a fashion, and happened not to have a sixpence with which to buy others? Well, we all know your command of strong language, so I do not think I need ask you to answer."

"I should have said——" began Good, bracing himself to the occasion, but Allan cut him short with a wave of his hand.

"Something about *Jupiter Tonans*, no doubt," he said.

Then he went on.

Well, what I said was only overheard by the recording angel, though perhaps Hans guessed it, for he screamed at me:

"It might have been *us*, Baas. When the sky is angry, it will have *something*; better the oxen than us, Baas."

"The cave, you idiot!" I roared. "Shut your mouth and take us to the cave, if there is one, for here comes the hail."

Hans grinned and nodded, then hastened by a large hailstone which hit him on the head, began to skip up the hill at a surprising rate, beckoning to the rest of us to follow. Presently we came to a tumbled pile of rocks through which we dodged and scrambled in the gloom that now, when the hail had begun to fall, was denser than ever between the flashes. At the back of the biggest of these rocks Hans dived among some bushes, dragging me after him between two stones that formed a kind of natural gateway to a cavity beyond.

"This is the place, Baas," he said, wiping the blood that ran down his forehead from a cut in the head made by the hailstone.

As he spoke, a particularly vivid flash showed me that we were in the mouth of a cavern of unknown size. That it must be large, however, I guessed from the echoes of the thunder that followed the flash, which seemed to reverberate in that hollow place from unmeasured depths in the bowels of the mountain.

CHAPTER II

THE PICTURE IN THE CAVE

We did not reach the cave too soon, for as the boys scrambled into it after us the hail began to come down in earnest, and you fellows know, or at any rate have heard, what African hail can be, especially among the mountains of the Berg. I have known it to go through sheets of galvanized iron like rifle bullets, and really I believe that some of the stones which fell on this occasion would have pierced two of them put together, for they were as big as flints and jagged at that. If anybody had been caught in that particular storm on the open veldt without a wagon to creep under or a saddle to put over his head, I doubt whether he would have lived to see a clear sky again.

The driver, who was already almost weeping with distress over the loss of Kaptein and Deutchmann, as the two pole oxen were named, grew almost crazed because he thought that the hail would kill the others, and actually wanted to run out into it with the wild idea of herding them into some shelter. I told him to sit still and not be a fool, since we could do nothing to help them. Hans, who had a habit of growing religious when there was lightning about, remarked sententiously that he had no doubt that the "Great-Great" in the sky would look after the cattle since my Reverend Father (who had converted him to the peculiar faith, or mixture of faiths, which, with Hans, passed for Christianity) had told him that the cattle on a thousand hills were His especial property, and, here in the Berg, were they not among the thousand hills? The Zulu driver who had not "found religion," but was just a raw savage, replied with point that if that were so the "Great-Great" might have protected Kaptein and Deutchmann, which He had clearly neglected to do. Then, after the fashion of some furious woman, by way of relieving his nerves, he fell to abusing Hans, whom he called "a yellow jackal," adding that the tail of the worst of the oxen was of more value than his whole body, and that he wished his worthless skin were catching the hailstones instead of their inestimable hides.

These nasty remarks about his personal appearance irritated Hans, who drew up his lips as does an angry dog, and replied in suitable language, which involved reflections upon that Zulu's family, and especially on his mother. In short, had I not intervened there would have been a very pretty row that might have ended in a blow from a kerry or a knife thrust. This, however, I did with vigour, saying that he who spoke another word should be kicked out of the cave to keep company with the hail and the lightning, after which peace was restored.

That storm went on for a long while, for after it had seemed to go away it returned again, travelling in a circle as such tempests sometimes do, and when the hail was finished, it was followed by torrential rain. The result was that by the time the thunder had ceased to roar and echo among the mountain-tops darkness was at hand, so it became evident that we must stop where we were for the night, especially as the boys, who had gone out to look for the oxen, reported that they could not find them. This was not pleasant, as the cave was uncommonly cold and the wagon was too soaked with the rain to sleep in.

Here, however, once more Hans's memory came in useful. Having borrowed my matches, he crept off down the cave and presently returned, dragging a quantity of wood after him, dusty and worm-eaten-looking wood, but dry and very suitable for firing.

"Where did you get that?" I asked.

"Baas," he replied, "when I lived in this place with the Bushmen, long before those black children," (this insult referred to the driver and the voorlooper, Mavoon and Induka by name) "were begotten of their unknown fathers, I hid away a great stock of wood for the winter, or in case I should ever come back here, and there it is still, covered with stones and dust. The ants that run about the ground do the same thing, Baas, that their children may have food when they are dead. So now if those Kaffirs will help me to get the wood we may have a good fire and be warm."

Marvelling at the little Hottentot's foresight that was bred into his blood by the necessities of a hundred generations of his forefathers, I bade the others to accompany him to the cache, which they did, glowering, with the result that presently we had a glorious fire. Then I fetched some food, for luckily I had killed a Duiker buck that morning, the flesh of which we toasted on the embers, and with it a bottle of Square-face from the wagon, so that soon we were eating a splendid dinner. I know that there are many who do not approve of giving spirits to natives, but for my part I have found that when they are chilled and tired a "tot" does them no harm and wonderfully improves their tempers. The trouble was to prevent Hans from getting more than one, to do which I made a bedfellow of that bottle of Square-face.

When we were filled I lit my pipe and began to talk with Hans, whom the grog had made loquacious and therefore interesting. He asked me how old the cave was, and I told him that it was as old as the mountains of the Berg. He answered that he had thought so because there were footprints stamped in the rock floor farther down it, and turned to stone, which were not made by any beasts that he had ever heard of or seen, which footprints he would show me on the morrow if I cared to look at them. Further, that there were queer bones lying about, also turned to stone, that he thought must have belonged to giants. He believed that he could find some of these bones when the sun shone into the cave in the early morning.

Then I explained to Hans and the Kaffirs how once, thousands of thousands of years ago, before there were any men in the world, great creatures had lived there, huge elephants and reptiles as large as a hundred crocodiles made into one, and, as I had been told, enormous apes, much bigger than any gorilla. They were very interested, and Hans said that it was quite true about the apes, since he had seen a picture of one of them, or of a giant that looked like an ape.

"Where?" I asked. "In a book?"

"No, Baas, here in this cave. The Bushman made it ten thousand years ago." By which he meant at some indefinite time in the past.

Now I bethought me of a fabulous creature called the *Ngoloko* which was said to inhabit an undefined area of swamps on the East Coast and elsewhere. This animal, in which, I may add, I did not in the least believe, for I set it down as a native bogey, was supposed to be at least eight feet high, to be covered with gray hair and to have a claw in the place of toes. My chief authority for it was a strange old Portuguese hunter whom I had once known, who swore that he had seen its footprints in the mud, also that it had killed one of his men and twisted the head off his body. I asked Hans if he had ever heard of it. He replied that he had, under another name, that of *Milhoy*, I think, but that the devil painted in the cave was larger than that.

Now I thought that he was pitching me a yarn, as natives will, and said that if so he had better show me the picture forthwith.

"Best wait until the sun shines in the morning, Baas," he replied, "for then the light will be good. Also this devil is not nice to look at at night."

"Show it me," I repeated with asperity; "we have lanterns from the wagon."

So, somewhat unwillingly, Hans led the way up the cave for fifty paces or more, for the place was very big, he carrying one lantern and I another, while the two Zulus followed with candles in their hands. As we went I saw that on the walls there were many Bushmen paintings, also one or two of the carvings of this strange people. Some of these paintings seemed quite fresh, while others were faded or perhaps the ochre used by the primitive artist had flaked off. They were of the usual character, drawings of elands and other buck being hunted by men who shot at them with arrows; also of elephants and a lion charging at some spearmen.

One, however, which oddly enough was the best preserved of any of the collection, excited me enormously. It represented men whose faces were painted white and who seemed to wear a kind of armour and queer pointed caps upon their heads, of the sort that I believe are known as Phrygian, attacking a native kraal of which the reed fence was clearly indicated, as were the round huts behind. Moreover, to the left some of these men were dragging away women to what from a series of wavy lines, looked like a rude representation of the sea.

I stared and gasped, for surely here before me was a picture of Phoenicians carrying out one of their women-hunting raids, as ancient writers tell us it was their habit to do. And if so, that picture must have been painted by a Bushman who lived at least two thousand years ago, and possibly more. The thing was amazing. Hans, however, did not seem to be interested, but pushed on as though to finish a disagreeable task, and I was obliged to follow him, fearing lest I should be lost in the recesses of that vast cave.

Presently he came to a crevice in the side of the cavern which I should have passed unnoticed, as it was exactly like many others.

"Here is the place, Baas," he said, "just as it used to be. Now follow me and be careful where you step, for there are cracks in the floor."

So I squeezed myself into the opening where, although I am not very large, there was barely room for me to pass. Within its lips was a narrow tunnel, either cut out by water or formed by the rush of explosive gases hundreds of thousands of years ago—I think the latter, as the roof, which was not more than eight or nine feet from the floor, had sharp points and roughnesses that showed no water-wear. But as I have not the faintest idea how these great African caves were formed, I will not attempt to discuss the matter. This floor, however, was quite smooth, as though for many generations it had been worn by the feet of men, which no doubt was the case.

When we had crept ten or twelve paces down the tunnel, Hans called to me to stand quite still—not to move on any account. I obeyed him, wondering, and by the light of my lantern saw him lift his own, which had a loop of hide fastened through the tin eye at the top of it for convenience in hanging it up in the wagon, and set it, or rather the hide loop, round his neck, so that it hung upon his back. Then he flattened himself against the side of the cavern with his face to the wall as though he did not wish to see what was behind him, and cautiously crept forward with sidelong steps, gripping the roughnesses in the rock with his hands. When he had gone some twenty or thirty feet in this crab-like fashion, he turned and said:

"Now, Baas, you must do as I did."

"Why?" I asked.

"Hold down the lantern and you will see, Baas."

I did so, and perceived that a pace or two farther on there was a great chasm in the floor of the tunnel of unknown depth, since the lamplight did not penetrate to its bottom. Also I noted that the ledge at the side that formed the bridge by which Hans had passed, was nowhere more than twelve inches, and in some places less than six inches wide.

"Is it deep?" I asked.

By way of answer Hans found a bit of broken rock and threw it into the gulf. I listened, and it was quite a long while before I heard it strike below.

"I told the Baas," said Hans in a superior tone, "that he had better wait until to-morrow when some light comes down this hole, but the Baas would not listen to me and doubtless he knows best. Now would the Baas like to go back to bed, as I think wisest, and return to-morrow?"

If the truth were known there was nothing that I should have liked better, for the place was detestable. But I was in such a rage with Hans for playing me this trick that even if I thought that I was going to break my neck I would not give him the pleasure of mocking me in his sly way.

"No," I answered quietly, "I will go to bed when I have seen this picture you talk about, and not before."

Now Hans grew alarmed and begged me in good earnest not to try to cross the gulf, which reminded me vaguely of the parable of Abraham and Dives in the Bible, with myself playing the part of Dives, except that I was not thirsty, and Hans did not in any way resemble Abraham.

"I see how it is," I said, "there is not any picture and you are simply playing one of your monkey tricks on me. Well, I'm coming to look, and if I find you have been telling lies I'll make you sorry for yourself."

"The picture is there or was when I was young," answered Hans sullenly, "and for the rest, the Baas knows best. If he breaks every bone in his body presently, don't let him blame me, and I pray that he will tell the truth, all of it, to his Reverend Father in the sky who left him in my charge, saying that Hans begged him not to come but that because of his evil temper he would not listen. Meanwhile, the Baas had better take off his boots, since the feet of those Bushmen whose spooks I feel all about me have made the ledge very slippery."

In silence I sat down and removed my boots, thinking to myself that I would gladly give all my savings that were on deposit in the bank at Durban, to be spared this ordeal. What a strange thing is the white man's pride, especially if he be of the Anglo-Saxon breed, or what passes by that name. There was no need for me to take this risk, yet, rather than be secretly mocked at by Hans and those Kaffirs, here I was about to do so just for pride's sake. In my heart I cursed Hans and the cave and the hole and the picture and the thunderstorm that brought me there, and everything else I could remember. Then, as it had no strap like that of Hans, although it smelt horribly, I took the tin loop of my lantern in my teeth because it seemed the only thing to do, put up a silent but most earnest prayer, and started as though I liked the job.

To tell the truth, I remember little of that journey except that it seemed to take about three hours instead of under a minute, and the voices of woe and lamentation from the two Zulus behind, who insisted upon bidding me a tender farewell as I proceeded, amidst other demonstrations of affection, calling me their father and their mother for four generations.

Somehow I wriggled myself along that accursed ridge, shoving my stomach as hard as I could against the wall of the passage as though this organ possessed some prehensile quality, and groping for knobs of rock on which I broke two of my nails. However, I did get over all right, although just towards the end one of my feet slipped and I opened my mouth to say something, with the result that the lantern fell into the abyss, taking with it a loose front tooth. But Hans stretched out his skinny hand, and, meaning to catch me by the coat collar, got hold of my left ear, and, thus painfully supported, I came to firm ground and cursed him into heaps. Although some might have thought my language pointed, he did not resent it in the least, being too delighted at my safe arrival.

"Never mind the tooth, Baas," he said. "It is best that it should be gone without knowing it, as it were, because you see you can now eat crusts and hard biltong again, which you have not been able to do for months. The lantern, however, is another matter, though perhaps we can get a new one at Pretoria or wherever we go."

Recovering myself, I peered over the edge of the abyss. There, far, far below, I saw my lantern, which was a sort that burns oil, flaring upon a bed of something white, for the container had burst and all the oil was on fire.

"What is that white stuff down there?" I asked. "Lime?"

"No, Baas, it is the broken bones of men. Once when I was young, with the help of the Bushmen I let myself down by a rope that we twisted out of rushes and buckskins, just to look, Baas. There is another cave underneath this one, Baas, but I didn't go into it because I was frightened."

"And how did all those bones come there, Hans? Why, there must be hundreds of them!"

"Yes, Baas, many hundreds, and they came this way. Since the beginning of the world the Bushmen lived in this cave and set a trap here by laying branches over the hole and covering them with dust so that they looked like rock, just as one makes a game pit, Baas—yes, they did this until the last of them were killed not so long ago by the Boers and Zulus, whose sheep and beasts they stole. Then when their enemies attacked them, which was often, for it has always been right to kill Bushmen—they would run down the cave and into the cleft and creep along the narrow edge of rock, which they could do with their eyes shut. But the silly Kaffirs, or whoever it might be, running after them to kill them would fall through the branches and get killed themselves. They must have done this quite often, Baas, since there are such a lot of their skulls down there, many of them quite black with age and turned to stone.

"One might have thought that the Kaffirs would have grown wiser, Hans."

"Yes, Baas, but the dead keep their wisdom to themselves, for I believe that when all the attackers were in the passage, then other Bushmen, who had been hiding in the cave, came up behind and shot them with poisoned arrows and drove them on into the hole so that none went back; indeed, the Bushmen told me that this used to be their father's plan. Also, if any did escape, in a generation or two all was forgotten, and the same thing happened again because, Baas, there are always plenty of fools in the world and the fool who comes after is just as big as the fool who went before. Death spills the water of wisdom upon the sand, Baas, and sand is thirsty stuff that soon grows dry again. If it were not so, Baas, men would soon stop falling in love with women, and yet even great ones—like you, Baas—fall in love."

Having delivered this thrust, in order to prevent the possibility of answer Hans began to chat with the driver and the voorlooper on the other side of the gulf.

"Be quick and come over, you brave Zulus there," he said, "for you are keeping your Chief waiting and me also."

The Zulus, holding their candles forward, peered into the pit below.

"*Ow!*" said one of them, "are we bats that we can fly over a hole like that or baboons that we can climb on a shelf no wider than a spear, or flies that we can walk upon a wall? *Ow!* we are not coming, we will wait here. That road is only for yellow monkeys like you or for those who have the white man's magic like the Inkoos Macumazahn."

"No," replied Hans reflectively, "you are none of these creatures which are all of them good in their way. You are just a couple of low-born Kaffir cowards, black skins blown up to look like men. I, the 'yellow jackal,' can walk the gulf, and the Baas can walk the gulf, but you, Windbags, cannot even float over it for fear lest you should burst in the middle. Well, Windbags, float back to the wagon and fetch the coil of small rope that is in the *voorkissie*, for we may want it."

One of them replied in a humbled voice that they did not take orders from him, a Hottentot, whereon I said:

"Go and fetch the rope and return at once."

So they went with a dejected air, for Hans's winged words had gone home, and again they learned that at the end he always got the best of a quarrel. The truth is that they were as brave as men can be, but no Zulu is any good underground and least of all in the dark in a place that he thinks haunted.

"Now, Baas," said Hans, "we will go and look at the picture—that is, unless you are quite sure I am lying and that there is no picture, in which case it is not worth while to take the trouble, and you had better sit here and cut your broken nails until Mavoon and Induka come back with the rope."

"Oh, get on, you poisonous little vermin!" I said, exasperated by his jeers, emphasizing my words with a tremendous kick.

Here, however, I made a great mistake, since I had forgotten that at the moment I lacked boots, and either Hans carried a collection of hard articles in the seat of his filthy trousers or his posterior was of a singularly stonelike nature. In short, I hurt my toes most abominably and him not at all.

"Ah, Baas," said Hans with a sweet smile, "you should remember what your Reverend Father taught me: always to put on your boots before you kick against the thorn pricks. I have a gimlet and some nails in my pistol pocket, Baas, that I was using this morning to mend that box of yours."

Then he bolted incontinently lest I should experiment on his head and see if there were nails in that also, and as he had the only lantern, I was obliged to limp, or rather to hop, after him.

The passage, of which the floor was still worn smooth by thousands of dead feet, went on straight for eight or ten paces and then bent to the right. When we came to this elbow in it I saw a light ahead of me which I could not understand till presently I found myself standing in a kind of pit or funnel—it may have measured some thirty feet across—that rose from the level at which we stood, right through the strata to the mountain-side eighty or a hundred feet above us. What had formed it thus I cannot conceive, but there it was—a funnel, as I have said, in shape exactly like those that are used when beer is poured into barrels or port wine into a decanter, the place on which we were, being, of course, its narrower end. The light that I had seen came, therefore, from the sky, which, now that the tempest had passed away, was clean-washed and beautiful, sown with stars also, for at the moment a dense black cloud remaining from the storm hid the moon, now just past its full.

For a little way, perhaps five-and-twenty feet, the sides of this tunnel were almost sheer, after which they sloped outwards steeply to the mouth of the pit in the mountain flank. One other peculiarity I noticed—namely, that on the western face of the tunnel which, as it chanced, was in front of us as we stood, just where it began to expand, projected a sloping ridge of rock like to the roof of a lean-to shed, which ridge ran right across this face.

"Well, Hans," I said, when I had inspected this strange natural cavity, "where is your picture? I don't see it."

"*Wacht een beetje,*" (that is, "Wait a bit,"), "Baas. The moon is climbing up that cloud; presently she will get to the top of it and then you will see the picture, unless someone has rubbed it out since I was young."

I turned to look at the cloud and to witness a sight of which I never have grown tired: the uprising of the glorious African moon out of her secret halls of blackness. Already silver rays of light were shooting across the vastness of the firmament, causing the stars to pale. Then suddenly her bent edge appeared and with extraordinary swiftness grew and grew till the whole splendid orb emerged from a bed of inky vapour and for a while rested on its marge, perfect, wonderful! In an instant our hole was filled with light so strong and clear that by it I could have read a letter.

For a few moments I stood thrilled with the beauty of the scene, and forgetting all else in its contemplation, till Hans said with a hoarse cackle:

"Now turn round, Baas, and look at the pretty picture."

I did so, and followed the line of his outstretched hand, which pointed to that face of the rock with the pent roof that looked towards the east. Next second—my friends, I am not exaggerating—I nearly fell backwards. Have any of you fellows ever had a nightmare in which you dreamed you were in hell and suddenly met the devil tete-a-tete, all by your little selves? At any rate, I have, and there in front of me was the devil, only much worse than fond fancy can paint him even with the brush of the acutest indigestion.

Imagine a monster double life size—that is to say, eleven or twelve feet high—brilliantly portrayed in the best ochres of which these Bushmen have always had the secret, namely, white, red, black, and yellow, and with eyes formed apparently of polished lumps of rock crystal. Imagine this thing as a huge ape to which the biggest gorilla would be but a child, and yet not an ape but a man, and yet not a man, but a fiend.

It was covered with hair like an ape, long gray hair that grew in tufts. It had a great, red, bushy beard like a man; its limbs were tremendous, the arms being of abnormal length like to the arms of a gorilla, but, mark this, it had no fingers, only a great claw where the thumb should be. The rest of the hand was all grown together into one piece like a duck's foot, although what should have been the finger part was flexible and could grip like fingers, as shall be seen.

At least, that is what the picture suggested, though it occurred to me afterwards that it might represent the creature as wearing fingerless gloves such as men in this country use when cutting fences. The feet however, which were certainly shown as bare, were the same; I mean that there were no toes, only one terrible claw where the big toe should be. The carcass was enormous; supposing it to have been drawn from life, the original, I should guess, would have weighed at least thirty stone; the chest was vast, indicating strength, and the paunch beneath wrinkled and protuberant. But—and here came one of the human touches—about its middle the thing wore a moocha or, rather, a hide tied round it by the leg skins, which hide seemed to have been dressed.

So much for the body. Now for the head and face. These I know not how to describe, but I will try. The neck was as that of a bull, and perched horribly on the top of it was quite a small head, which—notwithstanding the great red beard whereof I have spoken that grew upon the chin, and a wide mouth from whose upper jaw projected yellow tusks like to those of a baboon that hung over the lower lip—was curiously feminine in appearance; indeed, that of an old, old she-devil with an aquiline nose. The brow, however, was disproportionate to the rest of the face, being prominent, massive, and not unintellectual, while set deep in it and unnaturally far apart were those awful glaring crystal eyes.

That was not all, for the creature seemed to be laughing cruelly, and the drawing showed by it laughed. One of its feet was set upon the body of a man into which the great claw was driven deep. One of its hands held the head of the man, that evidently it had just twisted from the body. The other hand grasped by the hair a living naked girl badly drawn, as though this detail had not interested the artist, whom apparently it was about to drag away.

"Isn't it a pretty picture, Baas?" sniggered Hans. "Now the Baas will not say that I tell lies, no, not for quite a week."

CHAPTER III

THE OPENER-OF-ROADS

I stared and stared, then was overcome with faintness and sat down upon the ground.

I see you laughing at me, young man [this was addressed to me, the recorder of the tale] who no doubt have already decided that this drawing was the work of some imaginative Bushman who had gone mad and set down upon the rock the hellish dream of a mind diseased. Of course, that was the conclusion I came to myself next morning, but at the time it did not strike me like that.

The place was lonesome and eerie, a horrible place with the pit full of bones near by; heavily silent also except for a distant hyena or jackal howling at the moon, and I had gone through some trials that day—the passage of the death-pit, for instance, which reminded me of the oubliettes in ancient Norman castles that I have read of down which prisoners were hurled to doom. Also, as you may have observed, even in your short career, moonlight differs from sunlight and we, or some of us, are much more affected by horrible things at night than we are by day. At any rate, I sat down because I felt faint and thought that I was going to be ill.

"What is it, Baas?" queried the observant Hans, still mocking. "If you want to be sick, Baas, please don't mind me, for I'll turn my back. I remember that I was sick myself when first I saw Heu-Heu—just there," he added reminiscently, pointing to a certain spot.

"Why do you call that thing 'Heu-Heu,' Hans?" I asked, trying to master the reflex action of my interior arrangements.

"Because that is his nice name, Baas, given him by his Mammie when he was little, perhaps."

(Here I nearly *was* sick, the idea of that creature with a mother almost finished me—like the sight and smell of a bit of fat bacon in a gale at sea.)

"How do you know that?" I gurgled.

"Because the Bushmen told me, Baas. They said that their fathers, a thousand years ago, knew this Heu-Heu far away, and that they left that part of the country because of him as they never slept well at night there, just like a Boer when another Boer comes and builds a house within six miles of him, Baas. I think they meant that they heard Heu-Heu when he talked, for they told me that their great-great-grandfathers could hear him doing it and beating his breast when he was miles away. But I daresay they lied, for I don't believe they really knew anything about Heu-Heu, or who painted his portrait on the rock, Baas."

"No," I answered, "nor do I. Well, Hans, I think I have had enough of your friend Heu-Heu for this evening, and should like to go back to bed."

"Yes, Baas, so should I, Baas. Still, take another good look at him before you leave. You don't see a picture like that every night, Baas, and you know you wanted to come."

Now I would have kicked Hans again, but luckily I remembered those nails in his pocket in time, so, after one lingering glance, I only rose and loftily motioned to him to lead on.

This was the last that I saw of the likeness of Heu-Heu or Beelzebub, or whoever the monster may have been. Somehow, although I intended to return to examine it more closely by the light of day, when morning came I thought that I would not risk another scramble over that ledge but would be satisfied with the memory of first impressions. These they say, are always the best—like first kisses, as Hans added when I explained this to him.

Not that I could forget Heu-Heu; on the contrary, it is not too much to say that this devilish creature haunted me. I could not dismiss that picture as some mere flight of distorted savage imagination. From a hundred characteristics I knew or thought I knew it, erroneously as I now believe, to be Bushmen's work and was certain that no Bushman, even if he had *delirium tremens*—not a complaint from which these people ever suffered, because they lacked the opportunity of doing so, could have evolved this monstrous creation out of his own soul—if a Bushman has a soul. No, Bushman or not, that artist was drawing something that he had seen, or thought that he had seen.

Of this there were several indications. Thus, on Heu-Heu's right arm the elbow joint was much swollen as though he had once suffered an injury there. Again, the claw of one of his horrible hands—the left, I think—was broken and divided at the point. Further, there was a wart or protuberance upon the brow, just beneath where the long iron-gray tufts of hair parted in the middle and hung down on each side of the demoniacal, womanish face. Now the painter must have remembered these blemishes and set them down faithfully, copying from some original, real or imagined. Certainly, I reflected, he would not have invented them.

Where, then, did he get his model? I have mentioned that I had heard rumours of creatures called *Ngolokos*, which I took it, if they existed at all, were peculiarly terrific apes of an unknown variety. Heu-Heu, then, might be a most distinguished and improved specimen of these apes. Yet that could scarcely be, for this beast was more man than monkey, notwithstanding his huge claws where the thumbs and big toes should be. Or perhaps I should say that he was more devil than either.

Another idea occurred to me: he might have been the god of these Bushmen, only I never heard that they had any god except their own stomaches. Afterwards I questioned Hans on this point but he replied that he did not know, as the Bushmen he lived with in the cave had never told him anything to that effect. It was true, however, that they did not go to the place where the picture was except through fear of enemies, and that when they did they would not look or speak about it more than they could help. Perhaps, he suggested with his usual shrewdness, Heu-Heu might be the god of some other people with whom the Bushmen had nothing to do.

Another question—when was this work executed? Owing to its sheltered position the colours were still fairly bright, but it must have been a long while ago. Hans said that the Bushmen told him that they did not know who painted it or what it represented, but that it was "*old, old, old!*" which might mean anything or nothing, since to a people without writing five or six generations become remote antiquity. One thing was certain, however, that another of the paintings in the cave was undoubtedly old, that of the Phoenicians raiding a kraal of which I have spoken, which can scarcely have been executed since the time of Christ. Of this I am sure, for I examined it carefully on the following morning and it was not more faded than that of the Monster. Further, in this picture a piece of the rock had scaled off just above the left knee, and I had noticed that the surface thus exposed seemed as much weathered as that of the surrounding rock outside the limits of the painting.

On the other hand, it must be remembered that the Phoenician picture was under cover, while that of Heu-Heu was exposed to the air and would therefore age more rapidly.

Well, all that night I dreamed of this horrid Heu-Heu, dreamed that he was alive and challenging me to fight him, dreamed that someone was calling to me to rescue her—it was certainly her—not him—from the power of the beast; dreamed that I did fight him and that he got me down and was about to twist my head off as he had done to the man in the picture, when something happened—I do not know what—and I woke up covered with perspiration and in a most pitiable fright.

Now at the time I visited this cave I was not far from the borders of Zululand on one of my trading expeditions, the wagon being laden with blankets, beads, iron pots, knives, hoes, and such other articles as the simple savage loves, or in those days loved to pay for in cattle. Before the storm overtook us, however, I was contemplating leaving the Zulus alone on this trip and trying to break new ground somewhere north of Pretoria among less sophisticated natives who might put a higher value on my wares. After seeing Heu-Heu, as it chanced, I changed my mind for two reasons. The first of these was that the lightning had killed my two best oxen and I thought that I could replace these without cash expenditure in Zululand, where debts were owing to me that I might collect in kind. The second was connected with that confounded and obsessing Heu-Heu. I felt convinced that only one man in the world could tell me about this monster, if, indeed, there were anything to tell, namely, old Zikali, the wizard of the Black Kloof, the *Thing-that-should-never-have-been-born*, as Chaka, the great Zulu king, named him.

I think that I have told you all about Zikali before, but in case I have not, I will say that he was the greatest witch doctor who ever lived in Zululand and the most terrible. No one knew when he was born, but undoubtedly he was very ancient and under his native name of "Opener-of-Roads" had been known and dreaded in the land for some generations. For many years, since my boyhood, indeed, he and I had been friends in a fashion, though of course I was aware that from the first he was using me for his own ends, as, indeed, became very clear before all was done and he had triumphed over and brought about the fall of the Zulu Royal House, which he hated.

However, Zikali, like a wise merchant, always paid those who served him with a generous hand, in one coin or another, as he paid those he hated. My coin was information, either historical or concerning the hidden secrets of the strange land of Africa, of which, for all our knowledge, we white men really understand so little. If any one could give information about the picture in the cave and its origin, it would be Zikali, and therefore to Zikali I would go. Curiosity about such matters, as perhaps you have guessed, was always one of my besetting sins.

We had great trouble in recovering our remaining fourteen oxen since some of them had wandered far to find cover from the storm. At last, however, they were found uninjured except for some bruises from the hailstones, for it is wonderful, if they are left alone, how cattle manage to protect themselves against the forces of nature. In Africa, however, they seldom take shelter beneath trees during a thunderstorm, as is their habit here in England, perhaps because, such tempests being so frequent, they have inherited from their progenitors an instinctive knowledge that lightning strikes trees and kills anything that happens to be underneath them. At least, that is my experience.

Well, we inspanned and trekked away from that remarkable cave. Many years afterwards, by the way, when Hans was dead, I tried to find it again and could not. I thought that I reached the same mountain slope in which it was, but I suppose that I must have been mistaken, since in that neighbourhood there are multitudes of such slopes and on the one that I identified I could discover no trace of the cave.

Perhaps this was because there had been a landslide and, with the funnel-like shaft in the mountain side down which the moonlight poured on to the picture of Heu-Heu, the orifice that, it will be remembered, was very small, had been covered up with rocks. Or it may be that I was searching the wrong slope, not having taken my bearings sufficiently when I visited the place at a time of tempest and hurry.

Further, I was pressed and, desiring to reach a certain outspan before night fell, could only give about an hour to the quest and when it failed was obliged to get on. Nor have I ever met any one who was acquainted with this cave, so I suppose that it must have been known to the Bushmen and Hans only, dead now all of them, which is a pity because of the wonderful paintings that it contains or contained.

You will remember I told you that just before the storm broke we were overtaken by a party of Kaffirs going to or returning from some feast. When we had gone about half a mile we found one of those Kaffirs again quite dead, but whether he (the body was that of a young man) had been killed by the lightning or by the hail, I was not sure. Evidently his companions were so frightened that they had left him where he lay, proposing, I suppose, to return and bury him later. So you will see that when it gave us shelter, this cave did us a good turn.

Now I will skip all the details of my trek into Zululand, which was as are other treks, only slower, because it was a hard job to get that heavily laden wagon along with but fourteen oxen. Once, indeed, we stuck in a river, the White Umfolozi, quite near to the Nongela Rock or Cliff which frowns above a pool of the river. I shall never forget that accident because it caused me to be the unwilling witness of a very dreadful sight.

Whilst we were fast in the drift a party of men appeared upon the brow of this Nongela Rock, about two hundred and fifty yards away, dragging with them two young women. Studying them through my glasses, I came to the conclusion from the way they moved their heads and stared wildly about them, that these young women were blind or had been blinded. As I looked at them, wondering what to do, the men seized the women by the arms and hurled them over the edge of the cliff. With a piteous wail the poor creatures rolled down the stratified rock into the deep pool below and there the crocodiles got them, for distinctly I saw the rush of the reptiles. Indeed, in this pool they were always on the look-out, as it was a favourite place of execution under the Zulu kings.

When their horrible business was finished the party of "slayers"—there were about fifteen of them—came down to the ford to interview us. At first I thought there might be trouble, and to tell the truth, should not have been sorry, for the sight of this butchery had made me furious and reckless. As soon as they found out, however, that the wagon belonged to me, Macumazahn, they were all amiability, and wading into the water, tackled on to the wheels, with the result that by their help we came safe to the farther bank.

There I asked their leader who the two murdered girls might be. He replied that they were the daughters of Panda, the King. I did not question this statement although, knowing Panda's kindly character, I doubted very much whether they were actually his children. Then I asked why they were blind, and what crime they had committed. The captain replied that they had been blinded by the order of Prince Cetywayo, who even then was the real ruler of Zululand, because "they had looked where they should not."

Further inquiry elicited the fact that these unhappy girls had fallen in love with two young men, and run away with them against the King's orders, or Cetywayo's, which was the same thing. The party were overtaken before they could reach the Natal border, where they would have been safe; the young men were killed at once and the girls brought up for judgment, with the result that I have described. Such was the end of their honeymoon!

Moreover, the captain informed me cheerfully that a body of soldiers had been sent out to kill the fathers and mothers of the young men and all who could be found in their kraals. This kind of free love must be put a stop to, he said, as there had been too much of it going on; indeed, he did not know what had come to the young people in Zululand, who had grown very independent of late, contaminated, no doubt, by the example of the Zulus in Natal, where the white men allowed them to do what they liked without punishment.

Then with a sigh over the degeneracy of the times, this crusted old conservative took a pinch of snuff, bade me a hearty farewell, and departed, singing a little song which I think he must have invented, as it was about the love of children for their parents. If it had been safe I should have liked to let him have a charge of shot behind to take away as a souvenir, but it was not. Also, after all, he was but an executive officer, a product of the iron system of Zululand in the day of the kings.

Well, I trekked on, trading as I went, and getting paid in cows and heifers, which I sent back to Natal, but could come by no oxen that were fit for the yoke, and much less any that had been broken in, since in those days such were almost unknown in Zululand. However, I did hear of some that had been left behind by a white trader because they were sick or footsore, I forget which, who took young cattle in exchange for them. These were said now to be fat again, but no one seemed to know exactly where they were. One friendly chief told me, however, that the "Opener-of-Roads," that is, old Zikali, might be able to do so, as he knew everything and the oxen had been traded away in his district.

Now by this time, although I was still obsessed about Heu-Heu, I had almost made up my mind to abandon the idea of visiting Zikali on this trip, because I had noticed that whenever I did so, always I became involved in arduous and unpleasant adventures as an immediate consequence. Being, however, badly in need of more oxen, for, not to mention the two that were dead, others of my team seemed never to have recovered from the effects of the hailstorm and one or two showed signs of sickness, this news caused me to revert to my original plan. So after consultation with Hans, who also thought it the best thing to be done, I headed for the Black Kloof, which was only two short days' trek away.

Arriving at the mouth of that hateful and forbidding gulf on the afternoon of the second day, I outspanned by the spring and, leaving the cattle in charge of Mavoon and Induka, walked up it accompanied by Hans.

The place, of course, was just as it had always been, and yet, as it ever did, struck me with a fresh sense of novelty and amazement. In all Africa I scarcely know a gorge that is so eerie and depressing. Those towering cliffsides that look as though they are about to fall in upon the traveller, the stunted, melancholy aloe plants which grow among the rocks; the pale vegetation; the jackals and hyaenas that start away at the sound of voices or echoing footsteps; the dense dark shadows; the whispering winds that seem to wail about one even when the air is still over-head, draughts, I suppose, that are drawing backwards and forwards through the gulley; all of these are peculiar to it. The ancients used to declare that particular localities had their own genii or spirits, but whether these were believed to be evolved by the locality or to come thither because it suited their character and nature, I do not know.

In the Black Kloof and some other spots to which I have wandered, I have often thought of this fable and almost found myself accepting it as true. But, then, what kind of a spirit would it be that chose to inhabit this dreadful gorge? I think some embodiment—no, that word is a contradiction—some impalpable essence of Tragedy, some doomed soul whereof the head was bowed and the wings were leaded with a weight of ineffable and unrepented crime.

Well, what need was there to fly to fable and imagine such an invisible inhabitant when Zikali, the *Thing-that-should-never-have-been-born*, was, and for uncounted years had been, the Dweller in this tomb-like gulf? Surely he was Tragedy personified, and that hoary head of his was crowned with ineffable and unrepented crime. How many had this hideous dwarf brought down to doom and how many were yet destined to perish in the snares that year by year he wove for them? And yet this sinner had been sinned against and did but pay back his sufferings in kind, he whose wives and children had been murdered and whose tribe had been stamped flat beneath the cruel feet of Chaka, whose House he hated and lived on to destroy. Even for Zikali allowances could be made; he was not altogether bad. Is any man *altogether* bad, I wonder.

Musing thus, I tramped on up the gorge, followed by the dejected Hans, whom the place always depressed, even more than it did myself.

"Baas," he said presently, in a hollow whisper, for here he did not dare to speak aloud, "Baas, do you think that the Opener-of-Roads was once Heu-Heu himself who has now shrunk to a dwarf with age, or at any rate, that Heu-Heu's spirit lives in him?"

"No, I don't," I answered, "for he has fingers and toes like the rest of us, but I do think that if there is any Heu-Heu he may be able to tell us where to find him."

"Then, Baas, I hope that he has forgotten, or that Heu-Heu has gone to heaven where the fires go on burning of themselves without the need for wood. For, Baas, I do not want to meet Heu-Heu; the thought of him turns my stomach cold."

"No, you would rather go to Durban and meet a gin bottle that would turn your stomach warm, Hans, and your head, too, and land you in the Trunk for seven days," I replied, improving the occasion.

Then we turned the corner and came upon Zikali's kraal. As usual, I appeared to be expected, for one of his great silent body servants was waiting, who saluted me with uplifted spear. I suppose that Zikali must have had a look-out man stationed somewhere who watched the plain beneath and told him who was approaching. Or possibly he had other methods of obtaining information. At any rate, he always knew of my advent and often enough why I came and whence, as, indeed, he did on this occasion.

"The Father of Spirits awaits you, Lord Macumazahn," said the body servant. "He bids the little yellow man who is named Light-in-Darkness, to accompany you and will see you at once."

I nodded and the man led me to the gate of the fence that surrounded Zikali's great hut, on which he tapped with the handle of his spear. It was opened, by whom I did not see, and we entered, whereon someone slipped out of the shadows and closed the gate behind us, then vanished. There in front of the door of his hut, with a fire burning before him, crouched the dwarf wrapped in a fur kaross, his huge head, on either side of which the gray locks fell down much as they did in the picture of Heu-Heu, bent forward, and the light of the fire into which he was staring shining in his cavernous eyes. We advanced across the shiny beaten floor of the courtyard and stood in front of him, but for half a minute or more he took no notice of our presence. At length, without looking up, he spoke in that hollow, resounding voice which was unlike to any other I ever heard, saying:

"Why do you always come so late, Macumazahn, when the sun is off the hut and it grows cold in the shadows? You know I hate the cold, as the aged always do, and I was minded not to receive you."

"Because I could not get here before, Zikali," I answered.

"Then you might have waited until to-morrow morning unless, perhaps, you thought that I should die in the night, which I shall not do. No, nor for many nights. Well, here you are, little white Wanderer who hops from place to place like a flea."

"Yes, here I am," I replied, nettled, "to visit you who do not wander but sit in one spot like a toad in a stone, Zikali."

"Ho, ho, ho!" he laughed—that wonderful laugh of his which echoed from the rocks and always made me feel cold down the back, "Ho, ho, ho! how easy it is to make you angry. Keep your temper, Macumazahn, lest it should run away with you as your oxen did before the storm in the mountains the other day. What do you want? You only come here when you want something from him whom once you named the Old Cheat. So I don't wander, don't I, but sit like a toad in a stone? How do you know that? Is it only the body that wanders? Cannot the spirit wander also, far, oh, far, even to the 'Heaven Above' sometimes, and perhaps to that land which is under the earth, the place where they say the dead are to be found again? Well, what do you want? Stay, and I will tell you, who explain yourself so badly, who, although you think that you speak Zulu like a native, have never really learned it properly because to do that you must think in it and not in your own stupid tongue, that has no words for many things. Man, my medicines."

A figure darted out of the hut, set down a cat-skin bag before him, and was gone again. Zikali plunged his claw-like hand into the bag and drew out a number of knuckle bones, polished, but yellow with age, which he threw carelessly on to the ground in front of him, then glanced at them.

"Ha," he said, "something about cattle, I see; yes, you want to get oxen, broken oxen, not wild ones, and think that I can tell you where to do it cheap. By the way, what present have you brought for me? Is it a pound of your white man's snuff?" (As a matter of fact, it was a quarter of a pound.) "Now am I right about the oxen?"

"Yes," I replied, rather amazed.

"That astonishes you. It is wonderful, isn't it, that the poor Old Cheat should know what you want? Well, I'll tell you how it is done. You lost two oxen by lightning, did you not? You therefore, naturally would want others, especially as some of those which remain"—here he glanced at the bones once more—"were hurt, yes, by hailstones, very large hailstones, and others are showing signs of sickness, red-water, I think. Therefore, it isn't strange that the poor Old Cheat should guess that you needed oxen, is it? Only a silly Zulu would put such a thing down to magic. About the snuff, too, which I see you have taken from your pocket—a very little parcel, by the way. You've brought me snuff before, haven't you? Therefore, it isn't strange that I should guess that you would do so again, is it? No magic there."

"None, Zikali, but how did you learn of the lightning killing the cattle and of the hailstorm?"

"How did I learn that the lightning killed your pole-oxen, Kaptein and Deutchmann? Why, are you not a very great man in whom all are interested, and is it wonderful that I should be told of accidents that happen a hundred miles or so away? You met a party going to a wedding, did you not, just before the storm, and found one of them dead afterwards? By the way, he wasn't killed either by lightning or by hail. The flash fell near and stunned him, but really he died of the cold during the night. I thought that you might like to know that, as you are curious on the point. Of course, those Kaffirs would have told me about it, would they not? No magic, again you see. That's how we poor witch doctors gain repute, just by keeping our eyes and ears open. When you are old you might set up in the trade yourself, Macumazahn, since you do the same thing, even at night, they say."

Now while he went on mocking me he had gathered up the bones out of the dust and suddenly threw them again with a curious spiral twist that caused them to fall in a little heap, perched on one another. He looked at them, and said:

"Why, what do these silly things remind me of? They are some of the tools of my trade, you know, Macumazahn, used to impress the fools that come to see us witch doctors, who think that they will tell us secrets, and to take off their attention while we read their hearts. Somehow or other they remind me of rocks piled one on another as on a mountain slope, and look! there is a hollow in the middle like the mouth of a cave.

"Did you chance to take refuge from that storm in a cave, Macumazahn? Oh, you did! Well, see how cleverly I guessed it. No magic there again, only just a guess. Isn't it likely that you would go to a cave to escape from such a tempest, leaving the wagon outside? Look at that bone there, lying a little distance off the others, that's what made me think of the wagon being outside. But the question is, what did you see in the cave? Anything out of the way, I wonder? The bones can't tell me that, can they? I must guess that somehow else, mustn't I? Well, I'll try to do so, just to give you, the wise white man, another lesson in the manner that we poor rascals of witch doctors do our work and take in fools. But won't you tell me, Macumazahn?"

"No, I won't," I answered crossly, who knew that the old dwarf was making a butt of me.

"Then I suppose that I must try to discover for myself, but how, how? Come here, you little yellow monkey of a man, and sit between me and the fire so that its light shines through you, for then perchance I may be able to see something of what is going on in that thick head of yours, Light-in-Darkness, as you are called, and get some light in my darkness."

Hans advanced unwillingly enough and squatted down at the spot that Zikali indicated with his bony finger, being very careful that none of the magic bones should touch any portion of his anatomy, for fear lest they should bewitch him, I suppose. There he sat, holding his ragged felt hat upon the pit of his stomach as though to ward off the gimlet-like glances of Zikali's burning eyes.

"Ho-ho! Yellow Man," said the dwarf after a few seconds of inspection, which caused Hans to wriggle uncomfortably and even to colour beneath his wrinkled skin, like a young woman being studied by her prospective husband, who desires to ascertain whether she will or will not do for a fifth wife. "Ho-ho! it seems to me that you knew this cave before you went there in the storm, but of course I should guess that, for how otherwise would you have found it in such a hurry; also that it had something to do with Bushmen, as most caves have in this land.

"The question is, what was in it? No, don't tell me. I want to find out for myself. It is strange that the thought comes to me of pictures. No, it isn't strange, since the Bushmen often used to paint pictures in caves. Now, you shouldn't nod your head, Yellow Man, because it makes the riddle too easy. Just stare at me and think of nothing at all. Pictures, lots of them, but one principal picture, I think; something that was difficult to come at. Yes, dangerous, even. Was it perchance a picture of yourself that a Bushman drew long ago when you were young and handsome, Yellow Man?

"There, again you are shaking your head. Keep it quite still, will you, so that the thoughts in it don't ripple like water beneath a wind. At least it was a picture of something hideous, but much bigger than you. Ah! it grows and grows. I am getting it now. Macumazahn, come and stand by me, and you, Yellow Man, turn your back so that you face the fire. Bah! it burns badly, does it not, and the air is so cold, so cold! I must make it brighter.

"Are you there, Macumazahn? Yes. Now look at this stuff of mine; see what a fine blaze it causes," and putting his hand into the bag, he drew out some kind of powder, only a little of it, which he threw on to the embers. Then he stretched his skinny fingers over them as though for warmth, and slowly lifted his arms high into the air. It is a fact that after him the flames sprang up to a height of three or four feet. He dropped his arms again and the flames sank down. He lifted them once more and once more they rose, only this time much higher. A third time he repeated this performance, and now the sheet of flame sprang fully fifteen feet into the air and so remained burning steadily, like the flame of a lamp.

"Look at that fire, Macumazahn, and you also, Yellow Man," he said, in a strange new voice, a sort of dreamy far-off voice, "and tell me if you see anything in it, for I can't—I can't."

I looked, and for a moment perceived nothing. Then some shape began to grow upon the blazing background. It wavered; it changed; it became fixed and definite, yes, clear and real. There before me, etched in flame, I saw Heu-Heu—Heu-Heu as he had been in the painting on the cave wall, only, as it seemed to me, alive, for his eyes blinked—Heu-Heu, looking like a devil in hell. I gasped but stood firm. As for Hans, he ejaculated in his vile Dutch:

"*Allemaghte! Da is die leeliker auld deil!*" (that is, "Almighty! There is the ugly old devil!") and having said this, rolled over on to his back and lay still, frozen with terror.

"Ho, ho, ho!" laughed Zikali. "Ho, ho, ho!" and from a dozen places the walls of the kloof echoed back, "Ho, ho, ho!"

CHAPTER IV

THE LEGEND OF HEU-HEU

Zikali stopped laughing and contemplated us with his hollow eyes.

"Who was it who first said that all men are fools?" he asked. "I do not know, but I think it must have been a woman, a pretty woman who played with them and found that it was so. If so, she was wise, as all women are in their narrow way, which the saying shows, since they are left out of it. Well, I will add to the proverb; all men are cowards also in one matter or another, though in the rest they may be brave enough. Further, they are all the same, for what is the difference between you, Macumazahn, wise White Man who have dared death a hundred times, and yonder little yellow ape?" Here he pointed to Hans lying upon his back, with rolling eyes and muttering prayers to a variety of gods between his chattering teeth. "Both of you are afraid, one as much as the other; the only difference being that the White Lord tries to conceal his fear, whilst the Yellow Monkey chatters it out, as monkeys do.

"Why are you so frightened? Just because by a common trick I show to your eyes a picture of that which is in the minds of both of you. Mark you again, not by magic but by a common trick which any child could learn, if somebody taught it to him. I hope that you will not behave like this when you see Heu-Heu himself, for if you do I shall be disappointed in you and soon there will be two more skulls in that cave of his. But then, perhaps, you will be brave; yes, I think so, I think so, since never would you like to die remembering how long and loud I should laugh when I heard of it."

Thus the old wizard rambled on, as was his fashion when he wished to combine his acrid mockery with the desire to gain space for thought, till presently he grew silent and took some of the snuff which I had brought him, for he had been engaged in opening the packet while he talked, all the while continuing to watch us as though he would search out our very souls.

Now, because I thought that I must say something, if only to show that he had not frightened me with his accursed manifestations, or whatever they were, I answered:

"You are right, Zikali, when you say that all men are fools, seeing that you are the first and biggest fool among them."

"I have often thought it, Macumazahn, for reasons that I keep to myself. But why do you say so? Let me hear, who would learn whether yours are the same as my own."

"First, because you talk as though there were such a creature as Heu-Heu, which, as you know well, does not live and never did; and secondly, because you speak as though Hans and I would meet it face to face, which we shall never do. So cease from such nonsense and show us how to make pictures in the fire—an art, you tell us, any child could learn."

"If they are taught, Macumazahn, *if* they are taught how. But were I to do this, I should indeed be the first of fools. Do you think that I wish to establish two rival cheats—you see, between ourselves, I give myself my right name—in the land to trade against me? No, no, let each keep the knowledge he has gained for himself, for if it becomes common to all, who will pay for it? But why do you believe that you will never stand face to face with Heu-Heu except in pictures on rock or fire?"

"Because he doesn't exist," I answered with irritation; "and if he does, I suppose his home is a long way off and I cannot trek without fresh oxen."

"Ah!" said Zikali, "that reminds me of how you refuged in the cave from the storm and the rest said that you wanted more oxen. So, knowing that you would be in as great a hurry to get to Heu-Heu as a young man is to find his first wife, I made ready. The story you heard was quite true. A white trader did leave a very fine team of footsore oxen in this neighbourhood, salted, every one of them, which after three moons' rest, are now fat and sound. I will have them driven up to-morrow morning and take care of yours while you are away."

"I have no money to pay for more oxen," I said.

"Is not the promise of Macumazahn better than any money, even the red English gold? Does not the whole land know it? Moreover," he added slowly, "when you return from visiting Heu-Heu you ought to have plenty of money—or, rather, of diamonds, which is the same thing—and perhaps of ivory, though of that I am not so sure. No, I am not sure whether you will be able to carry the ivory. If I do not speak truth I will pay for the oxen myself."

Now at the word "diamonds" I pricked up my ears, for just then all Africa was beginning to talk about these stones; even Hans rose from the ground and began once more to take interest in earthly things.

"That's a fair offer," I said, "but stop blowing dust," (i.e. talking nonsense) "and tell me straight out what you mean before it grows dark. I hate this kloof in the dark. Who is Heu-Heu? And if he or it lives, or lived, where is Heu-Heu, dead or alive? Also, supposing that there was or is a Heu-Heu, why do you, Zikali, wish me to find him, as I perceive you do, who always have a reason for what you wish?"

"I will answer the last question first, Macumazahn, who, as you say, always have a reason for what I want you or others to do."

Here he stopped and clapped his hands, whereon instantly one of his great serving men appeared from the hut behind, to whom he gave some order. The man darted away and presently was back with more of the skin bags such as witch doctors use to carry their medicines. Zikali opened one of these and showed me that it was almost empty, there being in it but a pinch of brown powder.

"This stuff, Macumazahn," he said, "is the most wonderful of all drugs, even more wonderful than the herb called *taduki* that can open the paths of the past, with which herb you will become acquainted one day. By means of it—I speak not of *taduki*, but of the powder in the bag—I do most of my tricks. For instance, it was with a dust of it that I was able to show you and the little yellow man the picture of Heu-Heu in the flames just now."

"You mean that it is a poison, I suppose."

"Oh, yes, among other things, by adding another powder it can be made into a very deadly poison; so deadly that as little of it as will lie upon the point of a thorn will kill the strongest man and leave no trace. But it has other properties also that have to do with the mind and the spirit; never mind what they are; if I tried to tell you, you would not understand. Well, the Tree of Visions from the leaves of which this medicine is ground grows only in the garden of Heu-Heu and nowhere else in Africa, and I got my last supply of it thence many years ago, long before you were born, indeed, Macumazahn; never mind how.

"Now I must have more, of those leaves, or what these Zulus call my magic, which wise white men like you know to be but my tricks, will fail me, and the world will say that the Opener-of-Roads has lost his strength and turn to seek wiser doctors."

"Then why do you not send and get some, Zikali?"

"Whom can I send that would dare to enter the land of Heu-Heu and rob his garden? No one but yourself, Macumazahn. Ah! I read your mind. You are wondering now if that be so, why I do not order that the leaves should be brought to me from the place of Heu-Heu. For this reason, Macumazahn. The dwellers there may not leave their hidden land; it is against their law. Moreover, if they might they would not part even with a handful of that drug, except at a great price. Once, a hundred years ago," (by which, I suppose, he meant a long time), "I paid such a price and bought a quantity of the stuff of which you see the last in that bag. But that is an old story with which I will not trouble you. Oh! many went and but two returned, and they mad, as those are apt to be who have looked on Heu-Heu and left him living. If ever you see Heu-Heu, Macumazahn, be sure to destroy him and all that is his, lest his curse should follow you for the rest of your days. Fallen, he will be powerless, but standing, his hate is very strong and reaches far, or that of his priests does, which is the same thing."

"Rubbish!" I said. "If there is any Heu-Heu, he is but a big ape, and living or dead, I am not afraid of any ape."

"I am glad to hear that, Macumazahn, and hope that you will always be of the same mind. Doubtless it is only his picture painted on rock or in the fire that frightens you, just as a dream is more terrible than anything real. Some day you shall tell me which was the worse, Heu-Heu's picture or Heu-Heu himself. But you asked me other questions. The first of them was, Who is Heu-Heu?

"Well, I do not know. The legend tells that once, in the beginning, there was a people white, or almost white, who lived far away to the north. This people, says the old tale, were ruled over by a giant, very cruel and very terrible; a great wizard also, or cheat, as you would call him. So cruel and terrible was he, indeed, that his people rose against him, and strong as he might be, forced him to fly southwards with some who clung to him or could not escape him.

"So south he came with them, thousands of miles, until he found a secret place that suited him to dwell in. That place is beneath the shadow of a mountain of a sort that I have heard spouted out fire when the world was young, which even now smokes from time to time. Here this people, who are named Walloo, built them a town after their northern fashion out of the black stone which flowed from the mountain in past ages. But their king, the giant wizard, continued his cruelties to them forcing them to labour night and day at his city and Great House and a cave in which he was worshipped as a god, till at last they could bear no more and murdered him by night.

"Before he died, however, which he took long to do because of his magic, he mocked them, telling them that not thus would they be rid of him since he would come back in a worse shape than before and still rule over them from generation to generation. Moreover, he prophesied disaster to them and laid this curse upon them, that if they strove to leave the land that he had chosen, and to cross the ring of mountains by which it is enclosed, they should die, every one of them. This, indeed, happened, or so I have heard, since if even one of them travels down the river, by which alone that country can be approached from the desert, and sets foot in the desert, he dies, sometimes by sudden sickness, or sometimes by the teeth of lions and other wild beasts that live in the great swamp where the river enters the desert, whither the elephants and other game come to drink from hundreds of miles around."

"Perhaps fever kills them," I suggested.

"Maybe so, or poison, or a curse. At least, soon or late they die, and therefore it comes about that now none of them leaves that land."

"And what happened to the Walloos after they had finished off this kind king of theirs?" I asked, for Zikali's romantic fable interested me. Of course, I knew that it was a fable, but in such tales, magnified by native rumour, there is sometimes a grain of truth. Also Africa is a great country, and in it there are very queer places and peoples.

"Something very bad happened, Macumazahn, for scarcely was their king dead when the mountain began to belch out fire and hot ashes, which killed many of them and caused the rest to fly in boats across the lake that makes an island of the mountain, to the forest lands that lie around. There they live to this day upon the banks of the river which flows through the forest, the same that passes through the gorge of the mountains into the swamp, and there loses itself in the desert sands. So, at least, my messengers told me a hundred years ago, when they brought me the medicine that grows in Heu-Heu's garden."

"I suppose that they were afraid to go back to their town after the eruption was over," I said.

"Yes, they were afraid, at which you will not wonder when you see it, for when the mountain blew up the gases killed very many of them and what is more, turned them to stone. Aye, there they sit, Macumazahn, to this day, turned to stone, and with them their dogs and cattle."

Now at this amazing tale I burst out laughing, and even Hans grinned.

"I have noted, Macumazahn," said Zikali, "that in the beginning it is you who always laugh at me, while in the end it is I who laugh at you, and so I believe it will be in this case also. I tell you that there those people sit turned to stone, and if it is not so, you need not pay me for the oxen that I bought from the white man even should you come back with your pockets full of diamonds."

Now I bethought me of what happened at Pompeii, and ceased to laugh. After all, the thing was possible.

"That is one reason why they did not return to their town, even when the mountain went to sleep again, but there was another, Macumazahn, that was stronger still. Soon they found that it was haunted."

"Haunted! By what? By the stone men?"

"No, they are quiet enough, though what their spirits may be I cannot tell you. Haunted by their king who they had killed, turned into a gigantic ape, turned into Heu-Heu."

Now at this statement I did not laugh, although at first sight it seemed much more absurd than that of the dead people who had been petrified. For this reason: as I knew well, it is the commonest of beliefs among savages, and especially those of Central Africa, that dead chiefs, notably if they have been tyrants during their life, are metamorphosed into some terrible animal, which thenceforward persecutes them from generation to generation. The animal may be a rogue elephant or a man-killing lion, or perhaps a very poisonous snake. But whatever shape it takes, it always has this characteristic, that it does not die and cannot be killed—at any rate, by any of those whom it afflicts. Indeed, in my own experience I have come across sundry examples of this belief among natives. Therefore, it did not strike me as strange that these people should imagine their country to be cursed by the spirit of a legendary tyrant turned into a monster.

Only in the monster itself I put no faith. If it existed at all probably it would resolve itself into a large ape, or perhaps a gorilla living upon an island in the lake where it had become marooned, or drifted upon a tree in a flood.

"And what does this spirit do?" I asked Zikali incredulously. "Throw nuts or stones at people?"

"No, Macumazahn. According to what I have been told, it does much more. At times it crosses to the mainland—some say on a log, some say by swimming, some say as spirits can. There, if it meets any one, it twists off his or her head," (here I bethought me of the picture in the cave), "for no man can fight against its strength, or woman either, because if she be old and ugly, it serves her in the same fashion, but if she be young and well favoured, then it carries her away. The island is said to be full of such women who cultivate the garden of Heu-Heu. Moreover, it is reported that they have children who cross the lake and live in the forest—terrible, hairy creatures that are half human, for they can make fire and use clubs and bows and arrows. These savage people are named Heuheua. They dwell in the forests, and between them and the Walloos there is perpetual war."

"Anything else?" I asked.

"Yes, one thing. At a certain time of the year the Walloos must take their fairest and best-born maiden and tie her to an appointed rock upon the shore of the island upon a night of full moon. Then they go away and leave her alone, returning at sunrise."

"And what do they find?"

"One of two things, Macumazahn; either that the maiden has gone, in which case they are well pleased, except those of them to whom she is related, or that she has been torn to pieces, having been rejected by Heu-Heu, in which case they weep and groan, not for her but for themselves."

"Why do they rejoice, and why do they weep, Zikali?"

"For this reason. If the maiden has been taken, Heu-Heu, or his servants, the Heuheua, will spare them and his priests for that year. Moreover, their crops will prosper and they be free from sickness. If she has been killed, he or his servants haunt them, snatching away other women, and they will have bad harvests; also fever and other ills fall upon them. Therefore, the Offering of the Maiden is their great ceremony, which, should she be taken, is followed by the Feast of Rejoicing, and should she be rejected and slain, by the Fast of Lamentation and the sacrifice of her parents or others."

"A pleasant religion, Zikali. Tell me, is it one that pleases these Walloos?"

"Does any religion please any man, Macumazahn, and do tears, want, sickness, bereavement, and death please those who are born into the world? For example, like the rest of us, you white people suffer these things, or so I have heard; also you have your own Heu-Heu or devil who claims such sacrifices and yet avenges himself upon you. You are not pleased with him, still you go on making your sacrifices of war and blood and all wickedness in return for what he did to you, thereby binding yourselves to him afresh and confirming his power over you, and as you do, so do we all. Yet if you and the rest of us would but stand up against him, perhaps his strength might be broken, or he might be slain. Why, then, do we continue to sacrifice our maidens of virtue, truth, and purity to him, and how are we better than those who worship Heu-Heu, who do so to save their lives?"

I considered his argument, which was subtle for a savage, however old and instructed, to have evolved from his limited opportunities of observation, and answered rather humbly:

"I do not suppose that we are better at all." Then to change the subject to something more practical, I added, "But what about those diamonds?"

"The diamonds! Oho! the diamonds, which, by the way, I believe are one of the offerings that you white people make to your own Heu-Heu. Well, these people seem to have plenty of them. Of course, they are useless to them, as they do not trade. Still, the women know that they are pretty, and fasten them about themselves in little nets of hair after polishing them upon stone, because they do not know how to make holes in them, being so hard, and cannot set them in metals. Also they stick them in the clay of their eating dishes before these are dried, making pretty patterns with them. It seems that these stones and others that are red, are washed down by the river from some desert across which it flows above, through a tunnel in the mountains, I believe. At any rate, they find them in plenty in the gravel on its banks, which they set the children to sift in a closely woven sieve of human hair, or in some such fashion. Stay, I will show you what they are like, for my messengers brought me a fistful or two many years ago," and he clapped his hands.

Instantly, as before, one of his servants appeared, to whom he gave certain instructions. The man went, and presently returned with a little packet of ancient, wrinkled skin that looked like a bit of an old glove. This he untied and gave to me. Within were a quantity of small stones that looked and felt like diamonds, very good diamonds, as I judged from their colour, though none of them were large. Also among them was a sprinkling of other stones that might have been rubies, though of this I could not be sure. At a guess I should have estimated the value of the parcel at 200 or 300 pounds. When I had examined them, I offered them back to Zikali, but he waved his hand and said:

"Keep them, Macumazahn, keep them. They are no good to me, and when you come to the land of Heu-Heu, compare them with those you will find there, just to show yourself that in this matter I do not lie."

"When I come to the land of Heu-Heu!" I exclaimed indignantly. "Where, then, is this land, and how am I to reach it?"

"That I propose to tell you to-morrow, Macumazahn, not to-night, since it would be useless to waste time and breath upon the business until I know two things: first, whether you will go there, and secondly, whether the Walloos will receive you if you do go."

"When I have heard the answer to the second question, we will talk of the first, Zikali. But why do you try to make a fool of me? These Walloos and the savage Heuheuas with whom they fight, I understand, dwell far away. How, then, can you have the answer by to-morrow?"

"There are ways, there are ways," he answered dreamily, then seemed to go into a kind of doze with his great head sunk upon his breast.

I stared at him for a while, till, growing weary of the occupation, I looked about me and noted that of a sudden it was growing dusk. Whilst I did so I began to hear screechings in the air: sharp, thin screechings such as are made by rats.

"Look, Baas," whispered Hans in a frightened voice, "his spirits come," and he pointed upwards.

I did look, and far above, as though they were descending from the sky, saw some wide-winged, flittering shapes, three of them. They descended in circles very swiftly, and I perceived that they were bats, enormous and evil-looking bats. Now they were wheeling about us so closely that twice their outstretched wings touched my face, sending a horrid thrill through me; and each time that a creature passed, it screeched in my ear, setting my teeth on edge.

Hans tried to beat away one of them from investigating him, whereon it clung to his hand and bit his finger, or so I judged from the yell he gave, after which he dragged his hat down over his head and plunged his hands into his pockets. Then the bats concentrated their attention upon Zikali. Round and round him they went in a dizzy whirl which grew closer and closer, till at last two of them settled on his shoulders just by his ears, and began to twitter in them, while the third hung itself on to his chin and thrust its hideous head against his lips.

At this point in the proceedings Zikali seemed to wake up, for his eyes opened and grew bright, also with his skinny hands he stroked the bats upon his shoulders as though they were pet birds. More, he seemed to speak with the creature that hung to his chin, talking in a language which I could not understand, while it twittered back the answers in its slate-pencil notes. Then suddenly he waved his arms and all three of them took flight again, wheeling outwards and upwards, till presently they vanished in the gloom.

"I tame bats and these are quite fond of me," he said by way of explanation, then added, "Come back to-morrow morning, Macumazahn, and perhaps I shall be able to tell you whether the Walloos wish for a visit from you, and if so, to show you a road to their country."

So we went, glad enough to get away, since the Opener-of-Roads, with his peculiar talk and manifestations, as I believe they call them in spiritualistic circles, was a person who soon got upon one's nerves, especially at nightfall. As we stumbled down that hateful gorge in the gloom, Hans asked:

"What were those things that hung to Zikali's shoulders and chin?"

"Bats, very large bats. What else?" I answered.

"I think a great deal else, Baas. I think that they are his familiars whom he is sending to those Walloos, just as he said."

"Do you believe in the Walloos and the Heuheua then, Hans? I don't."

"Yes, I do, Baas, and what is more, I believe that we shall visit them, because Zikali means that we should, and who is there that can fight against the will of the Opener-of-Roads?"

CHAPTER V

ALLAN MAKES A PROMISE

I never could sleep well in the neighbourhood of the Black Kloof. It always seemed to me to give out evil and disturbing emanations, nor was this night any exception to the rule. For hour after hour, cogitating the old wizard's marvellous tale of the Walloos and Heu-Heu, their devil-ghost, I lay in the midst of the intense silence of that lonely place which was broken only by the occasional scream of a night-hawk, or perhaps of the prey that it gripped, or the echoing bark of some baboon among the rocks.

The story was foolishness. And yet—and yet there were so many strange peoples hidden away in the vast recesses of Africa, and some of them had these extremely queer beliefs or superstitions. Indeed, I began to wonder whether it is not possible for these superstitions, persisted in through ages, to produce something concrete, at any rate to the minds of those whom they affect.

Also there were odd circumstances connected with this tale or romance that might, in a way, be called corroborative. For instance, the picture of Heu-Heu in the cave which Zikali, by his infernal arts or tricks, reproduced in the flame of fire; for instance, the diamonds and rubies, or crystals and spinels, whichever they might be, that at present reposed in the pocket of my shooting coat. These, presuming them to be the former, must have come from some very far-off or hidden spot, since I had never seen or heard of such in any place that I had visited, as they were entirely unlike those which, at that time, they were beginning to find at Kimberley, being, for one thing, much more water-worn.

Still, the presence of diamonds in a certain district had nothing to do with the possible existence of a Heu-Heu. Therefore, they proved nothing, one way or the other.

And if there were a Heu-Heu, did I wish to meet him face to face? In one sense, not at all, but in another, very much indeed. My curiosity was always great, and it would be wonderful to behold that which no white man's eyes had ever seen, and still more wonderful also to struggle with and kill such a monster. A vision rose before my eyes of Heu-Heu stuffed in the British Museum with a large painted placard underneath:

Shot in Central Africa by Allan Quatermain, Esq.

Why, then I, the most humble and unknown of persons, would become famous and have my likeness published in the *Graphic*, and probably the *Illustrated London News* also, perhaps with my foot set upon the breast of the prostrate Heu-Heu.

That, indeed, would be glory! Only Heu-Heu looked a very nasty customer, and the story might have a wrong ending; his foot might be set upon *my* breast, and he might be twisting off my head, as in the cave picture. Well, in that case the illustrated papers would publish nothing about it.

Then there was the story of the town full of petrified men and animals. This must either be true or false, since it lacked ghostly implications. Although I had never heard of anything of the sort, there might be such a place, and if so, it would be splendid to be its discoverer.

Oh, of what was I thinking? Zikali's yarn must be nonsense, and rank fiction. Yet it reminded me of something I had once heard in my youth, which for a long while I could not recall. At last, in a flash, it came back to me. My old father, who was a learned scholar, had a book of Grecian legends, and one of these about a lady called Andromeda, the daughter of a king who, in obedience to popular pressure and in order to avert calamities from his country, tied her up to a rock, to be carried off by a monster that rose out of the sea. Then a magically aided hero of the name of Perseus arrived at the critical moment, killed the monster and took away the lady to be his wife.

Why, this Heu-Heu story was the same thing over again. The maiden was tied to a rock; the monster came out of the sea, or rather, the lake, and carried her off, whereby calamities were duly averted. So similar was it, indeed, that I began to wonder whether it were not an echo of the ancient myth that somehow had found its way into Africa. Only hitherto there had been no Perseus in Heuheua Land. That role, apparently, was reserved for me. And if so, what should I do with the maiden? Restore her to a grateful family, I suppose, for certainly I had no intention of marrying her. Oh, I was growing silly with thinking! I would go to sleep; I *would, I wo*——

A minute or two later, or so it seemed, I woke up thinking, not of Andromeda, but of the prophet Samuel, and for a while wondered what on earth could have put this austere patriarch and priest into my head. Then, being a great student of the Old Testament, I remembered that autocratic seer's indignation when he heard the lowing of the oxen which Saul spared from the general "eating up" of the Amalekites, as the Zulus would describe it, by divine command. (What was the use of cutting the throats of all that good stock, personally, I could never understand.)

Well, in my ears also was the lowing of oxen, which, of course, formed the connecting link. I marvelled what they could be, for our own were grazing at a little distance, and poked my head out under the wagon-hood to perceive a really beautiful team of trek cattle, eighteen of them, for there were two spare beasts, which had just been driven up to my camp by two strange Kaffirs. Then, of course, I remembered about the oxen which Zikali had promised to sell me upon easy terms, or under certain circumstances to give me, and thought to myself that in this matter, at any rate, he had proved a wizard of his word.

Slipping on my trousers, I descended from the wagon to examine them, and with the most satisfactory results. They had quite recovered from their poverty and footsoreness that had caused their former owner to leave them behind in Zikali's charge, and were now as fat as butter, looking as though they would pull anything anywhere. Indeed, even the critical Hans expressed his unqualified approval of the beasts which, as he pointed out from various indications, really seemed to be "salted," and inoculated also, some of them, as could be seen from the loss of the ends of their tails.

Having sent them to graze in charge of the Kaffirs who had brought them, for I did not wish them to mix with my own beasts, which showed signs of sickness, I breakfasted in excellent spirits, as wherever I might go I was now set up with draught beasts, and then bethought me of my undertaking to revisit Zikali. Hans tried to excuse himself from accompanying me, saying that he wanted to study the new oxen which those strange Zulus might steal, etc.; the fact being, of course, that he was afraid of the old wizard, and would not go near him again unless he were obliged. However, I made him come, since his memory was first rate, and four ears were better than two when Zikali was concerned.

Off we trudged up the kloof, and as before, without delay, were admitted within the fence surrounding the witch doctor's hut, to find the Opener-of-Roads seated in front of it, as usual with a fire burning before him. However hot the weather, he always kept that fire going.

"What do you think of the oxen, Macumazahn?" he asked abruptly.

I replied with caution that I would tell him after I had proved them.

"Cunning as ever," said Zikali. "Well, you must make the best of them, Macumazahn, and as I told you, you can pay me when you get back."

"Get back from where?" I asked.

"From wherever you are going, which at present you do not know."

"No, I don't, Zikali," I said, and was silent.

He also was silent for a long while, so long that at last he outwore my patience, and I inquired sarcastically whether he had heard from his friend Heu-Heu, by bat-post.

"Yes, yes, I have heard, or think that I have heard—not by bats, but perchance by dreams or visions. Oho! Macumazahn, I have caught you again. Why do you always walk into my snare so easily? You see some bats, which in truth, as I told you, are but creatures that I have tamed by feeding them for many years, flitter about me and fly away, and you half believe that I have sent them a thousand miles to carry a message and bring back an answer, which is impossible.

"Now I will tell the truth. Not thus do I communicate with those who are afar. Nay, I send out my thought and it flies everywhere to the ends of the earth, so that the whole earth might read it if it could. Yet perchance it is attuned to one mind only among the millions, by which it can be caught and interpreted. But for the vulgar—yes, and even for the wise White Man who cannot understand—there remains the symbol of the bats and their message. Why will you always seek the aid of magic to explain natural things, Macumazahn?"

Now I reflected that my idea of nature and Zikali's differed, but knowing that he was mocking me after his custom, and declining to enter into argument as though it were beneath me, I said:

"All this is so plain that I wonder you waste breath in setting it out. I only desired to know if you have any answer to your message, however it was sent, and if so—what answer."

"Yes, Macumazahn, as it happens I have; it came to me just as I was waking this morning. This is its substance; that the chief of the Walloos, with whom my heart talked, and, as he believes, most of his people, will be very glad to welcome you in their land, though, as he believes again, the priests of Heu-Heu, who worship him as a god and are sworn to his service, will not be glad. Should you choose to come, the chief will give you all that you desire of the river diamonds or aught else that he possesses, and you can carry away with you, also, the medicine that *I* desire. Further, he will protect you from dangers so far as he is able. Yet for these gifts he requires payment."

"What payment, Zikali?"

"The overthrow of Heu-Heu at your hands."

"And if I cannot overthrow Heu-Heu, Zikali?"

"Then certainly you will be overthrown and the bargain will fall to the ground."

"Is it so? Well, if I go, shall I be killed, Zikali?"

"Who am I that I should dispense life or death, Macumazahn? Yet," he added slowly, separating his words by deliberate pinches of snuff—"yet I do not think that you will be killed. If I did I should not trust you to pay me for those oxen on your return. Also I believe that you have much work left to do in the world—my work, some of it, Macumazahn, that could not be carried out without you. This being so, the last thing I should wish would be to send you to your death."

I reflected that probably this was true, since always the old wizard was hinting of some great future enterprise in which we should be mixed up together; also I knew that he had a regard for me in his own strange way, and therefore wished me no evil. Moreover, of a sudden a great longing seized me to undertake this adventure in which perchance I might see remarkable new things—I who was wearying of the old ones. However, I hid this, if anything could be hid from Zikali, and asked in a businesslike fashion:

"Where do you want me to go, how far off is it, and if I went, how should I get there?"

"Now we begin to handle our assegais, Macumazahn," (by which he meant that we were coming to business). "Hearken, and I will tell you."

Tell me he did indeed for over an hour, but I will not trouble you fellows with all that he said, since geographical details are wearisome and I want to get on with my story. You, my friend [this was addressed to me, the Editor], are only stopping here over to-morrow night, and it will take me all that time to finish it—that is, if you wish to hear the end.

It is enough to say, therefore, that I had to trek about three hundred miles north, cross the Zambesi, and then trek another three hundred miles west. After this I must travel nor'west for a rather indefinite distance till I came to a gorge in certain hills. Here I must leave the wagon, if by this time I had any wagon, and tramp for two days through a waterless patch of desert till I came to a swamp-like oasis. Here the river of which Zikali had spoken lost itself in the sands of the desert, whence I could see on a clear day the smoke of the volcano of which he had also spoken. Crossing the swamp, or making my way round it, I must steer for this slope, till at length I came to a second gorge in the mountains, through which the river ran from Heuheua Land out into the desert. There, according to Zikali, I should find a party of Walloos waiting for me with canoes or boats, who would take me on into their country, where things would go as they were fated.

Before you leave, my friend, I will give you a map[*] of the route, which I drew after travelling it, in case you or anybody else should like to form a company and go to look for diamonds and fossilized men in Heuheua Land, stipulating, however, that you do not ask me to take shares in the venture.

[* If Allan ever gave me this map, of which, after the lapse of so many years, I am not sure, I have put it away so carefully that it is entirely lost, nor do I propose to hunt for it amidst the accumulated correspondence of some five-and-thirty years. Moreover, if it were found and published, it might lead to foolish speculation and probable loss of money among maiden ladies, the clergy, and other venturesome persons.—*Editor*.]

"So that's the trek," I said, when at last Zikali had finished. "Well, I tell you straight out that I am not going to make it through unknown country. How could I ever find my way without a guide? I'm off to Pretoria with your oxen or without them."

"Is it so, Macumazahn? I begin to think that I am very clever. I thought that you would talk like that and therefore have made ready by finding a man who will lead you straight to the House of Heu-Heu. Indeed, he is here, and I will send for him," and he summoned a servant in his usual way and gave an order.

"Whence does he come, who is he, and how long has he been here?" I asked.

"I don't quite know who he is, Macumazahn, for he does not talk much about himself, but I understand that he comes from the neighbourhood of Heuheua Land, or out of it, for aught I know, and he has been here long enough for me to be able to teach him something of our Zulu language, though that does not matter much since you know Arabic well, do you not?"

"I can talk it, Zikali, and so can Hans, a little."

"Well, that is his tongue, Macumazahn, or so I believe, which will make things easier. I may tell you at once that he is a strange sort of man, not in the least like any one you would expect, but of that you will judge for yourself."

I made no answer, but Hans whispered to me that doubtless he was one of the children of the Heu-Heu and just like a great monkey. Although he spoke in a low voice, and at a distance Zikali seemed to overhear him, for he remarked:

"Then you will feel as though you had found a new brother, is it not so, Light-in-Darkness?" which, if I have not said so before, was a title that Hans had earned upon a certain honourable occasion.

Thereon Hans grew silent, since he dared not show his resentment of this comparison of himself to a monkey to the mighty Opener-of-Roads. I, too, was silent, being occupied with my own reflections, for now, in a flash, as it were, I saw the whole trick laid bare of its mysterious and pseudo-magical trappings. A messenger from some strange and distant country had come to Zikali, demanding his help for reasons that I did not know.

This he had determined to give through me, whom he thought suited to the purpose. Hence his bribe of the oxen, the news of which he had conveyed to me while I was still far off, having in some way become acquainted with my dilemma. Indeed, it looked as though everything had been part of a plan, though of course this was not possible, since Zikali could not have arranged that I should take shelter in a particular cave during a thunderstorm.

The sum of it was, however, that I should serve his turn, though what exactly that might be I did not know. He said that he wanted to obtain the leaves of a certain tree, which perhaps was true, but I felt sure that there was more behind.

Possibly his curiosity was excited and he desired information about a distant, secret people, since for knowledge of every kind he had a perfect lust. Or perhaps in some occult fashion this Heu-Heu, if there were a Heu-Heu, might be a rival who stood between him and his plans, and therefore was one to be removed.

Allowing ninety per cent. of Zikali's supernatural powers to be pure humbug, without doubt the remaining ten per cent. were genuine. Certainly he lived and moved and had his being upon a different plane from that of ordinary mortals, and was in touch with things and powers of which we are ignorant. Also as I have reason to know, though I do not trouble you with instances, he was in touch with others of the same class or hierarchy throughout Africa—yes, thousands of miles distant—of whom some may have been his friends and some his enemies but all were mighty in their way.

While I was reflecting thus and old Zikali was reading my thoughts—as I am sure he did, for I saw him smile in his grim manner and nod his great head as though in approval of my acumen—the servant returned from somewhere, ushering in a tall figure picturesquely draped in a fur kaross that covered his head as well as his body. Arrived in front of us, this person threw off the kaross and bowed in salutation, first to Zikali and then to myself. Indeed, so great was his politeness that he even honoured Hans in the same way, but with a slighter bow.

I looked at him in amazement, as well I might, since before me stood the most beautiful man that I had ever seen. He was tall, something over six feet high, and superbly shaped, having a deep chest, a sinewy form, and hands and feet that would have done credit to a Greek statue. His face, too, was wonderful, if rather sombre, perfectly chiselled and almost white in colour, with great dark eyes, and there was something about it that suggested high and ancient blood. He looked, indeed, as though he had just stepped straight out of the bygone ages. He might have been an inhabitant of the lost continent of Atlantis or a sun-burned old Greek, for his hair, which was chestnut brown, curled tightly, even where it hung down upon his shoulders, though none grew upon his chin or about the curved lips. Perhaps he was shaven. In short, he was a glorious specimen of mankind, differing from any other I had seen.

His costume, too, was striking and peculiar, although dilapidated; indeed, it might have been rifled from the body of an Egyptian Pharaoh. It consisted of a linen robe that seemed to be twisted about him, which was broidered at the edges with faded purple, a tall and battered linen headdress shaped like the lower half of a soda-water bottle reversed and coming to a point, a leather apron narrow at the top but broadening towards the knees, also broidered, and sandals of the same material.

I stared at him amazed, wondering whether he belonged to some people unknown to me, or was another of Zikali's illusions, and so did Hans, for his muddy little eyes nearly fell out of his head and he asked me in a whisper:

"Is he a man, Baas, or a spirit?"

For the rest the stranger wore a plain torque or necklet apparently of gold, and about him was girdled a cross-hilted sword with an ivory handle and a red sheath.

For a while this remarkable person stood before us, his hands folded and his head bent in a humble fashion, though it was really I who should have been humble, owing to the physical contrast between us. Apparently he did not think it proper to speak first, while Zikali squatted there grimly, not helping me at all. At last, seeing that something must be done, I rose from the stool upon which I was seated and held out my hand. After a moment's hesitation the splendid stranger took it, but not to shake in the usual fashion, for he bent his head and gently touched my fingers with his lips, as though he were a French courtier and I a pretty lady. I bowed again with the best grace I could command, then putting my hand in my trouser pocket, said, "How do you do?" and as he did not seem to understand, repeated it in the Zulu word, "*Sakubona*." This also failing, I greeted him in the name of the Prophet in my best Arabic.

Here I struck oil, as an American friend of mine named Brother John used to say, for he replied in the same tongue, or something like it. Speaking in a soft and pleasing voice, but without alluding to the Prophet, he addressed me as "Great Lord Macumazahn, whose fame and prowess echo across the earth," and a lot of other nonsense, with which I could see that Zikali had stuffed him, that may be omitted.

"Thank you," I cut in, "thank you, Mr.———?" and I paused.

"My name is Issicore," he said.

"And a very nice name, too, though I never heard one like it," I replied. "Well, Issicore, what can I do for you?" An inadequate remark, I admit, but I wanted to come to the facts.

"Everything," he answered fervently, pressing his hands to his breast. "You can save from death a most beautiful lady who will love you."

"Will she?" I exclaimed. "Then I will have nothing to do with that business, which always leads to trouble."

Here Zikali broke in for the first time, speaking very slowly to Issicore in Zulu, which I remembered he said he had been teaching him, and saying:

"The Lord Macumazahn is already full of woman's love and has no room for more. Speak not to him of love, O Issicore, lest you should anger the ghost of one who haunts this spot, a certain royal Mameena whom once he knew too well."

Now I turned upon Zikali, promising to give him a piece of my mind, when Issicore, smiling a little, repeated:

"Who will love you—as a brother."

"That's better," I said, "though I don't know that I want to take on a sister at my time of life, but I suppose you mean that she will be much obliged?"

"That is so, O Lord. Also the reward will be great."

"Ah!" I replied, really interested. "Now be so good as to tell me exactly what you want."

Well, to cut a long story short, with variations he repeated Zikali's tale. I was to travel to his remote land, bring about the destruction of a nebulous monster, or fetish, or system of religion, and in payment to be given as many diamonds as I could carry.

"But why can't you get rid of your own devil?" I asked. "You look a warrior and are big and strong."

"Lord," he replied gently, spreading out his hands in an appealing fashion, "I am strong and I trust that I am brave, but it cannot be. No man of my people can prevail against the god of my people, if so he may be called. Even to revile him openly would bring a curse upon us; moreover, his priests would murder us——"

"So he has priests?" I interrupted.

"Yes, Lord, the god has priests sworn to his service, evil men as he is evil. O Lord, come, I beseech you, and save Sabeela the beautiful."

"Why are you so interested in this lady?" I asked.

"Lord, because she loves me—not as a brother—and I love her. She, the great Lady of my land and my cousin, is my betrothed and, if the god is not overthrown, as the fairest of all our maidens she will be taken by the god." Here emotion seemed to overcome him, very real emotion, which touched me, for he bowed his head and I saw tears trickle down from his dark eyes.

"Hearken, Lord," he went on, "there is an ancient prophecy in my land that this god of ours, whose hideous shape hides the spirit of a long-dead chief, can only be destroyed by one of another race who can see in the night, some man of great valour destined to be born in due season. Now through our dream-doctors I caused enquiry to be made of this Master of Spirits, who is named Zikali, for I was in despair and knew what must happen at the appointed time. From him I learned that there lived in the south such a man as is spoken of in the prophecy and that his name meant Watcher-by-Night. Then I dared the journey and the curse and came to seek you, and lo! I have found you."

"Yes," I answered, "you have found one whose native name means Watcher-by-Night, but who cannot see in the dark better than any one else, and is not a hero or very brave, but only a trader and a hunter of wild beasts. Yet I tell you, Issicore, that I do not wish to interfere with your gods and priests and tribal matters, or to give battle to some great ape, if it exists, on the chance of earning a pocketful of bright stones should I live to take them away, and of getting a bundle of leaves that this doctor desires. You had better seek some other white man with eyes like a cat's and more strength and courage, Issicore."

"How can I see another when, without doubt, you are the one appointed, Lord? If you will not come, then I return to die with Sabeela, and all is finished."

He paused a few moments, and continued, "Lord, I can offer you little, but is not a good deed its own reward, and will not the memory of it feed your heart through life and death? Because you are noble I beseech you to come, not for what you may gain, but just because you are noble and will save others from cruelty and wrong. I have spoken—choose."

"Why did you not bring Zikali his accursed leaves yourself?" I asked furiously.

"Lord, I could not come to the place where that tree grows in the garden of Heu-Heu; nor, indeed, did I know that this Master of Spirits needed that medicine. Lord, be noble according to your nature, which is known afar."

Now I tell you fellows when I heard this I felt flattered. We all think that we are noble at times, but there are precious few who tell us so, and therefore the thing came as a pleasant surprise from this extraordinarily dignified, handsome and, if it would appear in his own fashion, well-educated son of Ham—if he were a son of Ham. To my mind, he looked more like a prince in disguise, somebody of unknown but highly distinguished race who had walked out of a fairy book. But when I came to think of it, that was exactly what he said he was. Anyway, he was a most discriminating person with a singular insight into character. (It did not occur to me at the moment that Zikali was also a discriminating person with an insight into character which had induced him to bring us two together for secret purposes of his own. Or that, in order to impress me, he had stuffed Issicore with the story of a predestined white man, told of in prophecy, who could see in the dark, as, without doubt, he had done.)

Also the adventure proposed was of an order so wild and unusual that it drew me like a magnet. Supposing that I lived to old age, could I, Allan Quatermain, bear to look back and remember that I had turned down an opportunity of that sort and was departing into the grave without knowing if there was or was not a Heu-Heu who snatched away lovely Andromedas—I mean Sabeelas—off rocks, and combined in his hideous personality the qualities of a god or fetish, a ghost, a devil, and a super-gorilla?

Could I bury my two humble talents of adventure and straight shooting in that fashion? Really, I thought not, for if I did, how could I face my own conscience in those last failing years? And yet there was so much to be said on the other side into which I need not enter. In the end, being unable to make up my mind, I fell into weakness and determined to refer the matter to fate. Yes, I determined to toss up, using Hans for the spinning coin.

"Hans," I said in Dutch, a tongue which neither of the other two understood, "shall we travel to this man's country, or shall we stay in our own? You have heard all; speak and I will accept your judgment. Do you understand?"

"Yes, Baas," said Hans, twirling his hat in his vacant fashion, "I understand that the Baas, as is usual when he is in a deep pit, seeks the wisdom of Hans to get him out—of Hans who has brought him up from a child and taught him most of what he knows; of Hans upon whom his Reverend Father, the Predikant, used to lean as upon a staff, that is, after he had made him into a good Christian. But the matter is important, and before I give my judgment that will settle it one way or another, I would ask a few questions."

Then he wheeled round, and, addressing the patient Issicore in his vile Arabic, said:

"Long Baas with a hooked nose, tell me, do you know the way back to this country of yours, and if so, how much of it can be travelled in a wagon?"

"I do," answered Issicore, "and all of it can be travelled in a wagon until the first range of hills is reached. Also along it there is plenty of game and water, except in the desert of which you have been told. The journey should take about three moons, though, myself alone, I accomplished it in two."

"Good, and if my Baas, Macumazahn, comes to your country, how will he be received?"

"Well by most of the people, but not well by the priests of Heu-Heu, if they think he comes to harm the god, and certainly not well by the Hairy Folk who live in the forest, who are called the Children of the god. With these he must be prepared to war, though the prophecy says that he will conquer all of them."

"Is there plenty to eat in your country, and is there tobacco, and something better than water to drink, Long Baas?"

"There is plenty of all these things. There is wealth of every kind, O Counsellor of the White Lord, and all of them shall be his and yours, though," he added with meaning, "those who have to deal with the priests of the god and the Hairy Folk would do well to drink water, lest they should be found asleep."

"Have you guns there?" Hans asked, pointing to my rifle.

"No, our weapons are swords and spears, and the Hairy Folk shoot with arrows from bows."

Hans ceased from his questions and began to yawn as though he were tired, as he did so, staring up at the sky where some vultures were wheeling.

"Baas," he said, "how many vultures do you see up there? Is it seven or eight? I have not counted them but I think there are seven."

"No, Hans, there are eight; one, the highest, was hid behind a cloud."

"You are quite sure that there are eight, Baas?"

"Quite," I answered angrily. "Why do you ask such silly questions when you can count for yourself?"

Hans yawned again and said, "Then we will go with this fine, hook-nosed Baas to the country of Heu-Heu. That is settled."

"What the deuce do you mean, Hans? What on earth has the number of vultures got to do with the matter?"

"Everything, Baas. You see, the burden of this choice was too heavy for my shoulders, so I lifted my eyes and put up a prayer to your Reverend Father to help me, and in doing so saw the vultures. Then your Reverend Father in the heaven above seemed to say to me, 'If there are an even number of vultures, Hans, then go; if an odd number, then stop where you are. But, Hans, do not count the vultures. Make my son, the Baas Allan, count them, for then he will not be able to grumble at you if things turn out badly whether you go or whether you stay behind, and say that you counted wrong or cheated.' And now, Baas, I have had enough of this, and should like to return to our outspan and examine those new oxen."

I looked at Hans, speechless with indignation. In my cowardice I had left it to his cunning and experience to decide this matter, virtually tossing up, as I have said. And what had the little rascal done? He had concocted one of his yarns about my poor old father and tossed up in his turn, going odd or even on the number of the vultures which he made *me* count! So angry was I that I lifted my foot with meaning, whereon Hans, who had been expecting something of the sort, bolted, and I did not see him again until I got back to the camp.

"Oho! Oho!" laughed Zikali, "Oho!" while the dignified Issicore studied the scene with mild astonishment.

Then I turned on Zikali, saying, "A cheat I have called you before, and a cheat I call you again, with all your nonsense about bat-messengers and the tale you have taught to this man as to a prophecy of his people, and the rest. *There* is the bat who brought the message, or the dream, or the vision, or whatever you like to call it, and all the while he was hidden beneath your eaves," and I pointed to Issicore. "And now I have been tricked into saying that I will go upon this fool's errand, and as I do not turn my back upon my word, go I must."

"Have you, Macumazahn?" asked Zikali innocently. "You talked with Light-in-Darkness in Dutch, which neither I nor this man understood, and therefore we did not know what you said. But, as out of the honesty of your heart you have told us, we understand now, and of course we know, as everyone knows, that your word once spoken is worth all the writings of the white men put together, and that only death or sickness will prevent you from accompanying Issicore to his own country. Oho ho! It has all come about as I would have it, for reasons with which I will not trouble you, Macumazahn."

Now I saw that I was doubly tricked, hit, as it were, with the right barrel by Hans and with the left by Zikali. To tell the truth, I had quite forgotten that he did not understand Dutch, although I remembered it when I began to use that tongue, and that therefore it did not in the least matter what I had said privately to Hans. But if Zikali did not understand Dutch, of which after all I am not so sure, at any rate he understood human nature, and could read thoughts, for he went on:

"Do not boil within yourself, like a pot with a stone on its lid, Macumazahn, because your crafty foot has slipped and you have repeated publicly in one tongue what you had already said secretly in another, and therefore made a promise to both of us. For all the while, Macumazahn, you had made that promise and your white heart would not have suffered you to swallow it again just because we could not hear it with our ears. No, that great white heart of yours would have risen in your throat and shut it fast. So kick away the burning sticks from beneath the water of your anger and let it cease from boiling, and go forth as you have promised, to see wonderful things and do wonderful deeds and snatch the pure and innocent out of the hands of evil gods or men."

"Yes, and burn my fingers, scooping your porridge out of the blazing pot, Zikali," I said with a snort.

"Perhaps, Macumazahn, perhaps, for if I had no porridge to be saved, should I have taken all this trouble? But what does that matter to you, to the brave White Lord who seeks the truth as a thrown spear seeks the heart of the foe? You will find plenty of truth yonder, Macumazahn, new truth, and what does it matter if the spear is a little red after it has reached the heart of things? It can be cleaned again, Macumazahn, it can be cleaned, and amidst many other services, you will have done one to your old friend, Zikali the Cheat."

Here Allan glanced at the clock and stopped.

"I say—do you know what time it is?" he said. "Twenty minutes past one—by the head of Chaka. If you fellows want to finish the story to-night, you can do so for yourselves according to taste. I'm off, or out shooting to-morrow I shan't hit a haystack sitting."

CHAPTER VI

THE BLACK RIVER

On the following evening, pleasantly tired after a capital day's shooting and a good dinner, once more the four of us—Curtis, Good, myself (the Editor) and old Allan—were gathered round the fire in his comfortable den at "The Grange."

"Now then, Allan," I said, "get on with your tale."

"What tale?" he asked, pretending to forget, for he was always a bad starter where his own reminiscences were concerned.

"That about the monkey-man and the fellow who looked like Apollo," answered Good. "I dreamt about it all night, and that I rescued the lady—a dark girl dressed in blue—and that just as I was about to receive a well-earned kiss of thanks, she changed her mind and turned into stone."

"Which is just what she would have done if she had any sense in her head and you were concerned, Good," said Allan severely, adding, "Perhaps it was your dream that made you shoot more vilely than usual to-day. I saw you miss eight cock pheasants in succession at that last corner."

"And I saw you kill eighteen in succession at the first," replied Good cheerily, "so you see the average was all right. Now then, get on with the romance. I like romance in the evening after a dose of the hard facts of life in the shape of impossible cock pheasants."

"Romance!" began Allan indignantly. "Am I romantic? Pray do not confuse me with yourself, Good."

Here I intervened imploring him not to waste time in arguing with Good, who was unworthy of his notice, and at last, mollified, he began.

Now I am in a hurry and want to be done with this job that dries up my throat—who, having lived so much alone, am not used to talking like a politician—and makes me drink more whisky and water than I ought. You are in a hurry, too, all of you, especially Good, who wants to get to the end of the story in order that he may argue about it and try to show that he would have managed much better, and you, my friend, because you have to leave to-morrow morning early and must see to your packing before you get to bed. Therefore, I am going to skip a lot, all about our journey, for instance, although, in fact, it was one of the most interesting treks I ever made, and for much of the way through a country that was quite new to me, about which one might write a book.

I will simply say, therefore, that in due course after some necessary delay to re-pack the wagon, leaving behind all articles that were not wanted in Zikali's charge, we trekked from the Black Kloof. The oxen that I had bought—on credit—from Zikali were in the yokes, and we drove with us his two extra beasts as well as four of the best of my old team to serve as spares.

Also I took, in addition to my own driver and voorlooper, Mavoon and Induka, two other Zulus, Zikali's servants, who I knew would be faithful because they feared their terrible master, although I knew also that they would spy upon me and, if ever they returned alive, make report of everything to him.

Well, leaving out all the details of this remarkable trek in which we met with no fighting, disasters, or great troubles and always had plenty to eat, game being numerous throughout, I will take up the tale on our arrival, safe and sound, at the first line of hills that I show upon the map, of which Zikali had spoken as bordering the desert. Here we were obliged to leave the wagon, for it was impossible to get it over the hills or through the desert beyond.

This, fortunately, we were able to do at a little village of peaceable folk who lived in a charming and well-watered situation, and, having no near neighbours, were able to cultivate their lands unmolested. I placed it in the charge of Mavoon and Induka, whom I could trust and who would not run away, also the oxen, of which, by good fortune, we had only lost three. With them, as Issicore declared that we must go on alone, I left Zikali's servants, knowing that they would keep an eye on my men, and my men on them, and promised the headman of the village a good present if we found everything safe on our return.

He said that he would do his best, but added impressively—he was a melancholy person—that if we were going to the country of Heu-Heu we never should return, as it was a land of devils. In that event he asked what was to happen to the wagon and goods. I replied that I had given orders that if I did not reappear within a year, it was to trek back to whence we came and announce that we were gone, but that he need not be afraid as, being a great magician, I knew that we should be back long before that time.

He shrugged his shoulders, looking doubtfully at Issicore, and there the conversation ended. However, I persuaded him to lend us three of his people to guide us across the mountains and to carry water through the desert on the understanding that they should be allowed to return as soon as we sighted the swamp. Nothing would induce them to go nearer to the country of Heu-Heu.

So in due course off we started, leaving Mavoon and Induka almost in tears, for the gloom of the headman had spread to them and they too believed that they would see us no more. Hans, it is true, they never would have missed, since they hated him as he hated them, but in my case the matter was different because they loved me in their own way.

Our baggage was light: rifles (I took a double-barrelled Express), as much ammunition as we could manage, some medicines, blankets, etc., a few spare clothes and boots for myself, a couple of revolvers and as many vessels of one sort or another as possible to carry water, including two paraffin tins slung at either end of a piece of wood after the fashion of a milkman's yoke. Also we had tobacco, a good supply of matches, candles, and a bundle of dried biltong to eat in case we found no game. It doesn't sound much, but before we got across that desert I felt inclined to throw away half of it; indeed, I don't think we could have got the stuff over the mountain pass, which proved to be precipitous, without the assistance of the three water-bearers.

It took us twelve hours to reach and cross that mountain's crest, just beneath which we camped, and another six to descend the other side next day. At its foot was thin, tussocky grass with occasional thorn trees growing in a barren veldt that by degrees merged into desert. By the last water we camped for the second night; then, having filled up all our vessels, started out into the arid, sandy wilderness.

Now, you fellows know what an African desert is, for we went through a worse one than this on our journey to Solomon's Mines. Still, the particular specimen I am speaking of was pretty bad. To begin with, the heat was tremendous. Then, in parts, it consisted of rolling slopes or waves of sand, up which we must scramble and down which we must slide—a most exhausting process. Further, there grew in it a variety of thick-leaved plant with sharp spines that, if touched, caused a painful soreness, which abominable and useless growths made it impossible to travel at night, or even if the light were low, when they could not be seen and avoided.

We spent three days crossing that wretched desert, that had another peculiarity. Here and there in its waste, columns of stones, polished by blowing sand, stood up like obelisks, sometimes in one piece, monoliths, and sometimes in several, piled on each other. I suppose that they were the remains of strata: hard cores that had resisted the action of wind and water, which in the course of thousands or millions of years had worn away the softer rock, grinding it to dust.

Those obelisk-like columns gave a very strange appearance to that wilderness, suggesting the idea of monuments; also, incidentally, they were useful, since it was by them that our water-bearing guides, who were accustomed to haunt the place to kill ostriches or to steal their eggs, steered their path. Of these ostriches we saw a good number, which showed that the desert could not be so very wide, since in it there seemed to be nothing for them to live on, unless they ate the prickly plants. There was no other life in the place.

Fortunately, by dint of economy and self-denial, our water held out, until on the afternoon of the third day, as we trudged along parched and weary, from the crest of one of the sand waves we saw far off a patch of dense green that marked the end, or, rather, the beginning, of the swamp. Now our agreement with the guides was that when they came in sight of this swamp they should return, for which purpose we had saved some of the water for them to drink on their homeward journey.

After a brief consultation, however, they determined to come on with us, and when I asked why, wheeled round and pointed to dense clouds that were gathering in the heavens behind us. These clouds, they explained, foretold a sand tempest in which no man could live in the desert. Therefore they urged us forward at all speed; indeed, exhausted as we were, we covered the last three miles between us and the edge of the swamp at a run. As we reached the reeds the storm burst, but still we plunged forward through them, till we came to a spot where they grew densely and where, by digging pits in the mud with our hands, we could get water which, thick as it was, we drank greedily. Here we crouched for hours while the storm raged.

It was a terrific sight, for now the face of the desert behind was hidden by clouds of driven sand, which even among the reeds fell upon us thickly, so that occasionally we had to rise to shake its weight off us. Had we still been in the desert, we should have been buried alive. As it was we escaped, though half choked and with our skins fretted by the wear of the particles of sand.

So we squatted all night till before dawn the storm ceased and the sun rose in a perfectly clear sky. Having drunk more water, of which we seemed to need enormous quantities, we struggled back to the edge of the swamp and from the crest of a sand wave looked about us. Issicore stretched out his arm towards the north and touched me on the shoulder. I looked, and far away, staining the delicate blue of the heavens, perceived a dark, mushroom-shaped patch of vapour.

"It is a cloud," I said. "Let us go back to the reeds; the storm is returning."

"No, Lord," he answered, "it is the smoke from the Fire Mountain of my country."

I studied it and said nothing, reflecting, however, that in this particular, at any rate, Zikali had not lied. If so, was it not possible that he had spoken truth about other matters also? If there existed a volcano as yet unreported by any explorer, might there not also be a buried city filled with petrified people, and even a Heu-Heu? No, in Heu-Heu I could not believe.

Here, after they had filled themselves and their gourds with water, the three natives from the village left us, saying that they would go no farther and that they could now depart safely as the sandstorm would not return for some weeks. They added that our magic must be very strong, since had we delayed even for a few hours we should certainly all have been killed.

So they departed, and we camped by the reeds, hoping to rest after our exhausting journey. In this, however, we were disappointed, for as soon as the sun went down we became aware that this vast area of swampy land was the haunt of countless game that came thither, I suppose, from all the country round in order to drink and to fill themselves with its succulent growths.

By the light of the moon I saw great herds of elephants appearing out of the shadows and marching majestically towards the water. Also there were troops of buffalo, some of which broke out of the reeds showing that they had hidden there during the day, and almost every kind of antelope in plenty, while in the morass itself we could hear sea cows wallowing and grunting, and great splashes which I suppose were caused by frightened crocodiles leaping into pools.

Nor was this all, since so much animal life upon which they could prey attracted many lions that coughed and roared and slew according to their nature. Whenever one of them sprang on to some helpless buck, a stampede of all the game in the neighbourhood would follow.

The noise they made crashing through the reeds was terrific, so much so that sleep was impossible. Moreover, there was always a possibility that the lions might be tempted to try a change of diet and eat us, especially as we had no bushes with which to form a *boma*, or fence. So we made a big fire of dry, last year's reeds, of which, fortunately, there were many standing near, and kept watch.

Once or twice I saw the long shape of a lion pass us, but I did not fire for fear lest I should wound the beast only and perhaps cause it to charge. In short, the place was a veritable sportsman's paradise, and yet quite useless from a hunter's point of view, since, if he killed elephants, it would be impossible to carry the ivory across the desert, and only a boy desires to slaughter game in order to leave it to rot. At dawn, it is true, I did shoot a reed buck for food, which was the only shot I fired.

As amidst all this hubbub the idea of sleep must be abandoned, I took the opportunity to question Issicore about his country and what lay before us there. During our journey I had not talked much to him on the matter, since he seemed very silent and reserved, all his energies being concentrated upon pushing forward as quickly as possible; also, there was no object in doing so while we were still far away. Now, however, I thought that the time had come for a talk.

In answer to my queries, he said that if we travelled hard, by marching round the narrow western end of the swamp, in three days we should arrive at the mouth of the gorge down which the river ran that flowed through the mountains surrounding his country. These mountains, I should add, we had sighted as a black line in the distance almost as soon as we entered the desert, which showed that they were high. Here, if we reached it without accident, he hoped to find a boat waiting in which we could be paddled to his town, though why anybody should be expecting us I could not elicit from him.

Leaving that question unsolved, I asked him about this town and its inhabitants. He replied that it was large and contained a great number of people, though not so many as it used to do in bygone generations. The race was dwindling, partly from intermarriage and partly because of the terror in which they lived, that made the women unwilling to bear children lest these should be snatched away by the Hairy Folk who dwelt in the surrounding forest, or perhaps sacrificed to the god himself. I inquired whether he really believed that there was such a god, and he replied with earnestness that certainly he did, as once he had seen him, though from some way off, and he was so awful that description was impossible. I must judge of him for myself when we met—an occasion that I began to wish might be avoided.

I cross-examined him persistently about this god, but with small result, for the subject seemed to be one on which he did not care to dwell. I gathered, however, that he, Issicore, had been in a canoe when he saw Heu-Heu on a rock at dawn, surrounded by women, upon the occasion of some sacrifice, and that he had not looked much at him because he was afraid to do so. He noted, however, that he was taller than a man and walked stiffly. He added that Heu-Heu never came to the mainland, though his priests did.

Then, dropping the subject of Heu-Heu, he went on to tell me of the system of government amongst the Walloos, which, it appeared, was an hereditary chieftainship that could be held either by men or women. The present chief, an old man, like the people was named Walloo, as indeed were all the chiefs of the tribe in succession, for "Walloo" was really a title which he thought had come with them from whatever land they inhabited in the dark, forgotten ages. He had but one child living, a daughter, the lady Sabeela, of whom he had spoken to me at the hut of the Opener-of-Roads, she who was doomed to sacrifice. He, Issicore, was her second cousin, being descended from the brother of her grandfather, and therefore of the pure Walloo blood.

"Then if this lady died, I suppose you would be the chief, Issicore?" I said.

"Yes, Lord, by descent," he answered; "yet perhaps not so. There is another power in the land greater than that of the kings or chiefs—the power of the priests of Heu-Heu. It is their purpose, Lord, should Sabeela die, to seize the chieftainship for themselves. A certain Dacha, who is also of the pure Walloo blood, is the chief priest, and he has sons to follow him."

"Then it is to this Dacha's interest that Sabeela should die?"

"It is to his interest, Lord, that she should die and I also, or, better still, both of us together, for then his part would be clear."

"But what of her father, the Walloo? He cannot desire the death of his only child."

"Nay, Lord, he loves her much and desires that she should marry me. But, as I have said, he is an old man and terror-haunted. He fears the god, who already has taken one of his daughters; he fears the priests, who are the oracles of the god, and, it is said, murdered his son as they have striven to murder me. Therefore, being frozen by fear, he is powerless, and without his leadership none can act, since all must be done in the name of the Walloo and by his authority. Yet it was he also who sent me to seek for help from the great wizard of the South with whom he and his fathers have had dealings in bygone years. Yes, because of the ancient prophecy that the god could only be overthrown and the tyranny of the priests be broken by a white man from the South, he sent me, who am the betrothed of his daughter, secretly and without the knowledge of Dacha, and because of Sabeela I dared the curse and went, for which deed perchance I must pay dearly. He it is also who watches for my return."

"And if he exists, which you have not proved to me, how am I to kill this god, Issicore? By shooting him?"

"I do not know, Lord. It is believed that he cannot be harmed by weapons, over whom only fire and water have power, since legend tells that he came out of the fire and certainly he lives surrounded by water. The prophecy does not say how he will be killed by the stranger from the South."

Now, listening to this weird talk in that wild-beast-peopled wilderness from the mouth of a man who evidently was very frightened, and wearied as I was, I confess that I grew frightened also, and wished most heartily that I had never been beguiled into this adventure. Probably the terrible god, of whom I could learn no details, question as I would, was nothing but an invention of the priests, or perhaps one of their number disguised. But, however this might be, no doubt I was travelling to a fetish-ridden land in which witchcraft and murder were rampant; in short, one of Satan's peculiar possessions. Yes, I, Allan Quatermain, was brought here to play the part of a modern Hercules and clean out this Augean stable of bloodshed and superstitions, to say nothing of fighting the lion in the shape of Heu-Heu, always supposing that there was a Heu-Heu, a creature taller than a man that "walked stiffly," whom Issicore believed he had once seen from a distance at dawn.

However, I was in for it, and to show fear would be as useless as it was undignified, since, unless I turned and ran back into the desert, which my pride would never suffer me to do, I could see no escape. Having put my hand to the plough I must finish the furrow. So I sat silent, making no comment upon Issicore's rather nebulous information. Only after a while I asked him casually when this sacrifice was to take place, to which he replied with evident agitation:

"On the night of the full harvest moon, which is this moon, fourteen days from now; wherefore we must hurry, since at best it will take us five days to reach the town of Walloo, three in travelling round the swamp and two upon the river. Do not delay, Lord, I pray you do not delay, lest we should be too late and find Sabeela gone."

"No," I answered, "I shall not be late, and I can assure you, my friend Issicore, that the sooner I am through with this business one way or another, the better I shall be pleased. And now that all those beasts in the swamp seem to have grown a little quieter I will try to go to sleep."

Happily I was successful in this effort and obtained several hours' sound rest, which I needed sorely, before the sun appeared and Hans woke me. I rose, and, taking my rifle, shot a fat reed-buck, which I selected out of a number which stood quite close by, a young female off which we breakfasted, for, as you know, if the meat of antelopes is cooked before it grows cold it is often as tender as though it had been hung for a week. The odd thing was that the sound of the shot did not seem to disturb the other beasts at all; evidently they had never heard anything of the sort before, and thought that their companion was just lying down.

An hour later we started on our long tramp round the edge of that swamp. I did not like to march before for fear lest we should get into complications with the herds of elephants and other animals that were trekking out of it in all directions with the light, though where they went to feed I am sure I do not know. In all my life I never saw such quantities of game as had collected in this place, which probably furnished the only water for many miles round.

However, as I have said, it was of no use to us, and therefore our object was to keep as clear of it as possible. Even then we stumbled right on to a sleeping white rhinoceros with the longest horn that ever I saw. It must have measured nearly six feet, and anywhere else would have been a great prize. Fortunately the wind was blowing from it to us, so it did not smell us and charged off in another direction, for, as you know, the rhinoceros is almost blind.

Now I am not going to give all the details of that interminable trudge through sand, for in the mud of the swamp we could not walk at all. During the day we were scorched by the heat and at night we were tormented by mosquitoes and disturbed by the noise of the game and the roaring of lions, which fortunately, being so full fed, never molested us. By the third night, bearing always to the right, we had come quite close to the mountain range, which, although it was not so very lofty, seemed to be absolutely precipitous, faced, indeed, by sheer cliffs that rose to a height of from five to eight hundred feet. To what extraordinary geological conditions these black cliffs and the desert by which they were surrounded owe their origin, I am sure I do not know, but there they were, and no doubt are.

Before sunset on this third day, by Issicore's direction, we collected a huge pile of dried reeds, which we set upon the crest of a sand mound, and after dark fired them, so that for a quarter of an hour or so they burned in a bright column of flame. Issicore gave no explanation of this proceeding, but as Hans remarked, doubtless it was a signal to his friends. Next morning, at his request, we started on before the dawn, taking our chances of meeting with elephants or buffaloes, and at sunrise found ourselves right under the cliffs.

An hour later, following a little bay in them where there was no swamp, because here the ground rose, of a sudden we turned a corner and perceived a tall, white-robed man with a big spear standing upon a rock, evidently keeping a look-out. As soon as he saw us he leapt down from his rock with the agility of a *klip-springer* and came towards us.

After one curious glance at me he went straight to Issicore, knelt down and, taking his hand, pressed it to his forehead, which showed me that our guide was a venerated person. Then they conversed together in low tones, after which Issicore came to me and said that so far all was well, as our fire had been seen and a big canoe awaited us. We went on, guided by the sentry, and after one turn suddenly came on quite a large river, which had been hidden by the reeds. To the left appeared this deep, slow-flowing river; to the right, within a hundred paces, indeed, it changed into swamp or morass, of which the pools were fringed with very tall and beautiful papyrus plants, such open water as there was being almost covered by every kind of wild fowl that rose in flocks with a deafening clamour. This stream, the Black River, as the Walloos called it, was bordered on either side by precipices through which I suppose it had cut its way in the course of millenniums, so high and impending that they seemed almost to meet above, leaving the surface of the water nearly dark. It was a stream gloomy as the Roman Styx, and, glancing at it, I half expected to see Charon and his boat approaching to row us to the Infernal fields. Indeed, into my mind there floated a memory of the poet's lines, which I hope I quote correctly:

In Kubla Khan a river ran Through caverns measureless to man, Down to a sunless sea.

I confess honestly that the aspect of the place filled me with fear: it was forbidding—indeed, unholy—and I marvelled what kind of a sunless sea lay beyond this hell gate. Had I been alone, or with Hans only, I admit that I should have turned tail and marched back round that swamp, upon which, at any rate, the sun shone, and, if I could, across the desert beyond to where I had left the wagon. But in the presence of the stately Issicore and his myrmidon, this I could not do because of my white man's pride. No, I must go on to the end, whatever it might be.

If I was frightened, Hans was much more so, for his teeth began to chatter with terror.

"Oh, Baas," he said, "if this is the door, what will the house beyond be like?"

"That we shall learn in due course," I answered, "so there is no good in thinking about it."

"Follow me, Lord," said Issicore, after some further talk with his companion.

I did so, accompanied by Hans, who stuck to me as closely as possible. We advanced round the rock and discovered a little indent in the bank of the river where a great canoe, hollowed apparently from a single huge tree, or rather its prow, was drawn up on the sandy shore. In this canoe sat sixteen rowers or paddle-men—I remember there were sixteen of them because at the time Hans remarked that the number was the same as that of a wagon team and subsequently called these paddlers "water oxen."

As we approached they lifted their paddles in salute, apparently of Issicore, since of me and my companion, except by swift, surreptitious glances, they took no notice.

With a kind of silent, unobtrusive haste Issicore caused our small baggage, which consisted chiefly of cartridge bags, to be stowed away in the prow of the canoe that for a few feet was hollowed out in such a fashion that it made a kind of cupboard roofed with solid wood, and showed us where to sit. Next he entered it himself, while the lookout man ran down the canoe and took hold of the steering oar.

Then at a word all the paddlers back-watered and the craft slid off the sandy beach into the river which was full to the banks, almost in flood indeed. It seemed that here the rain had been nearly incessant for some months and the lowering sky showed that ere long there was much more to come.

CHAPTER VII

THE WALLOO

In perfect stillness, except for the sound of the dipping of the paddles in the water, we glided away very swiftly up the placid river. I think that nothing upon this strange journey, or at any rate during the first part of it, struck me more than its quietness. The water was still, flowing peacefully between its rocky walls towards the desert in which it would be lost, just as the life of some good man flows towards death. The rocky precipices on either side were still; they were so steep that on them nothing which breathed could find a footing, except bats, perhaps, that do not stir in the daytime. The riband of grey sky above us was still, though occasionally a draught of air blew between the cliffs with a moaning noise, such as one might imagine to be caused by the passing wind of spiritual wings. But stillest of all were those rowers who for hour after hour laboured at their task in silence, and with a curious intentness, or, if speak they must, did so only in a whisper.

Gradually an impression of nightmare stole over me; I felt as though I were a sleeper taking part in the drama of a dream. Perhaps, in fact, this was so, since I was very tired, having rested but little for a good many nights and laboured hard during the day trudging through the sand with a heavy rifle and a load of cartridges upon my back. So really I may have been in a doze, such as is easily induced in any circumstances by the sound of lapping water. If so, it was not a pleasant dream, for the titanic surroundings in which I found myself and the dread possibilities of the whole enterprise oppressed my spirit with a sensation of departure from the familiar things of life into something unholy and unknown.

Soon the cliffs grew so high and the light so faint that I could only just see the stern, handsome faces of the rowers appearing as they bent forward to their ordered stroke, and vanishing into the gloom as they leant back after it was accomplished. The very regularity of the effort produced a kind of mesmeric effect which was unpleasant. The faces looked to me like those of ghosts peeping at one through cracks of the curtains round a bed, then vanishing, continually to return and peep again.

I suppose that at last I went to sleep in good earnest. It was a haunted sleep, however, for I dreamed that I was entering into some dim Hades where all realities had been replaced by shadows, strengthless but alarming.

At length I was awakened by the voice of Issicore, saying that we had come to the place where we must rest for the night, as it was impossible to travel in the dark and the rowers were weary. Here the cliffs widened out a little, leaving a strip of shore upon either side of the river, upon which we landed. By the last light that struggled to us from the line of sky above we ate such food as we had, supplemented by biscuits of a sort that were carried in the canoe, for no fire was lighted. Before we had finished, dense darkness fell upon us, for the moonbeams were not strong enough to penetrate into that place, so that there was nothing to be done except lie down upon the sand and sleep with the wailing of the night air between the cliffs for lullaby.

The night passed somehow. It seemed so long that I began to think or dream that I must be dead and waiting for my next incarnation, and when occasionally I half woke up, was only reassured by hearing Hans at my side muttering prayers in his sleep to my old father, of which the substance was that he should be provided with a half-gallon bottle of gin! At last a star that shone in the black riband far above vanished and the riband turned blue, or, rather, grey, which showed that it was dawn. We rose and stumbled into the canoe, for it was impossible to see where to place our feet, and started. Within a few hundred yards of our sleeping place suddenly the cliffs that hemmed in the river widened out, so that now they rose at a distance of a mile or more from either bank of flat, water-levelled land.

These banks, which here were steep, were clothed with great, dark-coloured, spreading trees of which the boughs projected far over the water and cut off the light almost as much as the precipices had done lower down the stream. Thus we travelled in gloom, especially as the sun was not yet up. Presently through this gloom, to which my trained eyes had grown accustomed, I thought that I caught sight of tall, dark-hued figures moving between the trees. Sometimes these figures seemed to stand upright and walk upon their feet, and sometimes to run swiftly upon all fours.

"Look, Hans," I whispered—everyone whispered in that place—"there are baboons!"

"Baboons, Baas!" he answered. "Were ever baboons such a size? No, they are devils."

Now from behind me Issicore also whispered:

"They are the Hairy Men who dwell in the forest, Lord. Be silent, I pray you, lest they should attack us."

Then he began to consult with the rowers in low tones, apparently as to whether we should go on or turn back. Finally we went on, paddling at a double pace. A moment later a sound arose in that dim forest, a sound of indescribable weirdness that was half an animal grunt and half a human cry, which to my ears shaped itself into the syllables, "*Heu-Heu!*" In an instant it was taken up upon all sides, and from everywhere came this wail of "*Heu-Heu!*" which was so horrid to hear that my hair stood up even straighter than usual. Listening to it, I understood whence came the name of the god I had travelled so far to visit.

Nor was this all, for there followed heavy splashes in the water, like to those made by plunging crocodiles, and in the deep shadow beneath the spreading trees I saw hideous heads swimming towards us.

"The Hairy Folk have smelt us," whispered Issicore again, in a voice that I thought perturbed. "Do nothing, Lord; they are very curious. Perhaps when they have looked they will go away."

"And if they don't?" I asked—a question to which he returned no answer.

The canoe was steered over towards the left bank and driven forward at great speed with all the strength of the rowers. Now in the space of open water, upon which the light began to shine more strongly, I saw a beast-like, bearded head that yet undoubtedly was human, yellow-eyed, thick-lipped, with strong, gleaming teeth, coming towards us at the speed of a very strong swimmer, for it had entered the water above us and was travelling downstream. It reached us, lifted up a powerful arm that was completely covered with brown hair like to that of a monkey, caught hold of the gunwale of the boat just opposite to where I sat, and reared its shoulders out of the water, thereby showing me that its great body was for the most part also covered with long hair.

Now its other hand was also on the gunwale, and it stood in the water, resting on its arms, the hideous head so close to me that its stinking breath blew into my face. Yes, there it stood and jabbered at me. I confess that I was terrified who never before had seen a creature like this. Still, for a while I sat quiet.

Then of a sudden I felt that I could bear no more, who believed that the brute was about to get into the boat, or perhaps to drag me out of it. I lost control of myself, and drawing my heavy hunting-knife—the one you see on the wall there, friends—I struck at the hand that was nearest. The blow fell upon the fingers and cut one of them right off so that it fell into the canoe. With an appalling yell the man or beast let go and plunged into the water, where I saw him waving his bleeding hand above his head.

Issicore began to say something to me in frightened tones, but just then Hans ejaculated:

"*Allemaghter!* here's another!" and a second huge head and body reared itself up, this time on his side.

"Do nothing!" I heard Issicore exclaim. But the appearance of the creature was too much for Hans, who drew his revolver and fired two shots in rapid succession into its body. It also tumbled back into the water, where it began to wallow, screaming, but in a thinner voice. I thought, and rightly, that it must be female.

Before the echo of the shots had died away there rose another hideous chorus of *Heu-Heus* and other cries, all of them savage and terrible. From both banks more of the creatures precipitated themselves into the water, but luckily not to attack us because they were too much occupied with the plight of their companion. They congregated round her and dragged her to the shore. Yes, I saw them lift the body out of the stream, for by this time I was sure from its hanging arms and legs that it was dead, an act which showed me that although they had the shape and the covering of beasts, in fact they were human.

"Elephants will do as much," interrupted Curtis.

"Yes," said Allan, "that is true. Sometimes they will; I have seen it twice. But everything about the behaviour of those Hairy Men was human. For instance, their wailing over the dead, which was dreadful and reminded me of the tales of banshees. Moreover, I had not far to look for proof. At my feet lay the finger that I had cut off. It was a human finger, only very thick, short, and covered with hair, having the nail worn down, too, doubtless in climbing trees and grubbing for roots."

Even then with a shock I realized that I had stumbled on the Missing Link, or something that resembled it very strongly. Here in this unknown spot still survived a people such as were our forefathers hundreds of thousands or millions of years ago. Also I reflected that I ought to be proud, for I had made a great discovery, although, to tell the truth, just then I should have been quite willing to resign its glory to someone else.

After this I began to reflect upon other things, for a large jagged stone whizzed within an inch of my head, and presently was followed by a rude arrow tipped with fish bone that stuck in the side of the canoe.

Amidst a shower of these missiles, which fortunately, beyond a bruise or two, did us no harm, we headed out into mid-stream again where they could not reach us, and as no more of the Hairy People swam from the banks to cut us off, soon were pursuing our way in peace. For once, however, the imperturbable Issicore was much disturbed. He came forward and sat by me and said:

"A very evil thing has happened, Lord. You have declared war upon the Hairy Men and the Hairy Men never forget. It will be war to the end."

"I can't help it," I answered feebly, for I was sick with the sight and sound of those creatures. "Are there many of them, and are they all over your country?"

"A good many, perhaps a thousand or more, Lord, but they only live in the forests. You must never go into the forest, Lord, at any rate, not alone; or on to the island where Heu-Heu lives, for he is their king and keeps some of them about him."

"I have no present intention of doing so," I answered.

Now, as we went, the cliffs receded farther and farther from the river, till at length they ceased altogether. We were through the lip of the mountains, if I may so call it, and had entered a stretch of unbroken virgin forest, a veritable sea of great trees that occupied the rich land of the plain and grew to an enormous size and tallness. Moreover, before us appeared clearly the cone of the volcano, broad but of no great height, over which hung the mushroom-shaped cloud of smoke.

All day long we travelled up this tranquil river, rejoicing in the comparative brightness in its centre, although, of course, the trees upon either edge overhung it much.

Late in the afternoon a bend of the banks brought us within sight of a great sheet of water from which apparently the river issued, although, as I learned afterwards, it flowed into it upon the other side, from I know not whence. This lake—for it was a big lake many miles in circumference—surrounded an island of considerable size, in the centre of which rose the volcano, now a mere grey-hued mountain that looked quite harmless, although over it hung that ominous cloud of smoke which, oddly enough, one could not see issuing from its crest. I suppose that it must have gone up in steam and condensed into smoke above. At the foot of the mountain, upon a plain between it and the lake, with the help of my glasses I could see what looked like buildings of some size, constructed of black stone or lava.

"They are ruins," said Issicore, who had observed that I was examining them. "Once the great city of my forefathers stood yonder until the fire from the mountain destroyed it."

"Then does nobody live on the island now?" I asked.

"The priests of Heu-Heu live there, Lord. Also Heu-Heu himself lives there in a great cave upon the farther side of the mountain, or so it is said, for none of us has ever visited that cave, and with him some of the Hairy People who are his servants. My grandfather did so, however, and saw him there. Indeed, as I have told you, once I saw him myself; but what he looked like you must not ask me, Lord, for I do not remember," he added hastily. "In front of the cave is his garden, where grows the magic tree of which the Master of Spirits yonder in the South desires leaves to mix with his medicines; the tree that gives dreams with long life and vision."

"Does Heu-Heu eat of this tree?" I asked.

"I do not know, but I know that he eats the flesh of beasts, because of these we must make offerings to him, and sometimes of men, or so it is said. Near the foot of the garden burn the eternal fires, and between them is the rock upon which the offerings are made."

Now I thought to myself I should much like to see this place of which it was evident that Issicore knew or would tell very little, where there was a great cave in which dwelt a reputed demon with his slaves and hierophants; and where too grew a tree supposed to be magical, flanked by eternal fires. What were these eternal fires, I wondered. I could only suppose that they had something to do with the volcano.

As it happened, however, whilst I was preparing to question Issicore upon the subject, we passed round a tree-clad headland, for here the river had widened into a kind of estuary, and on the shore of the bay beyond it discovered a town of considerable size, covering several hundred acres of ground. The houses of this town, most of which stood in their own gardens, though some of the smaller ones were arranged in streets, had an Eastern appearance, inasmuch as they were low and flat-roofed.

Only there was this difference: Eastern houses of the primitive sort as a rule are whitewashed, but these were all black, being built of lava, as I discovered afterwards. All round the town also, except on the lake side, ran a high wall likewise of black stone, the presence of which excited my curiosity and caused me to inquire its object.

"It is to defend us from the Hairy Folk who attack by night," answered Issicore. "In the daylight they never come, and therefore our fields beyond are not walled," and he pointed to a great stretch of cultivated land that I suppose had been cleared of trees, which extended for miles into the surrounding forest.

Then he went on to explain that they laboured there while the sun was up and at nightfall returned to the town, except certain of them who slept in forts or blockhouses to guard the crops and cattle kraals.

Now I looked at this place and thought to myself that never in my life had I seen one more gloomy, especially in the late afternoon under a sullen, rain-laden sky. The black houses, the high black walls that reminded me of a prison, the black waters of the lake, the outlook on to the black volcano and the black mass of the forest behind, all contributed to this effect.

"Oh, Baas, if I lived here I should soon go mad!" said Hans, and upon my word, I agreed with him.

Now we paddled towards the shore, and presently ran alongside a little jetty formed of stones loosely thrown together, on which we landed. Evidently our approach had been observed, for a number of people—forty or fifty of them, perhaps—were collected at the shore end of the jetty awaiting us. A glance showed me that although of varying ages and both sexes, in type they all resembled our guide, Issicore. That is to say, they were tall, well-shaped, light-coloured and extremely handsome, also clothed in white robes, while some of the men wore hats of the Pharaonic type that I have described. The women's headdress, however, consisted of a close-fitting linen cap with lappets hanging down on either side, and was extraordinarily becoming to their severe cast of beauty. From what race could this people have sprung, I wondered. I had not the faintest idea; to me they looked like the survivals of some ancient civilization.

Conducted by Issicore, we advanced, carrying our scanty baggage, a forlorn and battered little company. As we drew near, the crowd separated into two lines, men to the right and women to the left, like the congregation in a very high church, and stood quite silent, watching us intently with their large, melancholy eyes. Never a word did they say as we passed between them, only watched and watched till I felt quite nervous. They did not even offer any greeting to Issicore, although it seemed to me that he had earned one after his long and dangerous journey.

I observed, however, although at the time I took little notice of the matter, and afterwards forgot all about it until Hans brought the circumstance back to my mind, that a certain dark man of austere countenance, clothed rather differently from the rest, approached Issicore, addressed him, and thrust something into his hand. Issicore glanced at this object, whatever it might be, and distinctly I saw him tremble and turn pale. Then he hid it away, saying nothing.

Turning to the right, we marched along a roadway that bordered the lake, which was constructed about twelve feet above its level, perhaps to serve as a protection against inundation, till we came to a wall in which was a door built of solid balks of wood. This door opened as we approached, and, passing it, we found ourselves in a large garden cultivated with taste and refinement, for in it were beds of flowers, the only cheerful thing I ever saw in this town that, it appeared, was named Walloo after the tribe or its ruler. At the end of the garden stood a long, solid, flat-roofed house built of the prevailing lava rock.

Entering, we found ourselves in a spacious room which, as dusk was gathering, was lit with cresset-like lamps of elegant shape placed upon pedestals cut from great tusks of ivory.

In the centre of this room were two large chairs made of ebony and ivory with high backs and footstools, and in these chairs sat a man and a woman who were well worth seeing. The man was old, for his silver hair hung down upon his shoulders, and his fine, sad face was deeply wrinkled.

At a glance I saw that he must be the king or chief, because of his dignified if somewhat senile appearance. Moreover, his robes, with their purple borders, had a royal look, and about his neck he wore a heavy chain of what seemed to be gold, while in his hand was a black staff tipped with gold, no doubt his sceptre. For the rest, his eyes had a rather frightened air, and his whole aspect gave an idea of weakness and indecision.

The woman sat in the other chair with the light from one of the lamps shining full upon her, and I knew at once that she must be the Lady Sabeela, the love of Issicore. No wonder that he loved her, for she was beautiful exceedingly; tall, well developed, straight as a reed, great-eyed, with chiselled features that were yet rounded and womanly, and wonderfully small hands and feet. She, too, wore purple-bordered robes. About her waist hung a girdle thickly sewn with red stones that I took to be rubies, and upon her shapely head, serving as a fillet for her abundant hair, which flowed down her in long waving strands of a rich and ruddy hue of brown or chestnut, was a simple golden band. Except for a red flower on her breast she wore no other ornament, perhaps because she knew that none was needed.

Leaving us by the door of the chamber, Issicore advanced and knelt before the old man, who first touched him with his staff and then laid a hand upon his head. Presently he rose, went to the lady and knelt before her also, whereon she stretched out her fingers for him to kiss, while a look of sudden hope and joy, which even at that distance I could distinguish, gathered on her face. He whispered to her for a while, then turned and began to speak earnestly to her father. At length he crossed the room, came to me and led me forward, followed by Hans at my heels.

"O Lord Macumazahn," he said, "here sit the Walloo, the Prince of my people, and his daughter, the Lady Sabeela. O Prince my cousin, this is the white noble famous for his skill and courage, whom the Wizard of the South made known to me and who at my prayer, out of the goodness of his heart, has come to help us in our peril."

"I thank him," said the Walloo in the same dialect of Arabic that was used by Issicore. "I thank him in my own name, in that of my daughter who now alone is left to me, and in the name of my people."

Here he rose from his seat and bowed to me with a strange and foreign courtesy such as I had not known in Africa, while the lady also rose and bowed, or rather curtseyed. Seating himself again, he said:

"Without doubt you are weary and would rest and eat, after which perchance we may talk."

Then we were led away through a door at the end of the great room into another room that evidently had been prepared for me. Also there was a place beyond for Hans, a kind of alcove. Here water, which I noticed had been warmed—an unusual thing in Africa—was brought in a large earthenware vessel by two quiet women of middle age, and with it an undershirt of beautiful fine linen which was laid upon a bed, or cushioned couch, that was arranged upon the floor and covered by fur rugs.

I washed myself, pouring the warm water into a stone basin that was set upon a stand, and put on the shirt, also the change of clothes that I had with me, and, with the help of Hans and a pair of pocket scissors, trimmed my beard and hair. Scarcely had I finished when the women reappeared, bringing food on wooden platters—roast lamb, it seemed to be—and with it drink in jars of earthenware that were of elegant shape and powdered all over with the little rough diamonds of which Zikali had given me specimens, that evidently had been set in it in patterns before the clay dried. This drink, by the way was a kind of native beer, sweet to the taste but pleasant and rather strong, so that I had to be careful lest Hans should take too much of it.

After we had finished our meal, which was very welcome, for we had eaten no properly cooked food since we left the wagon, Issicore arrived and took us back to the large room, where we found the Walloo and his daughter seated as before, with several old men squatting about them on the ground. A stool having been set for me the talk began.

I need not enter into all its details, since in substance they set out what I had already heard from Issicore; namely, that there dwelt Something or Somebody on the island in the lake who required annually the sacrifice of a beautiful virgin. This was demanded through the head priest of a college, also established on the island which acknowledged the being, real or imaginary, that lived there as its god or fetish. Further, that creature (if he existed) was said to be the king of all the Hairy Folk who inhabited the forest. Lastly, there was a legend that he was the reincarnation of some ancient monarch of the Walloo folk, who had come to a bad end at the hands of his indignant subjects at some date undefined. Walloo, it seemed, was their correct name, that of Heuheua applying only to the Hairy Men of the woods.

This story I dismissed at once, being quite convinced that it was only a variant of a very common African fable. Doubtless Heu-Heu, if there really were a Heu-Heu, was the ruler of the savage hairy aboriginals of the place that once in the far past had been conquered by the invading Walloo, who poured into the country from the north or west, being themselves the survivors of some civilized but forgotten people. This conclusion, I may add, I never found any reason to doubt. Africa is a very ancient land, and in it once lived many races that have vanished, or survive only in a debased condition, dwindling from generation to generation until the day of their extinction comes.

Here I may state briefly the final opinions at which I have arrived about this people.

Almost certainly these Walloos were such a dying race, hailing, as names among them seemed to suggest from some region in West Africa, where their forefathers had been highly civilized. Thus, although they could not write, they had traditions of writing and even inscriptions graven upon stones, of which I saw several in a character that I did not know, though to me it had the look of Egyptian hieroglyphics. Also they still had knowledge of certain cultured arts such as the weaving of fine linen, the carving of wood and marble, the making of pottery, and the smelting of metals with which their land abounded, including gold that they found in little nuggets in the gravel of the streams.

Most of these crafts, however, were dying out except those that were necessary to life, such as the moulding of pottery and the building of houses and walls, and particularly agriculture, in which they were very proficient. When I saw them all the higher arts were practised only by the very old men. As they never intermarried with any other blood, their hereditary beauty, which was truly remarkable, remained to them, but owing to the causes I have mentioned already, the stock was dwindling, the total population being now not more than half of what it was within the memory of the fathers of their oldest men. Their melancholy, which now had become constitutional, doubtless was induced by their gloomy surroundings and the knowledge that as a race they were doomed to perish at the hands of the savage aboriginals who once had been their slaves.

Lastly, although they retained traces of some higher religion, since they made prayer to a Great Spirit, they were fetish-ridden and believed that they could continue to exist only by making sacrifice to a devil who, if they neglected to do so, would crush them with misfortunes and give them over to destruction at the hands of the dreadful Forest-dwellers. Therefore they, or a section of them, became the priests of this devil called Heu-Heu, and thereby kept peace between them and the Hairy Men.

Nor was this the end of their troubles, since, as Issicore had told me, these priests, after the fashion of priests all the world over, now aspired to the absolute rule of the race, and for this reason plotted the extinction of the hereditary chief and all his family.

Such, in substance, was the lugubrious story that the unhappy Walloo poured into my ears that night, ending it in these words:

"Now you will understand, O Lord Macumazahn, why in our extremity and in obedience to the ancient prophecy, which has come down to us from our fathers, we communicated with the great Wizard of the South, with whom we had been in touch in ancient days, praying him to send us the helper of the prophecy. Behold, he has sent you and now I implore you to save my daughter from the fate that awaits her. I understand that you will require payment in white and red stones, also in gold and ivory. Take as much as you want. Of the stones there are jars full hidden away and the fences of some of my courtyards at the back of this house are made of tusks of ivory, though it is black with age, and I know not how you would carry it hence. Also there is a quantity of gold melted into bars, which my grandfather caused to be collected, whereof we make little use except now and again for women's ornaments, but that, too, would be heavy to carry across the desert. Still, it is all yours. Take it. Take everything you wish, only save my daughter."

"We will talk of the reward afterwards," I said, for my heart was touched at the sight of the old man's grief. "Meanwhile, let me hear what can be done."

"Lord, I do not know," he answered, wringing his hands. "The third night from this is that of full moon, the full moon which marks the beginning of harvest. On that night we must carry my daughter, on whom the lot has fallen, to the island in the lake where stands the smoking mountain and bind her to the pillar upon the Rock of Offering that is set between the two undying fires. There we must leave her, and at the dawn, so it is said, Heu-Heu himself seizes her and carries her into his cavern, where she vanishes for ever. Or, if he does not come, his priests do, to drag her to the god, and we see her no more."

"Then why do you take her to the island? Why do you not call your people together and fight and kill this god or his priest?"

"Lord, because not one man among us, save perhaps Issicore yonder, who can do nothing alone, would lift a hand to save her. They believe that if they did the mountain would break into flames, as happened in the bygone ages, turning all upon whom the ashes fell into stone; also, that the waters would rise and destroy the crops, so that we must die of starvation, and that any who escaped the fire and the water and the want would perish at the hands of the cruel Wood-devils. Therefore, if I ask the Walloos to save the maiden from Heu-Heu, they will kill me and give her up in accordance with the law."

"I understand," I said, and was silent.

"Lord," went on the old Walloo presently, "here with me you are safe, for none of my people will harm you or those with you. But I learn from Issicore that you have stabbed a Hairy Man with a knife, and that your servant slew one of their women with the strange weapons that you carry. Therefore, from the Wood-devils you are not safe, for, if they can, they will kill you both and feast upon your bodies."

"That's cheerful," I thought to myself, but made no further answer, for I did not know what to say.

Just then the Walloo rose from his chair, saying that he must go to pray to the spirits of his ancestors to help him, but that we would talk again upon the morrow. After this he bade us good-night and departed without another word, followed by the old men, who all this while had sat silent, only nodding their heads from time to time like porcelain images of Chinese mandarins.

CHAPTER VIII

THE HOLY ISLE

When the door had closed behind him, I turned to Issicore and asked him straight out if he had any plan to suggest. He shook his noble-looking head and answered, "None," as it was impossible to resist both the will of the people and the law of the priests.

"Then what is the use of your having brought me all this way?" I inquired with indignation. "Cannot you think of some scheme? For instance, would it not be possible for you and this lady to fly with us down the river and escape to a land which is not full of demons?"

"It would not be possible," he answered in a melancholy voice. "Day and night we are watched and would be seized before we had travelled a mile. Moreover, could she leave her father, and could I leave all my relations to be murdered in payment for our sacrilege?"

"Have you no thought in your mind at all?" I asked again. "Is there nothing that would save the Lady Sabeela?"

"Nothing, Lord, except the end of Heu-Heu and his priests. It is to you, great Lord, that we look to find a way to destroy them, as the prophecy declares will be done by the White Deliverer from the South."

"Oh, dash the prophecy! I never knew prophecies to help anybody yet," I ejaculated in English, as I contemplated that beautiful but helpless pair. Then I added in Arabic, "I am tired and am going to bed. I hope that I shall find more wisdom in my dreams than I do in you, Issicore," I added, staring at the man in whom I seemed to detect some subtle change, some access of fatalistic helplessness, even of despair.

Now Sabeela, seeing that I was angry, broke in:

"O Lord, be not wrath, for we are but flies in the spider's web, and the threads of that web are the priests of Heu-Heu, and the posts to which it is fixed are the beliefs of my people, and Heu-Heu himself is the spider, and in my breast his claws are fixed."

Now, listening to her allegory, I thought to myself that a better one might have been drawn from a snake and a bird, for really, like the rest of them, this poor girl seemed to be mesmerized with terror and to have made up her mind to sit still waiting to be struck by the poisoned fangs.

"Lord," she went on, "we have done all we could. Did not Issicore make a great journey to find you? Yes, did he not even dare the curse which falls upon the heads of those who try to leave our country, and travel south to seek the counsel of the Great Wizard, who once sent messengers here to obtain the leaves of the tree that grows in Heu-Heu's garden, the tree that makes men drunk and gives them visions?"

"Yes," I answered, "he did that, Lady, and might I say to you that his health seems none the worse. Those curses of which you speak have not yet hurt him."

"It is true they have not hurt his body—yet," she said in a musing voice, as though a new thought had struck her.

"Well, if that is true, Sabeela, may it not be true also that all this talk about the power of Heu-Heu is nonsense? Tell me, have you ever spoken with or seen Heu-Heu?"

"No, Lord, no, though unless you can save me I shall soon see him."

"Well, and has any one else?"

"No, Lord, no one has ever spoken with him, except, of course, his priests, such as my distant cousin, Dacha, who is the head of them, but whom I used to know before he was chosen by Heu-Heu to be one of their company."

"Oh! So no one has seen him? Then he must be a very secret kind of god who does not take exercise, but lives, I understand, in a cave with priests."

"I did not say that no one had ever seen Heu-Heu, Lord. Many say that they have seen him, as Issicore has done, when he came out of the cave on a Night of Offering, but of what they saw it is death to speak. Ask me and Issicore no more of Heu-Heu, Lord I pray you, lest the curse should fall. It is not lawful that we should tell you of him, whose secrets are sacred even to his priests," she added with agitation.

Then in despair I gave up asking questions about Heu-Heu and inquired how many priests he had.

"About twenty, I believe, Lord," she answered, ceasing from evasions, "not counting their wives and families, and it is said that they do not live with Heu-Heu in the cave, but in houses outside of it."

"And what do they do when they are not worshipping Heu-Heu, Sabeela?"

"Oh, they cultivate the land and they rule the Wild People of the Woods, who, it is believed, are all Heu-Heu's children. Also they come here and spy on us."

"Do they indeed?" I remarked. "And is it true that they hope to rule over you Walloos also?"

"Yes, I believe that it is true. At least, should my father die and I die, it is said that Dacha means to make war upon the Walloos and take the chieftainship, setting aside or killing my cousin and betrothed Issicore. For Dacha was always one who desired to be first."

"So you used to know Dacha pretty well, Lady?"

"Yes, Lord, when I was quite young before he became a priest. Also," she added, colouring, "I have seen him since he became a priest."

"And what did he say to you?"

"He said that if I would take him for a husband perhaps I should escape from Heu-Heu."

"And what did you answer, Lady?"

"Lord, I answered that I would rather go to Heu-Heu."

"Why?"

"Because Dacha, it is reported, has many wives already. Also I hate him. Also from Heu-Heu at the last I can always escape."

"How?"

"By death, Lord. We have swift poison in this country, and I carry some of it hidden in my hair," she added with emphasis.

"Quite so. I understand. But, Lady Sabeela, as you have been so good as to ask my advice about these matters, I will give you some. It is that you should not taste that poison till all else has failed and there is no escape. While we breathe there is hope, and all that seems lost still may be won, but the dead do not live again, Lady Sabeela."

"I hear and will obey you, Lord," she answered, weeping. "Yet sleep is better than Dacha or Heu-Heu."

"And life is better than all three of them put together," I replied, "especially life with love."

Then I bowed myself off to bed, followed by Hans, also bowing—like a monkey for pennies on a barrel-organ. At the door I looked back, and saw these two poor people in each other's arms, thinking, doubtless, that we were already out of sight of them. Yes, her head was upon Issicore's shoulder, and from the convulsive motions of her form I guessed that she was sobbing, while he tried to console her in the ancient, world-wide fashion. I only hope that she got more comfort from Issicore than I did. To me he now seemed to be but a singularly unresourceful member of a played-out race, though it is true that he had courage, since otherwise he would not have attempted the journey to Zululand. Also, as I have said, quite suddenly he had changed in some subtle fashion.

When we were in our own room with the door bolted (it had no windows, light and ventilation being provided by holes in the roof) I gave Hans some tobacco and bade him sit down on the other side of the lamp, where he squatted upon the floor like a toad.

"Now, Hans," I said, "tell me all the truth of this business and what we are to do to help this pretty lady and the old chief, her father."

Hans looked at the roof and looked at the wall; then he spat upon the floor, for which I reproved him.

"Baas," he said at length, "I think the best thing we can do is to find out where those bright stones are, fill our pockets with them, and escape from this country which is full of fools and devils. I am sure that Beautiful One would be better off with the priest Dacha, or even with Heu-Heu, than with Issicore, who now has become but a carved and painted lump of wood made to look like a man."

"Possibly, Hans, but the tastes of women are curious, and she likes this lump of wood, who, after all, is brave, except where ghosts and spirits are concerned. Otherwise he would not have journeyed so far for her sake. Moreover, we have a bargain to keep. What should we say to the Opener-of-Roads if we returned, having run away and without his medicine? No, Hans, we must play out this game."

"Yes, Baas, I thought that the Baas would say that because of his foolishness. Had I been alone, by now, or a little later, I should have been in that canoe going down-stream. However, the Baas has settled that we must save the lady and give her to the Lump of Wood for a wife. So now I think I will go to sleep, and to-morrow or the next day the Baas can save her. I don't think very much of the beer in this country, Baas—it is too sweet; and all these handsome fools who talk about devils and priests weary me. Also, it is a bad climate and very damp. I think it is going to rain again, Baas."

Having nothing else at hand, I threw my tobacco-pouch at Hans's head. He caught it deftly, and in an absent-minded fashion, put it into his own pocket.

"If the Baas really wishes to know what I think," he said, yawning, "it is that the medicine man named Dacha wants the pretty lady for himself; also to rule alone over all these dull people. As for Heu-Heu, I don't know anything about him, but perhaps he is one of those Hairy

Men who came here at the beginning of the world. I think that the best thing we can do, Baas, would be to take a boat to-morrow morning and go to that island, where we can find out the truth for ourselves. Perhaps the Lump of Wood and some of his men can row us there. And now I have nothing more to say, so, if the Baas does not mind, I will go to sleep. Keep your pistol ready, Baas, in case any of the Hairy People wish to call upon us—just to talk about the one I shot."

Then he retired to a corner, rolling himself up in a skin rug, and presently was snoring, though, as I knew well enough, with one eye open all the time. No Hairy Man, or any one else, would have come near that place without Hans hearing him, for his sleep was like to that of a dog who watches his master.

As I prepared to follow his example, I reflected that his remarks, casual as they seemed, were full of wisdom. These folk were superstition-riddled fools and useless; probably the only ones that had wits among them became priests. But the Hairy aboriginals were an ugly fact, as the priests knew, since apparently they had obtained rule over them. For the rest, the only thing to do was to visit the Holy Island and find out the truth for ourselves, as Hans had said. It would be dangerous, no doubt, but at the least it would also be exciting.

Next morning I rose after an excellent night's rest and found my way into the garden, where I amused myself by examining the shrubs and flowers, some of which were strange to me. Also I studied the sky, which was heavy and lowering, and seemed full of rain. I could study nothing else because the high wall cut off the view upon every side so that little was to be seen except the top of the volcano, which rose from the lake at a distance of several miles, for it was a large sheet of water. Presently the door of the garden opened and Issicore appeared, looking weary and somewhat bewildered. It occurred to me that he had been sitting up late with Sabeela. As they were to be parted so soon, naturally they would see as much as they could of each other. Or for aught I knew, he might have been praying to his ancestral spirits and trying to make up his mind what to do, no doubt a difficult process under the circumstances. I went to the point at once.

"Issicore," I said, "as soon as possible after breakfast, will you have a canoe ready to take me and Hans to the island in the lake?"

"To the island in the lake, Lord!" he exclaimed, amazed. "Why, it is holy!"

"I daresay, but I am holy also, so that if I go there it will be holier."

Then he advanced all kinds of objections, and even brought out the Walloo and his grey-heads to reinforce his arguments. Hans and Sabeela also joined the party; the latter, I noted, looking even more beautiful by day than she did in the lamplight. Sabeela, indeed, proved my only ally, for presently, when the others had talked themselves hoarse, she said:

"The White Lord has been brought hither that we, who are bewildered and foolish, may drink of the cup of his wisdom. If his wisdom bids him visit the Holy Isle, let him do so, my father."

As no one seemed to be convinced, I stood silent, not knowing what more to say. Then Hans took up his parable, speaking in his bad coast-Arabic:

"Baas, Issicore, although he is so big and strong, and all these others are afraid of Heu-Heu and his priests. But we, who are good Christians, are not afraid of any devils because we know how to deal with them. Also we can paddle, therefore let the Chief give us quite a small canoe and show us which way to row, and we will go to the island by ourselves."

In sporting parlance, this shot hit the bull in the eye, and Issicore, who, as I have said, was a brave man at bottom, fired up and answered:

"Am I a coward that I should listen to such words from your servant, Lord Macumazahn? I and some others whom I can find will row you to the island, though on it we will not set our foot because it is not lawful for us to do so. Only, Lord, if you come back no more, blame me not."

"Then that is settled," I replied quietly, "and now, if we may, let us eat, for I am hungry."

About two hours later we started from the quay, taking with us all our small possessions, down to some spare powder in flasks which we had brought to reload fired cartridge cases, for Hans refused to leave anything behind with no one to watch it. The canoe which was given to us was much smaller than that in which we had come up the river, though, like it, hollowed from a single log; and its crew consisted of Issicore, who steered, and four other Walloos, who paddled, stout and determined-looking fellows, all of them. The island was about five miles away, but we made a wide circuit to the south, I suppose in the hope of avoiding observation, and therefore it took us the best part of two hours to reach its southern shore.

As we approached I examined the place carefully through my glasses, and observed that it was much larger than I had thought—several miles in circumference, indeed, for in addition to the central volcanic cone there was a great stretch of low-lying land all round its base, which land seemed not to rise more than a foot or two above the level of the lake. In character, except on these flats by the lake, it was stony and barren, being, in fact, strewn with lumps of lava ejected from the volcano during the last eruption.

Issicore informed me, however, that the northern part of the island where the priests lived, which had not been touched by the lava stream, was very fertile. I should add that the crater of the volcano seemed to bear out his statement as to the direction of the flow, since on the south it was blown away to a great depth, whereas the northern segment rose in a high and perfect wall of rock.

The day was very misty—a circumstance which favoured our approach—and the sky, which, as I have said, was black and pregnant with coming rain, seemed almost to touch the crest of the mountain. These conditions, until we were quite close, prevented us from seeing that a stream of glowing lava, not very broad, was pouring down the mountain-side. When they discovered this, the Walloos grew much alarmed, and Issicore told me that such a thing had not been known "for a hundred years," and that he thought it portended something unusual, as the mountain was supposed to be "asleep."

"It is awake enough to smoke, anyway," I answered, and continued my examination.

Among the stones, and sometimes half-buried by them, I saw what appeared to be the remains of those buildings of which I have spoken. There, Issicore said, had once been part of the city of his forefathers, adding that, as he had been told, in some of them the said forefathers were still to be seen turned to stone, which, you will remember, exactly bore out Zikali's story.

Anything more desolate and depressing than the aspect of this place seen on that grey day and beneath the brooding sky cannot be imagined. Still I burned to examine it, for this tale of fossilized people excited me, who have always loved the remains of antiquity and strange sights.

Forgetting all about Heu-Heu and his priests for the moment, I told the Walloos to paddle to the shore, and, after a moment of mute protest, they obeyed, running into a little bay. Hans and I stepped easily on to the rocks and, carrying our bags and rifles, started on our search. First, however, we arranged with Issicore that he should await our return and then row us back round the island so that we might have a view of the priests' settlement. With a sigh he promised to do so, and at once paddled out to about a hundred yards from the shore, where the canoe was anchored by means of a pierced stone tied to a cord.

Off went Hans and I towards the nearest group of ruins. As we approached them, Hans said:

"Look out, Baas! There's a dog between those rocks."

I stared at the spot he indicated, and there, sure enough, saw a large grey dog with a pointed muzzle, which seemed to be fast asleep. We drew nearer, and as it did not stir, Hans threw a stone and hit it on the back. Still it did not stir, so we went up and examined it.

"It is a stone dog," I said. "The people who lived here must have made statues," for as yet I did not believe the stories I had heard about petrified creatures, which, after all, must be very legendary.

"If so, Baas, they put bones into their carvings. Look," and he touched one of the dog's front paws which was broken off. There, in the middle of it, appeared the bone fossilized. Then I understood.

The animal had been fleeing away to the shore when the poisonous gases overcame it at the time of the eruption. After this, I suppose, some rain of petrifying fluid had fallen on it and turned it into stone. It was a marvellous thing, but I could not doubt the evidence of my own eyes. All the tale was true, and I had made a great discovery.

We hurried on to the houses, which, of course, now were roofless, and in some instances choked with lava, though the outer walls, being strongly built of rock, still stood. On certain of these walls were the faint remains of frescoes; one of people sitting at a feast, another of a hunting scene, and so forth.

We passed on to a second group of buildings standing at some distance against the flank of the mountain and more or less protected by an overhanging ledge or shelf of stone. These appeared to have been a palace or a temple, for they were large, with stone columns that supported the roofs. We went on through the great hall to the rooms behind, and in the furthermost, which was under the ledge of rock and probably had been used as a store chamber, we saw an extraordinary sight.

There, huddled together, and in some instances clasping each other, were a number of people, twenty or thirty of them—men, women, and children—all turned to stone. Doubtless the petrifying fluid had flowed into the chamber through the cracks in the rock above and done its office on them. They were naked, every one, which suggested that their clothing had either been burnt off them or had rotted away before the process was complete. The former hypothesis seemed to be borne out by the fact that none of them had any hair left upon their heads. The features were not easy to distinguish, but the general type of the bodies was certainly very similar to that of the Walloos.

Speechless with amazement, we emerged from that death chamber and wandered about the place. Here and there we found the bodies of others who had perished in the great catastrophe and once came across an arm projecting from a mass of lava, which seemed to show that many more were buried underneath. Also we found a number of fossilized goats in a kraal. What a place to dig in! I thought to myself. Given some spades, picks, and blasting-powder, what might one not find in these ruins?

All the relics of a past civilization, perhaps—its inscriptions, its jewellery, the statues of its gods; even, perhaps, its domestic furniture buried beneath the lava and the dust, though probably this had rotted. Here, certainly, was another Pompeii, and perhaps beneath that another Herculaneum.

Whilst I mused thus over glories passed away and wondered when they had passed, Hans dug me in the ribs and, in his horrible Boer Dutch, ejaculated a single word, "*Kek!*" which, as perhaps you know, means "Look!" at the same time nodding towards the lake.

I did look, and saw our canoe paddling off for all it was worth, going "hell for leather," as my old father used to say, towards the Walloo shore.

"Now why is it doing that?" I asked.

"I expect because something is behind it, Baas," he replied with resignation, then sat down on a rock, pulled out his pipe, filled it, and lit a match.

As usual, Hans was right, for presently from round the curve of the island there appeared two other canoes, very large canoes, rowing after ours with great energy and determination, and, as I guessed, with malignant intent.

"I think those priests have seen our boat and mean to catch it, if they can," remarked Hans, spitting reflectively, "though as Issicore has got a long start, perhaps they won't. And now, Baas, what are we to do? We can't live here with dead men, and stone goat is not good to eat."

I considered the situation, and my heart sank into my boots, for the position seemed desperate. A moment before I had been filled with enthusiasm over this ruined city and its fossilized remains. Now I hated the very thought of them, and wished that they were at the bottom of the lake. Thus do circumstances alter cases, and our poor variable human moods. Then an idea came to me, and I said boldly:

"Do! Why, there is only one thing to do. We must go to call on Heu-Heu, or his priests."

"Yes, Baas. But the Baas remembers the picture in the cave on the Berg. If it is a true picture, Heu-Heu knows how to twist off men's heads!"

"I don't believe there is a Heu-Heu," I said stoutly. "You will have noticed, Hans, that we have heard all sorts of stories about Heu-Heu, but that no one seems to have seen him clearly enough to give us an accurate description of what he is like or what he does—not even Zikali. He showed us a picture of the beast on his fire, but after all it was only what we had seen on the wall of the cave, and I think that he got it out of our own minds. At any rate, it is just as well to die quickly without a head, as slowly with an empty stomach, since I am sure those Walloos will never come back to look for us."

"Yes, Baas, I think so, too. Issicore used to have courage, but he seems to have changed, as though something had happened to him since he got back into his own country. And now, if the Baas is ready, I think we had better be trekking, unless, indeed, he would like to look at a few more stone men first. It is beginning to rain, Baas, and we have been much longer here than the Baas thinks, since it is a slow business crawling about these old houses. Therefore, if we are to get to the other side of the island before nightfall, it is time to go."

So off we went, keeping to the western side of the volcano, since there it did not seem to project so far into the flat lands. A while later we turned round and looked at the lake. There in the far distance our canoe appeared a mere speck, with two other specks, those of the pursuers, close upon its heels. As we watched, out of the mists on the Walloo shore came yet other specks, which were doubtless Walloo boats paddling to the rescue, for the priests' canoes gave up the chase and turned homewards.

"Issicore will have a very nice story to tell to the Lady Sabeela," said Hans; "but perhaps she will not kiss him after she has heard it."

"He was quite wise to go. What good could he have done by staying?" I answered, as we trudged on, adding, "Still, you are right, Hans, Issicore has changed."

It was a hard walk over rough ground, at least at first, for so soon as we got round the shoulder of the volcano the character of the country altered and we found ourselves in fertile, cultivated land that appeared to be irrigated.

"These fields must lie very low, Baas," said Hans, "since otherwise how do they get the lake water on to them?"

"I don't know," I replied crossly, for I was thinking of the sky water, which was beginning to descend in a steady drizzle upon ourselves. But all the same, the remark stuck in my mind and was useful afterwards. On we marched, till at length we entered a grove of palm trees that was traversed by a road.

Presently we came to the end of the road and found ourselves in a village of well-built stone houses, with one very large house in the middle of it, of which the back was set almost against the foot of the mountain. As there was nothing else to be done, we walked on into the village, at first without being observed, for everybody was under cover because of the rain. Soon, however, dogs began to bark, and a woman, looking out of the doorway of one of the houses, caught sight of us and screamed. A minute later men with shaven heads and wearing white, priestly-looking robes, appeared and ran towards us flourishing big spears.

"Hans," I said, "keep your rifle ready, but don't shoot unless you are obliged. In this case, words may serve us better than bullets."

"Yes, Baas, though I don't believe that either will serve us much."

Then he sat down on the trunk of a fallen tree that lay by the roadside, and waited, and I followed his example, taking the opportunity to light my pipe.

CHAPTER IX

THE FEAST

When they were within a few paces of us the men halted, apparently astonished at our appearance, which certainly did not compare favourably with their own, for they were all of the splendid Walloo type. Evidently what astonished them still more was the match with which I was lighting my pipe, and indeed the pipe itself, for although these people grew tobacco, they only took it in the form of snuff.

That match went out and I struck another, and at the sight of the sudden appearance of fire they stepped back a pace or two. At length one of them, pointing to the burning match, asked in the same tongue that was used by the Walloos:

"What is that, O Stranger?"

"Magic fire," I answered, adding by an inspiration, "which I am bringing as a present to the great god Heu-Heu."

This information seemed to mollify them, for, lowering their spears, they turned to speak to another man who at this moment arrived upon the scene. He was a stout, fine-looking man of considerable presence, with a hooked nose and flashing black eyes. Also he wore a priestly cap upon his head and his white robes were broidered.

"Very big fellow, this, Baas," Hans whispered to me, and I nodded, observing as I did so that the other priests bowed as they addressed him.

"Dacha in person," thought I to myself, and sure enough Dacha it was.

He advanced and, looking at the wax match, said:

"Where does the magic fire of which you speak live, Stranger?"

"In this case covered with holy secret writing," I replied, holding before his eyes a box labelled "Wax Vestas, Made in England," and adding solemnly, "Woe be to him that touches it or him that bears it without understanding, for it will surely leap forth and consume that foolish man, O Dacha."

Now Dacha followed the example of his companions and stepped back a little way, remarking:

"How do you know my name, and who sends this present of self-conceiving fire to Heu-Heu?"

"Is not the name of Dacha known to the ends of the earth?" I asked—a remark which seemed to please him very much; "yes, as far as his spells can travel, which is the sky and back again. As to who sends the magic fire, it is a great one, a wizard of the best, if not quite so good as Dacha, who is named Zikali, who is named the 'Opener-of-Roads,' who is named 'the Thing-that-should-never-have-been-born.'"

"We have heard of him," said Dacha. "His messengers were here in our father's day. And what does Zikali want of us, O Stranger?"

"He wants leaves of a certain tree that grows in Heu-Heu's garden, that is called the Tree of Visions, that he may mix them with his medicines."

Dacha nodded and so did the other priests. Evidently they knew all about the Tree of Visions, as I, or rather Zikali, had named it.

"Then why did he not come for them himself?"

"Because he is old and infirm. Because he is detained by great affairs. Because it was easier for him to send me, who, being a lover of that which is holy, was anxious to do homage to Heu-Heu and to make the acquaintance of the great Dacha."

"I understand," the priest replied, highly gratified, as his face shewed. "But how are you named, O Messenger of Zikali?"

"I am named 'Blowing-Wind,' because I pass where I would, none seeing me come or go, and therefore am the best and swiftest of messengers. And this little one, this small but great-souled one with me"—here I pointed to the smirking Hans, who by now was quite alive to the humours of the situation and to its advantages from our point of view—"is named 'Lord-of-the-Fire' and 'Light-in-Darkness'" (this was true enough and worked in very well) "because it is he who is guardian of the magic fire," (also true, for he had half a dozen spare boxes in his pockets that he had stolen at one time or another) "of which, if he is offended, he can make enough to burn up all this island and everyone thereon; yes, more than is hidden in the womb of that mountain."

"Can he, by Heu-Heu!" said Dacha, regarding Hans with great respect.

"Certainly he can. Mighty though I be, I must be careful not to anger him lest myself I should be burnt to cinders."

At this moment a doubt seemed to strike Dacha, for he asked:

"Tell me, O Blowing-Wind and O Lord-of-Fire, how you came to this island? We observed a canoe manned with some of our rebellious subjects who serve that old usurper the Walloo, which is being hunted that they may be killed for the sacrilege in approaching this holy place. Were you perchance in that canoe?"

"We were," I answered boldly. "When we arrived at yonder town I met a lady, a very beautiful lady, named Sabeela, and asked her where dwelt the great Dacha. She said here—more, that she knew you and that you were the most beautiful and noblest of men, as well as the wisest. She said also that with some of her servants, including a stupid fellow called Issicore, of whom she never can be rid wherever she goes, she herself would paddle us to the island on the chance of seeing your face again." (I may explain to you fellows that this lie was perfectly safe, as I knew Issicore and his people had escaped.) "So she brought us here and landed us that we might look at the ruined city before coming on to see you. But then your people roughly hunted her away, so that we were obliged to walk to your town. That is all."

Now Dacha became agitated. "I pray Heu-Heu," he said, "that those fools may not have caught and killed her with the others."

"I pray so also, since she is too fair to die," I answered, "who would be a lovely wife for any man. But stay, I will tell you what has chanced. Lord-of-the-Fire, make fire."

Hans produced a match and lit it on the seat of his trousers, which was the only part of him that was not damp. He held it in his joined hands and I stared at the flame, muttering. Then he whispered:

"Be quick, Baas, it is burning my fingers!"

"All is well," I said solemnly. "The canoe with Sabeela the Beautiful escaped your people, since other canoes, seven—no, eight of them," I corrected, studying the ashes of the match, also the blister on Hans's finger, "came out from the town and drove yours away just as they were overtaking the Lady Sabeela."

This was a most fortunate stroke, for at that moment a messenger arrived and gave Dacha exactly the same intelligence, which he punctuated with many bows.

"Wonderful!" said the priest. "Wonderful! Here we have magicians indeed!" and he stared at us with much awe. Then again a doubt struck him.

"Lord," he said, "Heu-Heu is the ruler of the savage Hairy People who live in the woods and are named Heuheuas after him. Now a tale has reached us that one of these people has been mysteriously killed with a noise by some strangers. Had you aught to do with her death, Lord?"

"Yes," I answered. "She annoyed the Lord-of-the-Fire with her attentions, so he slew her, as was right and proper. I cut off the finger of another who wished to shake hands with me when I had told him to go away."

"But how did he slay her, Lord?"

Now I may explain that there was one inhabitant of this place that greeted us with no cordiality at all, namely a large and particularly ferocious dog, that all this while had been growling round us and finally had got hold of Hans's coat, which it held between its teeth, still growling.

"*Scheet!* Hans, *scheet seen dood!*" ("Shoot! Hans, shoot him dead!") I whispered, and Hans, who was always quick to catch an idea, put his hand into his pocket where he kept his pistol, and pressing the muzzle against the brute's head, fired through the cloth, with the result that this dog went wherever bad dogs go.

Then there was consternation. Indeed, one of the priests fell down with fear and the others turned tail, all of them except Dacha, who stood his ground.

"A little of the magic fire!" I remarked airily, "and there is plenty more where that came from," at the same time, as though by accident, slapping Hans's pocket, which I saw was smouldering. "And now, noble Dacha, it is setting in wet and we are hungry. Be pleased to give us shelter and food."

"Certainly, Lord, certainly!" he exclaimed, and started off with us, keeping me well between himself and Hans, while the others, who had returned, followed with the dead dog.

Presently, recovering from his fear, he asked me whether the Lady Sabeela had said anything more about him.

"Only one thing," I answered: "that it was a pity that a maiden should be obliged to marry a god when there were such men as you in the world."

Here I stopped and watched the effect of my shot out of the corner of my eye.

His coarse but handsome face grew cunning, and he smacked his lips.

"Yes, Lord, yes," he said hurriedly. "But who knows? Things are not always what they seem, Lord, and I have noted that sometimes the faithful servant tithes the master's offering."

"By Jingo! I've got it!" thought I to myself. "*You*, my friend, are Heu-Heu, or at any rate his business part." But aloud, glancing at the redoubtable Hans, I only remarked something to the effect that Dacha's powers of observation were keen and that, like the Lord-of-the-Fire himself, as he said truly, things were not always what they seemed.

We crossed a bare platform of rock, to the right of which, beyond a space of garden, I observed the mouth of a large cave. At the edge of this platform a strange sight was to be seen, for here, just on the borders of the lake, at a distance of about twenty paces from each other, burned two columns of flame which hitherto had been hidden from us by the lie of the ground and trees, between which columns was a pillar or post of stone.

"The 'eternal fires,'" thought I to myself, and then inquired casually what they were.

"They are flames which have always burned in that place from the beginning; we do not know why," Dacha replied indifferently. "No rain puts them out."

"Ah!" I reflected, "natural gas coming from the volcano, such as I have heard of in Canada."

Then we turned to the right along the outer wall of the garden I have mentioned, and came to some fine houses, that, to my fancy, had a kind of collegiate appearance, all one-storied and built against the rock of the mountain. As a matter of fact, I was right, for these were the dwellings of the priests of Heu-Heu and their numerous female belongings. These priests, I should say, had their privileges, for whereas the people on the mainland for the most part married only one wife, they were polygamous, the ladies being supplied to them through spiritual pressure put upon the unfortunate Walloos, or, if that failed, by the simple and ancient expedient of kidnapping. Once, however, they had arrived upon the island and thus became dedicated to the god, they vanished so far as their kinsfolk were concerned, and never afterwards were they allowed to cross the water or even to attempt any communication with them. In short, those who became alive in Heu-Heu, became also dead to the world.

Hans and I were led to the largest of this group of houses, that abutting immediately on to the garden wall, the inhabitants of which apparently had already been advised of our coming by messenger, since we found them in a bustle of preparation. Thus I saw handsome, white-robed women flitting about and heard hurried orders being given. We were taken to a room where a driftwood fire had been lighted on the hearth because the night was damp and chill, at which we warmed and dried ourselves after we had washed. A while later a priest summoned us to eat and then retired outside the door awaiting our convenience.

"Hans," I said, "all has gone well so far; we are accepted as the friends of Heu-Heu, not as his enemies."

"Yes, Baas, thanks to the cleverness of the Baas about the matches and the rest. But what has the Baas in his mind?"

"This, Hans; that all must continue to go well, for remember what is our duty, namely, to save the lady Sabeela, if we can, as we have sworn to do. Now if we are to bring this about we must keep our eyes open and our wits sharp. Hans, I daresay that they have strange liquors in this place which will be offered to us to make us talk. But while we are here we must drink nothing but water. Do you understand, Hans?"

"Yes, Baas, I understand."

"And do you swear, Hans?"

Hans rubbed his middle reflectively, and replied:

"My stomach is cold, Baas, and I should like a glass of something more warming than water after all this damp and the sight of those stone men. Yet, Baas, I swear. Yes, I swear by your Reverend Father that I will only drink water, or coffee if they make it, which, of course, they don't."

"That is all right, Hans. You know that if you break your oath my Reverend Father will certainly come even with you, and so shall I in this world or the next."

"Yes, Baas. But will the Baas please remember that a gin bottle is not the only bait that the devil sets upon his hook. Different men have different tastes, Baas. Now if some pretty lady were to come and tell the Baas that he was oh! so beautiful and that she loved him, oh! ever so much, someone like that Mameena, for instance, of whom old Zikali is always talking as having been a friend of yours, will the Baas swear by his Reverend Father——"

"Cease from folly and be silent," I said majestically. "Is this the time and place to chatter of pretty women?"

Nevertheless, in myself I appreciated the shrewdness of Hans's repartee, and as a matter of fact an attempt was made to play off that trick on me, though if I am to get to the end of this story, I shall have no time to tell you about it.

Our compact sealed, we went through the door and found the priest waiting outside. He led us down a passage into a fine hall plentifully lit with lamps for now the night had fallen. Here several tables were spread, but we were taken to one at the head of the hall where we were welcomed by Dacha dressed in grand robes, and some other priests; also by women, all of them handsome and beautifully arrayed in their wild fashion, whom I took to be the wives of these worthies. One of them, I noticed, had a singular resemblance to the Lady Sabeela, although she appeared to be her elder by some years.

We sat down at the table in curious, carved chairs, and I found myself between Dacha and this lady, whose name, I discovered, was Dramana. The feast began, and I may say at once that it was a very fine feast, for it appeared that we had arrived upon a day of festival. Indeed, I had not eaten such a meal for years.

Of course, it was barbaric in its way. Thus the food was served in great earthenware dishes, already cut up; there were no knives or forks, the fingers of the eaters taking their place, and the plates consisted of the tough green leaves of some kind of waterlily that grew in the lake, which were removed after each course and replaced by fresh ones.

Of its sort, however, it was excellent and included fish of a good flavour, kid cooked with spices, wild fowl, and a kind of pudding made of ground corn and sweetened with honey. Also, there was plenty of the strong native beer, which was handed round in ornamented earthenware cups that were, however, inlaid not with small diamonds and rubies, but with pearls found, I was informed, in the shells of freshwater mussels, and set in the clay when damp.

These pearls were irregular in shape and for the most part not large, but the effect of them thus employed, was very pretty. Still, some attained to a considerable size, since Dramana and other women wore necklaces of them bored and strung upon fibres. Without going into further details, I may say that this feast and its equipment convinced me more than ever that these people had once belonged to some unknown but highly civilized race which was now dying out in its last home and sinking into barbarism before it died.

In pursuance of our agreement Hans, who squatted on a stool behind me, for he would not sit at the table, and I, saying that we were bound by a vow to touch nothing else, drank water only, although I heard him groan each time the beer cups went round. I may add that this happened frequently, and the amount of liquor consumed was considerable, as became evident by the behaviour of the drinkers, many of whom grew more or less intoxicated, with the usual unpleasant results that I need not describe. Also they grew affectionate, for they threw their arms about the women and began to kiss them in a way which I considered improper. I observed, however, that the lady called

Dramana drank but little. Also, as she sat between me and an extremely deaf priest who became sleepy in his cups, she was, of course, freed from any such unwelcome attentions.

All these circumstances, and especially the fact that Dacha was much occupied with a handsome female on his left, gave Dramana and myself opportunities of conversation which I think were welcome to her. After a few general remarks, presently she said in a low voice:

"I hear, Lord, that you have seen Sabeela, the daughter of the Walloo, chief of the mainland. Tell me of her, for she is my sister on whom I have not looked for a long while, for we never visit the mainland, and those who dwell there never visit us—unless they are obliged," she added significantly.

"She is beautiful but lives in great terror because she, who desires to be married to a man, must be married to a god," I answered.

"She does well to be afraid, Lord, for by you sits that god," and with a shiver of disgust and the slightest possible motion of her head, she indicated Dacha, who had become quite drunken and at the moment was engaged in embracing the lady on his left, who also seemed to be somewhat the worse for alcoholic wear, or to put it plainly, "half seas over."

"Nay," I answered, "the god I mean is called Heu-Heu, not Dacha."

"Heu-Heu, Lord! You will learn all about Heu-Heu before the night is over. It is Dacha whom she must marry."

"But Dacha is your husband, lady."

"Dacha is the husband of many, Lord," and she glanced at several of the most handsome women present, "for the god is liberal to his high priest. Since I was bound between the eternal fires there have been eight such marriages, though some of the brides have been handed on to others or sacrificed for crimes against the god, or attempting to escape, or for other reasons.

"Lord," she went on, dropping her voice till I could scarcely catch what she said, although my hearing is keen, "be warned by me. Unless you are indeed a god greater than Heu-Heu, and your companion also, whatever you may see or hear, lift neither voice nor hand. If you do, you will be rent to pieces without helping any one and perhaps bring about the death of many, my own among them. Hush! Speak of something else. He is beginning to watch us. Yet, O Lord, help me if you can. Yes, save me and my sister if you can."

I glanced round. Dacha, who had ceased embracing the lady, was looking at us suspiciously, as though he had caught some word. Perhaps Hans thought so as well, for he managed to make a great clatter, either by tumbling off his stool or dropping his drinking cup, I know not which, that drew away Dacha's half-drunken attention from us and prevented him from hearing anything.

"You see to find the Lady Dramana pleasant, O Lord Blowing-Wind," sneered Dacha. "Well, I am not jealous and I would give such guests of the best I have, especially when the god is going to be so good to me. Also the Lady Dramana knows better than to tell secrets and what happens here to those who do. So talk to her as much as you like, little Blowing-Wind, before you blow yourself away," and he leered at me in a manner that made me feel very uncomfortable.

"I was asking the Lady Dramana about the sacred tree of which the great wizard, Zikali, desires some of the leaves for his medicine," I said, pretending not to understand.

"Oh!" he answered, with a change of manner which suggested that his suspicions were in course of being dissipated, "oh, were you? I thought you were asking of other things. Well, there is no secret about that, and she shall show it to you to-morrow, if you like; also anything else you wish, for I and my brethren will be otherwise engaged. Meanwhile, here comes the Cup of Illusions that is brewed from the fruit of the tree of which you must taste though you be a water-drinker, yes, and the yellow dwarf, Lord-of-the-Fire, also, for in it we pledge the god into whose presence we must enter very soon."

I answered hurriedly that I was weary and would not trouble the god by paying my respects to him at present.

"All who come here must pass the god, Lord Blowing-Wind," he answered, glaring at me, and adding: "Either they must pass the god living, or, if they prefer it, they may pass him dead. Did not Zikali tell you that, O Blowing-Wind? Choose, then. Will you wait upon the god living, or will you wait upon him dead?"

Now I thought it was time to assert myself, and looking this ill-conditioned brute in the eyes, I said slowly:

"Who is this that talks to me of death, not knowing perchance that I am a lord of death? Does he seek such a fate as that which befell the hound without your doors? Learn, O Priest of Heu-Heu, that it is dangerous to use ill-omened words to me or to the Lord-of-the-Fire, lest we should answer them with lightnings."

I suppose that these remarks, or something in my eye, impressed him. At any rate, his manner became humble, almost servile indeed, especially as Hans had risen and stood at my side, holding in his extended hand the box of matches, at which all stared suspiciously. Well they might have stared, had they known that his other hand, innocently buried in his pocket, grasped the butt of an excellent Colt revolver. I should have told you, by the way, that as we could not bring them with us to the feast we had left our rifles hidden in our beds, loaded and full clocked, so that they would be sure to go off if any thief began to finger them.

"Pardon, Lord, pardon," said Dacha. "Could I wish to insult one so powerful? If I said aught to offend, why, this beer is strong."

I bowed benignantly, but remembered the old Latin saying to the effect that drink digs out the truth. Then, by way of changing the subject, he pointed to the end of the room. Here appeared two pretty women dressed in exceedingly light attire and with wreaths upon their heads, who bore between them a large bowl of liquor in which floated red flowers. (The whole scene, I should say, much resembled some picture I had seen of an ancient Roman—or perhaps it was Egyptian feast taken from a fresco.) They brought the bowl to Dacha, and with a simultaneous movement of their graceful forms lifted it up, whereon all of the company who were not too drunk rose, bowed towards the bowl and twice cried out together:

"The Cup of Illusions! The Cup of Illusions!"

"Drink," said Dacha to me. "Drink to the glory of Heu-Heu." Then observing that I hesitated, he added: "Nay, I will drink first to show that it is not poisoned," and muttering, "O Spirit of Heu-Heu, descend upon thy priest!" drink he did, a considerable quantity.

Then the women brought the bowl, which reminded me of the loving-cup at a Lord Mayor's feast, and held it to my lips. I took a pull at it, making motions of my throat as though it were a long one, though in reality I only swallowed a sip. Next it was handed to Hans to whom I murmured one Boer Dutch word over my shoulder. It was "*Beetje*," which means "little," and as I turned my head to watch him, I think he took the advice.

After this the bowl, in which, I should add, the liquor was of a greenish colour and tasted something like Chartreuse, was taken from one to another till all present had drunk of it, the girls who bore it finishing up the little that was left.

This I saw, but after it I did not see much else for a while, for, small as had been my draught, the stuff went to my head and seemed to cloud my brain. Moreover, all kinds of queer visions, some of them not too desirable, sprang up in my mind, and with them a sense of vastness that was peopled by innumerable forms; beautiful forms, grotesque forms, forms of folk that I had known, now long dead, forms of others whom I had never seen, all of whom had this peculiarity, that they seemed to be staring at me with a strange intentness. Also these forms grouped themselves together and began to enact dramas of one kind or another, dramas of war and love and death that had all the vividness of a nightmare.

Presently, however, these illusions passed away and I remained filled with a great calm and a wonderful sense of well-being, also with my powers of observation rendered most acute.

Looking about me, I noted that all who had drunk seemed to be undergoing similar experiences. At first they showed signs of excitement; then they grew very still and sat like statues with their eyes fixed on vacancy, speaking not a word, moving not a muscle.

This state lasted quite a long time, till at length those who had drunk first appeared to awake, for they began to talk to each other in low tones. I noted that every sign of drunkenness had vanished; one and all they looked as sober as a whole Bench of Judges; moreover, their faces had grown solemn and their eyes seemed to be filled with some cold and fateful purpose.

CHAPTER X

THE SACRIFICE

After a solemn pause, Dacha rose and said in an icy voice:

"I hear the god calling us. Let us pass into the presence of the god and make offering of the yearly sacrifice."

Then a procession was formed. Dacha and Dramana went first, Hans and I followed next, and after us came all who had been at the feast, to a total of about fifty people.

"Baas," whispered Hans, "after I had drunk that stuff, which was so nice and warming that I wished you had let me have more of it, your Reverend Father came and talked to me."

"And what did he say to you, Hans?"

"He said, Baas, that we were going into very queer company and had better keep our eyes skinned. Also that it would be wise not to interfere in matters that did not concern us."

I reflected to myself that within an hour I had received advice of the same sort from a purely terrestrial source, which was an odd coincidence, unless indeed Hans had overheard or absorbed it subconsciously. To him I only observed, however, that such mandates must be obeyed, and that whatever chanced he would do well to sit quite still, keeping his pistol ready, but only use it in case of absolute necessity to save ourselves from death.

The procession left the hall by a back entrance behind the table at which we had sat, and entered a kind of tunnel that was lit with lamps, though whether this was hollowed in the rock or built of blocks of stone I am not sure. After walking for about fifty paces down this tunnel, suddenly we found ourselves in a great cavern, also dimly lit with lamps, mere spots of light in the surrounding blackness.

Here all the priests, including Dacha, left us; at least, peering about, I could not see any of them. The women alone remained in the cave, where they knelt down singly and at a distance from each other like scattered worshippers in a dimly lit cathedral when no service is in progress.

Dramana, to whose charge we seemed to have been consigned, led us to a stone bench upon which she took her seat with us. I noted that she did not kneel and worship like the others. For a while we remained thus in silence, staring at the blackness in front where no lamps burned. It was an eerie business in such surroundings that I confess began to get upon my nerves. At length I could bear it no longer, and in a whisper asked Dramana whether anything was about to happen, and if so, what.

"The sacrifice is about to happen," she whispered back. "Be silent, for here the ears of the god are everywhere."

I obeyed, thinking it safer, and another ten minutes or so went by in an intolerable stillness.

"When does the play begin, Baas?" muttered Hans in my ear. (Once I had taken him to a theatre in Durban to improve his mind, and he thought that this was another, as indeed it was, if of an unusual sort.)

I kicked him on the shins to keep him quiet, and just then at a distance I heard the sound of chanting. It was a weird and melancholy music that seemed to swing backwards and forwards between two bands of singers, each strophe and antistrophe, if those are the right words, ending in a kind of wail or cry of despair which turned my blood cold. When this had gone on for a little while, I thought that I saw figures moving through the gloom in front of us. So did Hans, for he whispered:

"The Hairy People are here, Baas."

"Can you see them?" I asked in the same low voice.

"I think so, Baas. At any rate, I can smell them."

"Then keep your pistol ready," I answered.

A moment later I saw a lighted torch floating in the air in front of us, though the bearer of it I could not see. The torch was bent downwards, and I heard the sound of kindling taking fire. A little flame sprang up revealing a pile of logs arranged for burning, and beyond it the tall form of Dacha wearing a strange headdress and white, priestlike robes, different from those in which he had been clad at the feast. Between his hands, which he held in front of him, was a white human skull reversed, I mean that its upper part was towards the floor.

"Burn, Dust of Illusion, burn," he cried, "and show us our desires," and out of the skull he emptied a quantity of powder on to the pile of wood.

A dense, penetrating smoke arose which seemed to fill the cave, vast though it was, and blot out everything. It passed away and was followed by a blaze of brilliant flame that lit up all the place and revealed a terrific spectacle.

Behind the fire, at a distance of ten paces or so, was an awful object, an appalling black figure at least twelve feet in height, a figure of Heu-Heu as we had seen him depicted in the Cave of the Berg, only there his likeness was far too flattering. For this was the very image of the devil as he might have been imagined by a mad monk, and from his eyes shot a red light.

As I have said before, the figure was like to that of a huge gorilla and yet no ape but a man, and yet no man but a fiend. There was the long gray hair growing in tufts about the body. There was the great, red, bushy beard. There were the enormous limbs and the long arms and the hands with claws on them where the thumbs should be, and the webbed fingers. The bull neck on the top of which sat the small head that somehow resembled an old woman's with a hooked nose; the huge mouth from which the baboon-like tusks protruded, the round, massive, able-looking brow, the deepest glaring eyes, now alight with red fire, the cruel smile—all were there intensified. There, too, was the shape of a dead man into the breast of which the clawed foot was driven, and in the left hand the head that had been twisted from the man's body.

Oh! evidently the painter of the picture in the Berg can have been no Bushman as once I had supposed, but some priest of Heu-Heu whom fate or chance had brought thither in past ages, and who had depicted it to be the object of his private worship. When I saw the thing I gasped aloud and felt as though I should fall to the ground through fear, so hellish was it. But Hans gripped my arm and said:

"Baas, be not afraid. It is not alive; it is but a thing of stone and paint with fire set within."

I stared again; he was right.

Heu-Heu was but an idol! Heu-Heu did not live except in the hearts of his worshippers!

Only out of what Satanic mind had this image sprung?

I sighed with relief as this knowledge came home to me, and began to observe details. There were plenty to be seen. For instance, on either side of the statue stood a line of the hideous Hairy Folk, men to the right and women to the left, with white cloths tied about their middles. In front of this line behind their high priest, Dacha, were the other priests, Heu-Heu's clergy, and on a raised table behind them just at the foot of the base of the statue, which I now saw stood upon a kind of pedestal so as to make it more dominant, lay a dead body, that of one of the Hairy women, as the clear light of the flame revealed.

"Baas," said Hans again, "I believe that is the gorilla-woman I shot in the river. I seem to know her pretty face."

"If so, I hope we shall not join her on that table presently," I answered.

After this suddenly I went mad; everybody went mad. I suppose that the vapour from that accursed powder had got into our brains. Had not Dacha called it the "Dust of Illusions"? Certainly, of illusions there were plenty, most of them bad, like those of a nightmare.

Still, before they possessed me completely, I had the sense to understand what was happening to me and to grip hold of Hans, who I saw was going mad also, and command him to sit quiet. Then came the illusions which really I can't describe to you. You fellows have read of the effects of opium smoking; well, it was that kind of thing, only worse.

I dreamed that Heu-Heu got off his pedestal and came dancing down the hall, also that he bent over me and kissed me on the forehead. In fact, I think it was Dramana who kissed me, for she, too, had gone mad. Everything that I had done bad in my life re-enacted itself in my mind and, all put together, seemed to make me a sinner indeed, because you see the good was entirely omitted. The Hairy Folk began an infernal dance before the statue; the women round us raved and shouted with extraordinary expressions upon their faces; the priests waved their arms and set up yells of adoration as did those of Baal in the Old Testament. In short, literally there was the devil to pay.

Yet strangely enough it was all wildly, deliriously exciting and really I seemed to enjoy it. It shows how wicked we must be at bottom. A sight of hell while you remain on the *terra firma* of our earth is not uninteresting, even though you be temporarily affected by its atmosphere.

Presently the nightmare came to an end, suddenly as it had commenced, and I woke to find my head on Dramana's shoulder, or hers on mine, I forget which, with Hans engaged in kissing my boot under the impression that it was the chaste brow of some black maiden whom he had known about thirty years before. I kicked him on his snub nose, whereon he rose and apologized, remarking that this was the strongest *dacca*—the hemp which the natives smoke with intoxicating effects—that he had ever tasted.

"Yes," I answered, "and now I understand where Zikali's magic comes from. No wonder he wants more of the leaves of that tree and thought it worth while to send us so far to get them."

Then I ceased talking, for something in the atmosphere of the place absorbed my attention. A sudden chill seemed to have fallen upon it and its occupants who, in strange contrast to their recent excesses, now appeared to be possessed by the very spirit of Mrs. Grundy. There they stood, exuding piety at every pore and gazing with rapt countenance at the hideous image of their god. Only to me those countenances had grown very cruel. It was as though they awaited the consummation of some dreadful drama with a kind of cold joy, which, of course, may have been an aftermath of their unholy intoxication. It was the scene at the feast repeated but with a difference. There they had been drunken with liquor and sobered by the potent stuff they had swallowed after it; now they had been made drunken with fumes and were sobered by I knew not what. Their master Satan, perhaps!

The fire still burnt brightly though it gave off no more of these fumes, being fed I suppose with natural fuel, and by the light of it I saw that Dacha was addressing the image with impassioned gestures. What he said I do not know, for my ears were still buzzing and of it I could hear nothing. But presently he turned and pointed to us and then began to beckon.

"What is it he wants us to do?" I asked of Dramana who now was seated at my side, a perfect model of propriety.

"He says that you must come up and make your offering to the god."

"What offering?" I asked, thinking that perhaps it would be of a painful nature.

"The offering of the sacred fire that the Lord of Fire," and she pointed to Hans, "bears about with him."

I was puzzled for a moment till Hans remarked:

"I think she means the matches, Baas."

Then I understood, and bade him produce a new box of Best Wax Vestas and hold it out in his hand. Thus armed we advanced and, passing round the fire, bowed, as the Bible potentate whom the Prophet cured bargained he should be allowed to do in the House of Rimmon, to the beastly effigy of Heu-Heu. Then in obedience to the muttered directions of Dacha, Hans solemnly deposited the box of matches upon the stone table, after which we were allowed to retreat.

Anything more ridiculous than this scene it is impossible to imagine. I suppose that its intense absurdity was caused, or at any rate accentuated by its startling and indeed horrible contrasts. There was the towering and demoniacal idol; there were the rogue priests, their faces alight with a fierce fanaticism; there, looking only half human, were the long lines of savage Hairy Folk; there was the burning fire reflecting itself to the farthest recesses of the cavern and showing the forms of the scattered worshippers.

Finally there was myself, a bronzed and tattered individual, and the dirty, abject-looking Hans holding in his hand that absurd box of matches which finally he deposited in the exact middle of the stone table about six inches from the swollen body of the aboriginal whom he had shot in the river. In those vast surroundings this box looked so lonely and so small that the sight of it moved me to internal convulsions. Shaking with hysterical laughter I returned to my seat as quickly as I could, dragging Hans after me, for I saw that his case was the same, although fortunately it is not the custom of Hottentots to burst into open merriment.

"What will Heu-Heu do with the matches, Baas?" asked Hans. "Surely there must be plenty of fire where he is, Baas."

"Yes, lots," I replied with energy, "but perhaps of another sort."

Then I observed that Dacha was pointing to the right and that the eyes of all present were fixed in that direction.

"The sacrifice comes," murmured Dramana, and as she spoke a woman appeared, a tall woman covered with a white robe or veil, who was led forward by two of the Hairy People. She was brought to the front of the table on which lay the body and the matches, and there stood quite still.

"Who is this?" I asked.

"Last year's bride, with whom the priest has done and passes on into the keeping of the god," answered Dramana with a stony smile.

"Do you mean that they are going to kill the poor thing?" I said, horrified.

"The god is about to take her into his keeping," she replied enigmatically.

At this moment one of the savage attendants snatched away the veil which draped the victim, revealing a very beautiful woman clad in a white kirtle which was cut low upon her breast and reached to her knees. Tall and stately, she stood quite still before us, her black hair streaming down upon her shoulders. Then, as though at some signal, all the women in the audience stood up and screamed:

"Wed her to the god! Wed her to the god and let us drink of the cup that through her unites us to the god!"

Two of the Hairy Folk drew near to the girl, each of whom had something in his hand, though what it was at the moment I could not see, and stood still, as though waiting for a sign. Then followed a pause during which I glanced about me at the faces of the women, made hideous by the unholy passions that raged within them, who stood with outstretched arms pointing at the victim. They looked horrible, and I hated them, all except Dramana, who, I noted with relief, had not cried aloud and did not stretch out her hands like the rest.

What was I about to see? Some dreadful act of voodooism such as negroes practise in Haiti and on the West Coast? Perhaps. If so, I could not bear it. Whatever the risk might be I could not bear it; almost automatically my hand grasped the stock of my revolver.

Dacha seemed as though he were about to say something, a word of doom mayhap. I measured the distance between me and himself with my eyes, calculating where I should aim to put a bullet through his large head and give the god a sacrifice which it did not expect. Indeed, had he spoken such a word, without doubt I should have done it, for as you fellows know I am handy with a pistol, and probably, as a result, never have lived to tell you this story.

As this juncture, however, the victim waved her arms and said in a loud, clear voice:

"I claim the ancient right to make my prayer to the god before I am given to the god."

"Speak on," said Dacha, "and be swift."

She turned and curtseyed to the hideous idol, then wheeled about again and addressed it in form although really she was speaking to the audience.

"O Fiend Heu-Heu," she said in a voice filled with awful scorn and bitterness, "whom my people worship to their ruin, I who was stolen from my people come to thee because I would have none of yonder high-priest and therefore must pay the price in blood. So be it, but ere I come I have something to tell these priests who grow fat in wickedness. Hearken! A spirit is in me, giving me sight. I see this place a sea of water, I see flames bursting through the water, turning thy hideous effigy to dust and burning up thy evil servants, so that not one of them remains. The Prophecy! The Prophecy! Let all who hear me bethink them of the ancient prophecy, for at length its hour is fulfilled!"

Then she stared towards Hans and myself, waving her arms, and I thought was about to address us. If so, she changed her mind and did not.

So far the priests and the congregation had listened in the silence of amazement, or perhaps of fear. Now, however, a howl of furious execration broke from them, and when it died down I heard Dacha shouting:

"Let this blaspheming witch be slain. Let the sacrifice be accomplished!"

The two savages stepped towards her, and now I saw that what they held in their hands were coils of rope with which doubtless she was to be bound. If so, she was too swift for them, for with a great bound she sprang upon the table where lay the body of the Hairy woman and the box of matches. Next instant I saw a knife flashing in her hand; I suppose it had been concealed somewhere in her dress. She lifted it and plunged it to her heart, crying as she did so:

"My blood be on you, Priests of Heu-Heu!"

Then she fell down there upon the table and was still.

In the hush that followed I heard Hans say:

"That was a brave lady, Baas, and doubtless all she said will come true. May I shoot that priest, Baas, or will you?"

"No," I began, but before I could get out another word my voice was overwhelmed by a tumult of shouts:

"The god has been robbed of his sacrifice and is hungry. Let the strangers be offered to the god."

These and other like things said the shouts.

Dacha looked towards us, hesitating, and I saw that it was time to act. Rising, I called out:

"Know, O Dacha, that before one hand is laid upon us I will make you as my companion, Lord-of-the-Fire, made the dog without your doors."

Evidently Dacha believed me, for he grew quiet humble. "Have no fear, Lords," he said. "Are you not our honoured guests and the messengers of a Great One? Go in peace and safety."

Then at his command or sign the brightly burning fire was scattered, so that the cave grew almost dark, especially as some of the lights had gone out.

"Follow me swiftly—swiftly," said Dramana, and taking my hand she led me away through the gloom.

Presently we found ourselves in the passage, though for aught I know it was another passage; at any rate, it led to the hall where we had feasted. This was now empty, although in it lights still burned. Crossing it, Dramana conducted us back to the house, where a hasty examination shewed us that our rifles were just as we had left them; nothing had been touched. Here, seeing that we were quite alone, for all had gone to the sacrifice, I spoke to her.

"Lady Dramana," I said, "does my heart tell me truly or do I only dream that you desire to depart from out of the shadow of Heu-Heu?"

She glanced about her cautiously, then answered in a low voice: "Lord, there is nothing that I desire so much—unless perchance it be death," she added with a sigh. "Hearken! Seven years ago I was bound upon the Rock of Offering, where my sister will stand to-morrow, having been chosen by the god and dedicated to him by the mad terror of my people, which means, Lord, that I had been chosen by Dacha and dedicated to Dacha."

"Why, then, do you still live?" I asked, "seeing that she who was chosen last year must be sacrificed this year?"

"Lord, am I not the daughter of the Walloo, the ruler of the people of the Mainland, and might not the title to that rule be acquired through me while I breathe? It is not the best of titles, it is true, because I was born of a lesser wife of my father, the Walloo, whereas my sister Sabeela is born of the great wife. Still, at a pinch, it might serve. That is why I still live."

"What then is Dacha's plan, Lady Dramana?

"It stands thus, Lord. Hitherto for many generations, it is said since the great fire burned upon the island and destroyed the city, there have been two governments in this land: that of the priests of Heu-Heu, who govern the minds of its people, also the wild Wood Folk, and that of the Walloos, who govern their bodies and are kings by ancient right. Now Dacha, who, when he is not lost in drink or other follies, is far-seeing and ambitious, purposes to rule both minds and bodies and it may be to bring in new blood from outside our country and once more to build up a great people, such as tradition tells we were in the beginning, when we came here from the north or from the west. He does but wait until he has married my sister, the lawful heiress to the Walloo, my father, who by now must be an old and feeble man, to strike his blow, and in her name to seize the government and power.

"The priests, as you have seen, are but few and cannot do this of their own strength, but they command all the savage folk who are called the Children of Heu-Heu. Now these people are very angry because the other day one of their women was killed upon the river, she who lay on the altar before the god, and this they think was done by the Walloo, not understanding that it was your servant, the yellow man there, who slew her. Or if they understand, they believe that he did so by the order of Issicore who, we hear, is betrothed to my sister Sabeela.

"Therefore they wish to make a great war upon the Walloo under the guidance of the priests of Heu-Heu, whom they call their Father, because his image is like to them. Already their mankind are gathering on the island, rowing themselves hither upon logs or bundles of reeds, and by to-morrow night all will be collected. Then, after what is called the Holy Marriage, when my sister Sabeela has been brought as an offering by the Walloo and bound to the pillar between the Everlasting Fires, led by Dacha they will attack the city on the mainland, which they dare not do alone. It will surrender to them, and Dacha will kill my old father and the lord Issicore who stands next to him, and any of the ancient blood who cling to him, and cause himself to be declared Walloo. After this his purpose is to poison the Forest Folk as he well knows how to do and as I have told you, perhaps to bring new blood into the land which is rich and wide, and found a kingdom."

"A big scheme," I said, not without admiration, for on hearing it, to tell the truth, I began to conceive a certain respect for that villain Dacha, who, at any rate, had ideas and presented a striking contrast to the helpless and superstition-ridden inhabitants of the mainland.

"But, Lady," I went on, "what is to happen to me and to my companion who is named Lord-of-the-Fire?"

"I do not know, Lord, who have had little talk with Dacha since you came, or with any to whom he reveals his secrets. I think, however, that he is afraid of you, believing you to be magicians, or in league with the greatest of magicians, the prophet Zikali, who dwells in the south, with whom the priests of Heu-Heu communicate from time to time. Also it is probable that he holds that you may be able to help him to build up a nation and that therefore he would wish to keep you in his service in this country, only killing you if you try to escape. On the other hand, when the Wood Folk come to understand that it was really you, or one of you, who killed the woman, they may clamour for your lives. Then, if he thinks it wisest to please them, at the great feast which is called the finishing of the Holy Marriage, you may be tied upon the altar as a Sacrifice while the blood is drained from you, to be drunk by the priests with the lips of Heu-Heu. Perhaps that matter will be settled at the Council of the Priests to-morrow, Lord."

"Thank you," I said, "never mind the details."

"Meanwhile," she went on, "for the present you are safe. Indeed I, who by my rank am the Mistress of Households, have been commanded to honour you in every way, and to-morrow, when the priests are engaged in preparations for the Holy Marriage, to show you all that you would see, also to provide you with boughs from the Tree of Illusions which Zikali the prophet desires."

"Thank you," I said again, "we shall be most happy to take a walk with you, even if it rains, as I think from the sounds upon the roof it is doing at present. Meanwhile, I understand that you wish to get out of this place and to save your sister. Well, I may as well tell you at once, Lady Dramana, that my companion, who chooses to assume the shape of a yellow dwarf, and I, who choose to be as I am, *are* in fact great magicians with much more power than we seem to possess. Therefore, it is quite possible that we may be able to help you in all ways, and to do other things more remarkable. Yet we may need your aid, since generally that which is mighty works through that which is small, and what I want to know is whether we can count upon it."

"To the death, Lord," she answered.

"So be it, Dramana, for know that if you fail us certainly you will die."

CHAPTER XI

THE SLUICE GATE

All that night it poured, not merely in the usual tropical torrent, but positively in waterspouts. Seldom in my life have I heard such rain as that which fell upon the roof of the house where we were, which must have been wonderfully well built, for otherwise it would have given away. When we rose in the morning and went to the door to look out, all the place was swimming and a solid wall of water seemed to stretch from heaven to earth.

"I think there will be a flood after this, Baas," remarked Hans.

"I think so, too," I answered, "and if we were not here I wish that it might be deep enough to drown every human brute upon this island."

"It cannot do that, Baas, because at the worst they would climb up the mountain, though it might get into the cave and give Heu-Heu a washing —which he needs."

"If it got into the cave, it would probably get into the mountain as well," I began—then stopped, for an idea occurred to me.

I had noticed that this cave sloped downwards somewhat steeply, I mean into the base of the mountain and towards its centre. Probably, in its origin it was a vent blown through the rock at some time in the past when the volcano was very active, which, for aught I knew, remained unblocked, or only slightly blocked. Suppose now that a great volume of water ran down that cave and vanished into the interior of the mountain, was it not probable that something unusual would happen? The volcano was still alive—this I knew from the smoke that hung above it, also by the stream of red-hot lava that we had seen trickling down its southern face—and fire and water do not agree well together. They make steam, and steam expands. This thought took such a persistent hold on me that I began to wonder whether it did not partake of the nature of an inspiration. However, I said nothing of it to Hans, who, being a savage, did not understand such matters.

A little later food was brought to us by one of the serving priests. With it came a message from Dacha to the effect that he grieved he could not wait on us that day as he had many matters to which he must attend, but that the Lady Dramana would do so shortly and show us all there was to be seen, if the rain permitted.

In due course she arrived—alone, as I had hoped she would—and at once began to talk of the rainfall of the previous night, which she said was such as had never been known in their country. She added that all the priests had been out that morning, dragging the great stone sluice gate into its place so as to keep out the water of the lake, lest the arable land should be flooded and the crops destroyed.

I told her that I was much interested in such matters, and asked questions about this sluice which she could not answer as she knew little of its working. She said, however, that she would show it to me so that I might study the system.

I thanked her and inquired whether the lake had risen much. She answered, Not yet, but that probably it would do so during the day and the following night when it became filled with the water brought down by the flooded river which ran into it from the country to the north. At any rate, this was feared, and it had been thought best to set the sluice in place, a difficult task because of its weight. Indeed, a woman who had gone to help out of curiosity had been caught by a lever —I understood that was what she meant—and killed. She still lay by the sluice, since it was not lawful for the priests of Heu-Heu or their servants to touch a dead body between the Feast of Illusions, which had been held on the previous night, and the Feast of Marriage, which would be held on the night of the morrow, when, she added significantly, they often touched plenty.

"It is a Feast of Blood, then?" I said.

"Yes, Lord, a Feast of Blood, and I pray that it may not be of your blood also."

"Have no fear of that," I answered airily, though in truth I felt much depressed. Then I asked her to tell me exactly what was going to happen as to the delivery of the "Holy Bride."

"This, Lord," she said. "Before midnight, when the moon should be at its fullest, a canoe comes, bringing the bride from the City of the Walloos. Priests receive her and tie her to the pillar that stands on the Rock of Offerings between the Everlasting Fires. Then the canoe goes and waits at a distance. The priests go also and leave the bride alone. I know it all, Lord, for I have been that bride. So she stands until the first ray of the rising sun strikes upon her. Then from the mouth of the cave comes out the high priest dressed in skins to resemble the image of the god, and followed by women and some of the Hairy savage folk shouting in triumph. He looses the bride, and they bear her in the cave, and there, Lord, she vanishes."

"Do you think that she will be brought at all, Dramana?"

"Certainly she will be brought, since if my father, the Walloo, or Issicore, or any refused to send her, they would be killed by their own people, who believe that then disaster would overtake them. Unless you can save her by your arts, Lord, my sister Sabeela must become the wife of Heu-Heu, which means the wife of Dacha."

"I will think the matter over," I said. "But if I make up my mind to help, am I right in understanding that you also desire to escape from this island?"

"Lord, I have told you so already, and I will only add this. Dacha hates me and when I have served his purpose and he has in his hands Sabeela, the true heiress to the chieftainship over our people unless first I tread her road, certainly it will be my lot to stand where that poor woman stood last night, who slew herself to escape worse things. Oh, Lord, save me if you can!"

"I will save you—if I can," I replied, and I meant it—almost as much as I meant to save myself.

Then I impressed upon her that she must obey me in all things without question, and this she swore to do. Also I asked her if she could provide us with a canoe.

"It is impossible," she replied. "Dacha is clever; he has bethought him that you might depart in a canoe. Therefore, every one of them has been moved round to the other side of the island where they are kept under watch of the Savage Folk. That is why he gives you leave to roam about the place, because he knows that you cannot leave it, unless you have wings, for the lake is too wide for any man to swim, and if it were not, the Walloo shore is haunted by crocodiles."

Now, my friends, as you may guess, this was a blow indeed. However, I kept my countenance and said that as this was the case something else must be arranged, only asking casually if there were any crocodiles about this part of the island coast. She answered that there were none, because, as she supposed, the flames of the Everlasting Fires, or some smell from the smoke of the mountain, frightened them away.

Next, as the torrents of rain had ceased, at any rate for a while, I suggested that we should go out, and we did so. Also I did not mind much about the weather, as to protect us from it she had brought with her for our use and her own three of the strangest waterproofs that ever I saw. These consisted of two giant leaves from some kind of waterlily that grew on the borders of the lake, sewn together, with a hole at the top of the leaves, where the stalk comes, for the wearer's head to go through, and two openings left for his arms. For the rest no mackintosh ever turned wet so well as did these leaves, the only drawback about them, as I was informed, being that they must be renewed once in every three days.

Arrayed in these queer garments we went out in rain that here we should call fairly heavy, though it was but the merest drizzle compared to what had gone before. This rain I may explain, had great advantages so far as we were concerned, seeing that in it not even the most curious woman put her nose outside her own door. So it came about that we were able to examine the village of the priests of Heu-Heu quite unobserved and at our leisure.

This settlement was small since there were never more than fifty priests in the college, if so it may be called, to whom, of course, must be added their wives and women, on an average, perhaps, of three or four per man.

The odd thing was that there seemed to be no children and no old people. Either offspring did not arrive and folk died young upon the island, or in both cases they were made away with, perhaps as sacrifices to Heu-Heu. I am sorry to say that in the pressure of great dangers I do not remember making any inquiry upon the point, or if I did I cannot recall the answer given. It was only afterwards that I reflected upon this strange circumstance. The fact remains that on the island there were no young and no aged. Another possible explanation, by the way, is that both may have been exported to the mainland.

Here I will add that with the exception of Dramana and a few discarded wives who may have been doomed to sacrifice, the women were fiercer bigots and more cruel votaries of Heu-Heu than were the men themselves. So, indeed, I had observed when I sat among them at the Feast of Illusions in the cave.

For the rest they all lived in dwellings such as that which was given to us, and were waited upon by servants or slaves from the savage race that was called Heuheua. Low as these Heuheua were and disgusting as might be their appearance, like our South African Bushmen, they were clever in their way, and, when trained, could do many things. Also they were faithful to the commands of their god Heu-Heu, or rather to those of his priests, though they hated the Walloos, from whom these priests sprang, and waged continual war against them.

Soon we had left the houses and were among the cultivated lands, all of which Dramana informed us were worked by the Heuheua slaves. These laboured here in gangs for a year at a time, and then were returned to their women in the forests on the mainland, for, except as servants, none of them were allowed upon the island. Those lands were extraordinarily fertile, as was shewn by the crops on them, which, although much beaten down by the torrential rain, were now ready for harvest. They were enclosed by a kind of sea wall built of blocks of lava and must at some time have been reclaimed from the muddy shallows of the lake, which accounted for their richness. Everywhere about them ran irrigation channels that were used in the dry sowing season and controlled by the sluice gate that has been mentioned. That is all I have to say about the gardens, except that the existence of this irrigation system is to my mind another proof that these Walloos sprang originally from some highly civilized race. Their fields extended to that extremity of the island which was nearest to the Walloo coast, and I know not how far in the other direction, for I did not go there.

Standing upon this point we saw in the distance a number of moving specks upon the water. I asked Dramana if they were hippopotami, and she answered:

"No, Lord, they are the Hairy Folk who, in obedience to the summons of the god, cross the lake upon bundles of reeds that they may be ready to fight in the coming war against the Walloo. Already there are hundreds of them gathered upon the farther side of the mountain, and by to-night all their able-bodied men will have come, leaving only the females, the aged, and the children hidden away in the depths of the forests. On the third day from now they will paddle back across the lake, led by the priests under the command of Dacha, and attack Walloo."

"A great deal may happen in three days," I said, and dropped the subject.

We walked back towards the village and the cave mouth by the sea wall, upon the top of which ran a path, and thus at last came to the Rock of Offering, upon each side of which burned the two curious columns of flame that, I took it, were fed with natural gas generated in the womb of the volcano. They were not very large fires—at any rate, when I saw them—the flame may have been about eight or ten feet high, no more. But there they burned, and had done so, Dramana said, from the beginning of things. Between them, at a little distance, stood a post of stone with rings also of stone, to which the bride was bound. I noted that from these rings hung new ropes placed there to serve as the bonds of Sabeela during the coming night.

Having seen all there was to see on this Rock of Offering, including the steps by which the victim was landed, we went on to a long shed with a steep reed roof, which contained the machinery, if so I can call it, that regulated the irrigation sluice. It had a heavy wooden door which Dramana unlocked with an odd-shaped stone key that she produced from a bag she was wearing. This key, she told us, had been given to her by Dacha with strict orders that she was to return it after we had examined the place, should we wish to do so.

As it happened there was a good deal to examine. Near one end of the shed the main irrigation canal, which may have been twelve feet wide, passed beneath it. Here, under the centre of the roof, was a pit of which the water that stood in it prevented us from seeing the depth. On either side of this pit were perpendicular grooves cut in the solid rock, very deep grooves that were exactly filled by a huge slab of dressed stone six or seven inches thick. When this stone, or the upper part of it, was lifted out of the rock floor of the channel, where normally it stood in its niche, forming part of the bed of the channel, it entirely cut off the inflow of water from the lake, and was, moreover, tall enough to stop any possible additional inflow at a time of flood.

Perhaps I can make the thing clear in this way. When Good and I were last in London together we went to Madame Tussaud's and saw the famous guillotine that was used in the French Revolution. The knife of that guillotine, you will remember, was raised between uprights, and when brought into action, let fall again to the bottom of the apparatus, severing the neck of the victim in its course. Now imagine that those uprights were the rock walls of the pit, and that the knife, instead of being but a narrow thing, were a great sheet of steel, or rather stone. Then, when it was drawn to the top of the uprights from the niche at the bottom, it would entirely fill the space to the head of the grooves, and none of the water that normally passed over it could flow between the uprights, or rather walls, because the sheet of stone barred its passage. Now do you understand?

As Good, who was stupid about such matters, looked doubtful, Allan went on:

"Perhaps a better illustration would be that of a portcullis; even you, Good, have seen a portcullis, which, by the way, must mean a door in a groove. Imagine a subterranean or rather subaqueous, portcullis that, when it was desired to shut it, rose in its grooves from below instead of falling from above, and you will have an exact idea of the water door of the priests of Heu-Heu. I'd draw it for you if it wasn't so late."

"I see now," said Good, "and I suppose they wound the thing up with a windlass."

"Why not say with a donkey engine at once, Good? Windlasses had not occurred to the Walloos. No, they acted on a simpler and more ancient plan. They lifted it with a lever. Near the top of this slab of rock, or water door, was drilled a hole. Through this hole passed a bolt of stone, of which the ends went into the cut-out base of the lever, thus forming a kind of hinge. The lever itself was a bar of stone—evidently they would not trust to wood which rots—massive and about twenty feet long, so as to obtain the best possible purchase. When the door was quite down in its niche at the bottom of the bed of the channel, the end of the lever naturally rose high into the air, almost to the top of the pitched roof of the shed, indeed."

When it was desired to raise the door so as to regulate the amount of water passing into the irrigation channel beyond, or to cut if off altogether in case of flood, the lever was pulled down by ropes that were tied to its end by the strength of a number of men and that end was passed into, or rather under, one or other of half a dozen hooks of stone hollowed into a face of solid rock. Here, of course, it remained immovable until it was released, again by the united strength of a number of men, and flew back to the roof, letting the portcullis slab drop into its bed or groove at the bottom of the channel, thus admitting the lake water.

On the present occasion, as a great flood was anticipated, this slab was raised to its full extent, and when I saw it, the top of it stood five or six feet above the level of the water, while the end of the handle of the lever was made fast beneath the lowest hook of rock within a foot of the floor.

Hans and I examined this primitive but effective apparatus for preventing inundations very carefully. Supposing, thought I, that any one wanted to release that lever so that the door fell and water rushed in over it, how could it be done? Answer: it could only be done by the application of the united force of a great number of men pressing on the end of the lever till it was pushed clear of the point of the hook, when naturally it would fly upwards and the door would fall. Or, secondly, by breaking the lever in two, when, of course, the same thing would happen. Now two men, that is Hans and myself, could not possibly release this beam of stone from its hook; indeed, I doubt whether ten men could have done it. Nor could two men possibly break that beam of stone. Perhaps, if they had suitable marble saws, such as workers in stone use, and plenty of time, they might cut it in two, although it seemed to be made of a kind of rock that was as hard as iron. But we had no saw. Therefore, so far as we were concerned the task was impossible; that idea must be dismissed.

Still, there is a way out of most difficulties if only it can be hit upon. My own mental resources were exhausted, it is true, but Hans remained, and possibly he might have some suggestion of value to make. He was a curious creature, Hans, and often his concentrated primitive instincts led him more directly to the mark than did all my civilized reasonings.

So speaking without emphasis in Dutch, for I did not wish Dramana to guess my internal excitement, I put the problem to Hans in these words:

"Supposing and you and I, Hans, with none to help, except perhaps this woman, found it necessary to break that bar of stone and cause the water gate to fall, so as to let in the lake flood over it, how could we do it with such means as we have in this place?"

Hans stared about him, twiddling his hat in his usual vacuous fashion, and remarked:

"I don't know, Baas."

"Then find out, for I want to learn if your conclusions agree with my own," I answered.

"I think that if they agree with the Baas's, they will agree with nothing at all," said Hans, delivering this shrewd and perfectly accurate shot with such a wooden expression of utter stupidity that I could have kicked him.

Next, without more words, he removed himself from my neighbourhood and began to examine the lever in a casual fashion, especially the hook of rock which held it in its place. Presently he remarked in Arabic, so that Dramana might understand, that he wanted to see how deep the pit was, which we could not do from the floor of the shed, and instantly climbed up the slope of the beam-like lever with all the agility of a monkey, and sat himself, cross-legged, on the top of it, just below the stone hinge that I have described. Here he remained for a while, apparently staring into the darkness of the hole or pit on the farther side of the stone slab, where, of course, it was almost empty, as the door cut off the water from the irrigation channel on the island side.

"That hole is too dark to see into," he said, presently, and swarmed down the shaft again. Then he called my attention to the body of the dead woman who Dramana had told us was struck by the lever and killed while it was being dragged into place, which lay almost out of sight in the shadow by the wall of the shed. We went to look at her. She was a tall woman, handsome, like all these people, and young. Outwardly she showed no signs of injury, for her long white robe was unstained. I suppose that she had been crushed between the lever and the hook, or perhaps struck in the side of the head as it was being swung into place. Whilst we were examining the corpse of this unfortunate, Hans said to me, still speaking in Dutch:

"Does the Baas remember that we have two pound tins of the best rifle powder in our bag and that he scolded me because I did not take them out when we left the house of the Walloo, saying that it was foolish to bring them with us as they would be quite useless to us on the island?"

I replied that I had some recollection of the incident, and that, as a matter of fact, they had been heavy to carry. Then Hans proceeded to set a riddle in his irritating and sententious way, asking:

"Who does the Baas think knows most about things that are to happen—the Baas or the Baas's Reverend Father in Heaven?"

"My father, I presume, Hans," I replied airily.

"The Baas is right. The Baas's father in the sky knows much more than the Baas, but sometimes I think that Hans knows better than either, at any rate, here on the earth."

I stared at the little wretch, rendered speechless by his irreverent impudence, but he went on unabashed:

"I did not forget to leave that powder behind, Baas; I brought it with me thinking that it might be useful, because with powder you can blow up men and other things. Also, I did not wish it to stay where we might never see it again."

"Well, what about the powder?" I asked.

"Nothing much, Baas. At least, only this. These Walloo do not bore stones very well; they make the holes too big for what has to go through them. That in the water gate is so large that there would be room to put two pound flasks of powder beneath the pin, so that the strain lifts it up to the top of the hole."

"And what would be the use of putting two flasks of powder in such a place?" I inquired carelessly, for at the moment I was thinking about the dead woman.

"None at all, Baas; none at all. Only I thought the Baas asked me how we could loose that stone arm. If two pounds of powder were put into the hole, covered with a little mud, and fired, I think that they would blow out the bit of rock at the top of the hole, or break the pin, or both. Then, as there would be nothing to hold it, the stone door would fall down and the lake would come in and water the fields of the priests of Heu-Heu, if in his wisdom and kindness the Baas thinks they want it at harvest time, and after so much rain."

"You little wretch," I said; "you infernal, clever little wretch! Hang me if I don't think you have got hold of the right end of the stick this time. Only the business will take a lot of thinking out and arrangement."

"Yes, Baas, and we had better do that in the house, which, as the Baas knows, is quite close, only about a hundred paces away. Let us get out of this place, Baas, before the lady begins to smell rats; only, as you go, take a good squint at that hole in the top of the stone door and the rock pin that goes through it."

Then Hans, who all this while had been staring at the body of the woman and apparently talking about her, bowed towards it, remarking in Arabic, "Allah, I mean Heu-Heu, receive her into his bosom," and retreated reverentially.

So we went away, but I, lingering behind, examined the hole and the pin very carefully.

Hans was quite right: there was just room left in the former to accommodate two tin flasks of powder, also, there were not more than three inches of rock on the topside of the hole. Surely two pounds of powder would suffice to blow out this ring of stone and perhaps to shatter the pin as well.

CHAPTER XII

THE PLOT

We left the shed and, after she had locked its door very carefully and returned the stone key to her pouch, were taken by Dramana to see the famous Tree of Illusions, of which the juice and leaves, if powdered and burnt, could produce such strange dreams and intoxicating effects. It grew in a large walled space that was called Heu-Heu's Garden, though nothing else was planted there. Dramana assured us indeed that this tree had a poisonous effect upon all other vegetation.

Passing the wall by a door of which she also produced some kind of key out of her bag, we found ourselves standing in front of the famous tree, if so it can be called, for its growth was shrub-like and its topmost twigs were not more than twenty feet above the ground. On the other hand, it covered a great area and had a trunk two or three feet thick from which projected a vast number of branches whereof the extremities lay upon the soil, and I think rooted there, after the manner of wild figs, though of this I am not certain.

It was an unholy product of nature, inasmuch as it had no real foliage, only dark green, euphorbia-like and flesh fingers—indeed, I think it must have been some variety of euphorbia. At the extremities of these green fingers appeared purple-coloured blooms with a most evil smell that reminded me of the odour of something dead; also down their sides—for, like the orange, the tree appeared to have the property of flowering and fruiting at the same time—were yellow seed vessels about the size of those of a prickly pear. Except that the trunk was covered with corrugated gray bark and that the finger-like leaves were full of resinous white milk like those of other euphorbias, there is nothing more to say about it. I should add, however, that Dramana told us no other specimen existed, either on the mainland or the island, and that to attempt its propagation elsewhere was a capital offence. In short, the Tree of Illusions was a monopoly of the priests.

Hans set to work and cut a large faggot of the leaves, or fingers, which he tied up with a piece of string he had in his pocket, to be conveyed to Zikali, though there seemed to be such a small prospect of their ever reaching him. It was not an agreeable job, for when it was cut the white juice of the tree spurted out, and if it fell upon the flesh, burned like caustic.

I was glad when it came to an end because of the stench of the flowers, but before I left I took the opportunity, when Dramana was not looking, of picking some of the ripest of the fruits and putting them in my pocket, with the idea of planting the seeds should we ever escape from that country. I am sorry to say, however, that I never did so, as the sharp spines that grew upon the fruits wore a hole in the lining of my pocket, which already was thin from use, and they tumbled out unobserved. Evidently the Tree of Illusions did not intend to be reproduced elsewhere; at least, that was Hans's explanation.

On our way back to the house we had to pass round a lava boulder on the lake side of the sluice shed, crossing by a little bridge the water channel that ran beneath it, near to a flight of landing steps that were used by fishermen. I examined this channel which pierced the sea wall and here, outside the sluice gate, was about twenty feet wide. At the side of it, built into the wall, was a slab of stone on which were marks, cut there, no doubt, to indicate the height of the water level and the rate at which it rose. I noticed that the topmost of these marks was already covered, and that during the little while I stood and watched, it vanished altogether, showing that the water was rising rapidly.

Seeing that I was interested, Dramana remarked that the priests said that tradition never told of the water having reached that topmost mark before, even during the greatest rains. She added that she supposed it had done so now owing to the unprecedented wetness of the summer and great tempests farther up the river that fed the lake, of which we were experiencing the last.

"It is fortunate that you have such a strong door to keep out the water," I said.

"Yes, Lord," she answered, "since if it broke all this side of the island would be flooded. If you look you will see that already the lake stands higher than the cultivated lands and even than the mouth of the Cave of Heu-Heu. It is told in tradition that when first, hundreds of years ago, these lands were reclaimed from the mud of the lake and the wall was built to protect them, the priests of Heu-Heu trusted to the rain for their crops. Then came many dry seasons, and they cut a way through the wall and let in water to irrigate them, making the sluice gate that you have seen to keep it out if it rose too high. An old priest of that time said that this was madness and would one day prove their destruction, but they laughed at him and made the sluice. He was wrong also, since thenceforward their crops were doubled, and the gate is so well-fashioned that no floods, however great, have ever passed through or over it; nor can they do so, because the top of the stone gate rises to the height of a child above the level of the water wall which separates the lake from the reclaimed land."

"The lake might come over the crest of the wall," I suggested.

"No, Lord. If you look you will see that the wall is raised far above its level, to a height that no flood could ever reach."

"Then safety depends upon the gate, Dramana?"

"Yes, Lord. If the flood were high enough, which it never has been within the memory of man, the safety of the town would depend upon the gate, and that of the Cave of Heu-Heu also. Before the mountain broke into flame and destroyed the city of our ancestors, the new mouth was made on the level, for formerly, it is said, it was entered from the slope above. Moreover, there is no danger, because if any accident happened and the flood broke through, all could flee up the mountain. Only then the cultivated land would be ruined for a time and there might be scarcity, during which people must obtain corn from the mainland or draw it from that which is stored in pits in the hillside, to be used in case of war or siege."

I thanked her for her explanation of these interesting hydraulic problems, and after another glance at the scale rock, on which the marks had now vanished completely, showing me that the lake was still rising rapidly, we went to the house to rest and eat.

Here Dramana left us, saying that she would return at sundown. I begged her to do so without fail. This I did for her own sake, a fact that I did not explain. Personally, I was indifferent as to whether she came back or not, having learned all she could teach us, but as I was planning catastrophe, I was anxious, should it come, to give her any chance of escape that might offer for ourselves. After all, she had been a good friend to us and was one who hated Dacha and Heu-Heu and loved her sister Sabeela.

Hans led her to the door and in an awkward fashion made much ado in helping her to put on her leaf raincoat, which she had discarded and was carrying. For now suddenly the rain, which had almost ceased while we walked, had begun to fall again in torrents.

When we had eaten and were left alone within closed doors, Hans and I took counsel together.

"What is to be done, Hans?" I asked, wishing to hear his views.

"This, I think, Baas," he answered. "When it draws near to midnight we must go to hide near the steps, there by the Rock of Offerings, not the smaller ones near the sluice gate. Then when the canoe comes and lands the Lady Sabeela to be married, as soon as she has been taken and tied to the post we must swim out to it, get aboard, and go back to Walloo-town."

"But that would not save the Lady Sabeela, Hans."

"No, Baas, I was not troubling my head about the Lady Sabeela who I hope will be happy with Heu-Heu, but it would save *us*, though perhaps we shall have to leave some of our things behind. If Issicore and the rest wish to save Lady Sabeela, they had better cease from being cowards who are afraid of a stone statue and a handful of priests, and do so for themselves."

"Listen, Hans," I said. "We came here to get a bundle of stinking leaves for Zikali and to save the Lady Sabeela who is the victim of folly and wickedness. The first we have got, the second remains to be done. I mean to save that unfortunate woman, or to die in the attempt."

"Yes, Baas. I thought the Baas would say that, since we are all fools in our different ways, and how can any one dig out of his heart the folly that his mother put there before he was born? Therefore, since the Baas is a fool, or in love with Lady Sabeela because she is so pretty—I don't know which—we must make another plan and try to get ourselves killed in carrying it out."

"What plan?" I asked, disregarding his crude satire.

"I don't know, Baas," he said, staring at the roof. "If I had something to drink, I might be able to think of one, as all this wet has filled my head with fog, just as my stomach is full of water. Still, Baas, do I understand the Baas to say that if that stone gate were broken the lake would flow in and flood this place, also the Cave of Heu-Heu, where all the priests and their wives will be gathered worshipping him?"

"Yes, Hans, so I believe, and very quickly. As soon as the water began to run it would tear away the wall on either side of the sluice and enter in a mighty flood; especially now as the rain is again falling heavily."

"Then, Baas, we must let the stone fall, and as we are not strong enough to do it ourselves, we must ask this to help us," and he produced from his bag the two pounds of powder done up in stout flasks of soldered tin as it had left the maker in England. "As I am called Lord-of-the-Fire, the priests of Heu-Heu will think it quite natural," he added with a grin.

"Yes, Hans," I said, nodding, "but the question is—how?"

"I think like this, Baas. We must pack these two tins tight into that hole in the rock door beneath the pin with the help of little stones, and cover them over thickly with mud to give the powder time to work before the tins are blown out of the hole. But first we must bore holes in the tins and make slow matches and put the ends of them into the holes. Only how are we to make these slow matches?"

I looked about me. There on a shelf in the room stood the clay lamps with which it was lighted at night, and by them lay a coil of the wick which these people used, made of fine and dry plaited rushes, many feet of it.

"There's the very stuff!" I said.

We got it down, we soaked it in a mixture of the native oil, mixed with gunpowder that I extracted from a cartridge, and behold! in half an hour we had two splendid slow matches that by experiment I reckoned would take quite five minutes to burn before the fire reached the powder. That was all we could do for the moment.

"Now, Baas," said Hans, when we had finished our preparations and hidden the matches away to dry, "all this is very nice, but supposing that the stone falls and the water runs in and everything goes softly, how are we to get off the island? If we drown the priests of Heu-Heu—though I do not think we shall drown them because they will bolt up the mountain-side like rock rabbits—we drown ourselves also, and travel in their company to the Place of Fires of which your Reverend Father was so fond of talking. It will be very nice to try to drown the priests of Heu-Heu, Baas, but we shall be no better off, nor will the Lady Sabeela if we leave her tied to that post."

"We shall not leave her, Hans, that is if things go as I hope; we shall leave someone else."

Hans saw light and his face brightened.

"Oh, Baas, now I understand! You mean that you will tie to the post the Lady Dramana, who is older and not quite so nice-looking as the Lady Sabeela, which is why you told her she must stay with us all the time after she comes back? That is quite a good plan, especially as it will save us trouble with her afterwards. Only, Baas, it will be necessary to give her a little knock on the head first lest she should make a noise and betray us in her selfishness."

"Hans, you are a brute to think that I mean anything of the sort," I said indignantly.

"Yes, Baas, of course I am a brute who think of you and myself before I do of others. But then *who* will the Baas leave? Surely he does not mean to leave *me* dressed up in a bride's robe?" he added in genuine alarm.

"Hans, you are a fool as well as a brute, for, silly as you may be, how could I get on without you? I do not mean to leave any one living. I mean to leave that dead woman in the gate house."

He stared at me in evident admiration and answered:

"The Baas is growing quite clever. For once he has thought of something that I have not thought of first. It is a good plan—if we can carry her there without any one seeing us, and the Lady Sabeela does not betray us by making a noise, laughing and crying both together like stupid women do. But suppose that it all happens, there will be four of us, and how are we to get into that canoe, Baas, if those cowardly Walloos wait so long?"

"Thus, Hans. When the canoe lands the Lady Sabeela and she has been tied to the post, if Dramana speaks truth, it waits for the dawn at a little distance. While it is waiting you must swim out to it, taking your pistol with you, which you will hold above your head with one hand to keep the cartridges dry, but leaving everything else behind. Then you must get into the boat, telling the Walloo and Issicore, or whoever is there, who you are. Later, when all is quiet, the Lady Dramana and I will carry the dead woman to the post and tie her there in place of Sabeela. After this you will bring the canoe to the landing steps—the small landing steps by the big boulder which we saw near to the sluice mouth on the lake wall, those that Dramana told us were used by fishermen, because it is not lawful for them to set foot upon the Rock of Offerings. You remember them?"

"Yes, Baas. You mean the ones at the end of a little pier which Dramana also said was built to keep mud from the lake from drifting into the sluice mouth and blocking it."

"When I see you coming, Hans, I shall fire the slow matches and we will run down to the pier and get into the canoe. I hope that the priests and their women in the cave, which is at a distance, will not hear the powder explode beneath that shed, and that when they come out of the cave they will find the water running in and swamping them. This might give them something else to do besides pursuing us, as doubtless they would otherwise, for I am sure they have canoes hidden away somewhere near by, although Dramana may not know where they are. Now do you understand?"

"Oh, yes, Baas. As I said, the Baas has grown quite clever all of a sudden. I think it must be that Wine of Dreams he drank last night that has woke up his mind. But the Baas has missed one thing. Supposing that I get into the canoe safely, how am I to make those people row in to the landing steps and take you off? Probably they will be afraid, Baas, or say that it is against their custom, or that Heu-Heu will catch them if they do, or something of the sort."

"You will talk to them gently, Hans, and if they will not listen, then you will talk to them with your pistol. Yes, if necessary, you will shoot one or more of them, Hans, after which I think the rest will obey you. But I hope that this will not be necessary, since if Issicore is there, certainly he will desire to win back Sabeela from Heu-Heu. Now we have settled everything, and I am going to sleep for a while, with the slow matches under me to dry them, as I advise you to do also. We had little rest last night, and to-night we shall have none at all, so we may as well take some while we can. But first bring that mat and tie up the twigs from the stinking tree for Zikali, on whom be every kind of curse for sending us on this job."

"Settled everything!" I repeated to myself with inward sarcasm as I lay down and shut my eyes. In truth, nothing at all was ever less settled, since success in such a desperate adventure depended upon a string of hypotheses long enough to reach from where we were to Capetown. Our case was an excellent example of the old proverb:

If ifs and ands made pots and pans, There'd be no work for tinkers' hands.

If the canoe came; *if* it waited off the rock; *if* Hans could swim out to it without being observed and get aboard; *if* he could persuade those fetish-ridden Walloos to come to take us off; *if* we could carry out our little game about the powder undetected; *if* the powder went off all right and broke up the sluice-handle as per our plan; *if* we could free Sabeela from the post; *if* she did not play the fool in some female fashion; *if* blackguards of sorts did not manage to cut our throats during all these operations, and a score of other "ifs," why, then our pots and pans would be satisfactorily manufactured and perhaps the priests of Heu-Heu would be satisfactorily frightened away or drowned. As it was, it looked to me as though, so far from not getting any rest that night, we should slumber more soundly than ever we did before—in the last long sleep of all.

Well, it could not be helped, so I just fell back upon my favourite fatalism, said my prayers and went off to sleep, which, thank God, I can do at any time and under almost any circumstances. Had it not been for that gift I should have been dead long ago.

When I woke up it was dark, and I found Dramana standing over me; indeed, it was her entry that roused me. I looked at my watch and discovered to my surprise that it was past ten o'clock at night.

"Why did you not wake me before?" I said to Hans.

"What was the use, Baas, seeing that there was nothing to be done and it is dull to be idle without a drop to drink?"

That's what he said, but the fact was that he had been fast asleep himself. Well, I was thankful, as thus we got rid of many weary hours of waiting.

Suddenly I made up my mind to tell Dramana everything, and did so. There was something about this woman that made me trust her; also, obviously, she was mad with desire to escape from Dacha, whom she hated and who hated her and had determined to murder her as soon as he had obtained possession of Sabeela.

She listened and stared at me, amazed at the boldness of my plans.

"It may all end well," she said, "though there is the magic of the priests to be feared which may tell them things that their eyes do not see."

"I will risk the magic," I said.

"There is also another thing," she went on. "We cannot get into the place where the stone gate is which you would destroy. As I was bidden, when I went back to the cave, I gave up the bag in which I carried the key and that of Heu-Heu's Garden to Dacha, and he has put it away, I know not where. The door is very strong, Lord, and cannot be broken down, and if I went to ask Dacha for the key again he would guess all, especially as the water is rising more fast than it ever rose before in the memory of man, and priests have been to make sure that the stone gate is fixed so that it cannot be moved—yes, and bound down the handle with ropes."

Now I sat still, not knowing what to say, for I had overlooked this matter of the key. While I did so I heard Hans chuckling idiotically.

"What are you laughing at, you little donkey?" I asked. "Is it a time to laugh when all our plans have come to nothing?"

"No, Baas, or rather, yes, Baas. You see, Baas, I guessed that something of this sort might happen, so, just in case it should, I took the key out of the Lady Dramana's bag and put in a stone of about the same weight in place of it. Here it is," and from his pocket he produced that ponderous and archaic lock-opening instrument.

"That was wise. Only you say, Dramana, that the priests have been to the shed. How did they get in without the key?" I asked.

"Lord, there are two keys. He who is called the Watcher of the Gate has one of his own. According to his oath he carries it about him all day at his girdle and sleeps with it at night. The key I had was that of the high priest, who uses it, and others that he may look into all things when he pleases, though this he does seldom, if ever."

"So far so good, then, Dramana. Have you aught to tell us?"

"Yes, Lord. You will do well to escape from this island to-night, if you can, since at to-day's council an oracle has gone forth from Heu-Heu that you and your companion are to be sacrificed at the bridal feast to-morrow. It is an offering to the Wood-dwellers, who now know that the woman was killed by you on the river and say that if you are allowed to live they will not fight against the Walloos. I think also that I am to be sacrificed with you."

"Are we indeed?" I said, reflecting to myself that any scruples I might have had as to attempting to drown out these fanatical brutes were now extinct for reasons which quite satisfied my conscience. I did not intend to be sacrificed if I could help it, then or at any future time, and evidently the best way to prevent this would be to give the prospective sacrificers a dose of their own medicine. From that moment I became as ruthless as Hans himself.

Now I understood why we were being treated with so much courtesy and allowed to see everything we wished. It was to lull our suspicions. What did it matter how much we learned, if within a few hours we were to be sent to a land whence we could communicate it to no one else?

I asked more particularly about this oracle, but only got answers from Dramana that I could not understand. It appeared, however, that as she said, it had undoubtedly been issued in reply to prayers from the savage Hairy Folk, who demanded satisfaction for the death of their countrywoman on the river, and threatened rebellion if it were not granted. This explained everything, and really the details did not matter.

Having collected all the information I could, we sat down to supper, during which Dramana told us incidentally that it had been arranged that our arms, which were known "to spit out fire," should be stolen from us while we slept before dawn, so as to make us helpless when we were seized.

So it came to this: if we were to act at all, it must be at once.

I ate as much as I was able, because food gives strength, and Hans did the same. Indeed, I am sure that he would have made an excellent meal even in sight of the noose which his neck was about to occupy. Eat and drink, for to-morrow we die, would have been Hans's favourite motto if he had known it, as perhaps he did. Indeed, we did drink also of some of the native liquor which Dramana had brought with her, since I thought that a moderate amount of alcohol would do us both good, especially Hans, who had the prospect of a cold swim before him. Immediately I had swallowed the stuff I regretted it, since it occurred to me that it might be drugged. However, it was not; Dramana had seen to that.

When we had finished our food we packed up our small belongings in the most convenient way we could. One half of these I gave to Dramana to carry, as she was a strong woman, and, of course, as he had to swim, Hans could be burdened with nothing except his pistol and the bundle of twigs from the Tree of Illusions, which we thought might help both to support and to conceal him in the water.

Then about eleven o'clock we started, throwing over our heads goatskin rugs that had served for coverings on our beds, to make us resemble those animals if that were possible.

CHAPTER XIII

THE TERRIBLE NIGHT

Leaving the house very softly, we found that the torrential rain had dwindled to a kind of heavy drizzle which thickened the air, while on the surface of the lake and the low-lying cultivated land there hung a heavy mist. This, of course, was very favourable to us, since even if there were watchers about they could not see us unless we stumbled right into them.

As a matter of fact I think that there was none, all the population of the place being collected at the ceremony in the cave. We neither saw nor heard anybody; not even a dog barked, for these animals, of which there were few on the island, were sleeping in the houses out of the wet and cold. Above the mist, however, the great full moon shone in a clear sky which suggested that the weather was mending, as in fact proved to be the case, the tempest of rain, which we learned afterwards had raged for months with some intervals of fine weather, having worn itself out at last.

We reached the sluice house, and to our surprise found that the door was unlocked. Supposing that it had been left thus through carelessness by the inspecting priests, we entered softly and closed it behind us. Then I lit a candle, some of which I always carried with me, and held it up that we might look about us. Next moment I stepped back horror-struck, for there on the coping of the water shaft sat a man with a great spear in his hand.

Whilst I wondered what to do, staring at this man, who seemed to be half asleep and even more frightened than I was myself, with the greater quickness of the savage, Hans acted. He sprang at the fellow as a leopard springs. I think he drew his knife, but I am not sure. At any rate, I heard a blow and then the light of the candle shone upon the soles of the man's feet as he vanished backwards into the pit of water. What happened to him there I do not know; so far as we were concerned he vanished for ever.

"How is this? You told us no one would be here," I said to Dramana savagely, for I suspected a trap.

She fell upon her knees, thinking, probably, that I was going to kill her with the man's spear which I had picked up, and answered:

"Lord, I do not know. I suppose that the priests grew suspicious and set one of their number to watch. Or it may have been because of the great flood which is rising fast."

Believing her explanations, I told her to rise, and we set to work. Having fastened the door from within, Hans climbed up the lever, and by the light of the candle, which could not betray us, as there were no windows to the shed, fixed the two flasks of powder in the hole in the stone gate immediately beneath the pin of the lever. Then, as we had arranged, he wedged them tight with pebbles that we had brought with us.

This done, I procured a quantity of the sticky clay with which the walls of the shed were plastered, taking it from a spot where the damp had come through and made it moist. This clay we stuck all over the flasks and the stones to a thickness of several inches. Only immediately beneath the pin we left an opening, hoping thereby to concentrate the force of the explosion on it and on the upper rim of the hole that was bored through the sluice gate. The slow matches, which now were dry, we inserted in the holes we had made in the flasks, bringing them out through the clay encased in two long, hollow reeds that we had drawn from the roof of our house where we lodged, hoping thus to keep the damp away from them.

Thus arranged, their ends hung to within six feet of the ground, where they could easily be lighted, even in a hurry.

By now it was a quarter past eleven, and the most terrible and dangerous part of our task must be faced. Lifting the corpse of the dead woman who had been killed, presumably, by a blow from the lever that morning, Hans and I—Dramana would not touch her—bore her out of the shed. Followed by Dramana with all our goods, for we dared not leave them behind, as our retreat might be cut off, we carried her with infinite labour, for she was very heavy, some fifty yards to a spot I had noted during our examination in the morning at the edge of the Rock of Offering, which spot, fortunately, rose to a height of six feet or rather less above the level of the surrounding ground. Here there was a little hollow in the rock face washed out by the action of water; a small, roofless cavity large enough to shelter the three of us and the corpse as well.

In this place we hid, for there, fortunately, the shape of the surrounding rock cut off the glare from the two eternal fires, which in so much wet seemed to be burning dully and with a good deal of smoke, the nearer of them at a distance of not more than a dozen paces from us. The post to which the victim was to be tied was perhaps the length of a cricket pitch away.

In this hiding hole we could scarcely be discovered unless by ill fortune someone walked right on to the top of us or approached from behind. We crouched down and waited. A while later, shortly before midnight, in the great stillness we heard a sound of paddles on the lake. The canoe was coming! A minute afterwards we distinguished the voices of men talking quite close to us.

Lifting my head, I peered very cautiously over the top of the rock. A large canoe was approaching the landing steps, or rather, where these had been, for now, except the topmost, they were under water because of the flood. On the rock itself four priests, clad in white and wearing veils over their faces with eyeholes cut in them, which made them look like monks in old pictures of the Spanish Inquisition, were marching towards these steps. As they reached them, so did the canoe. Next, from its prow was thrust a tall woman, entirely draped in a white cloak that covered both head and body, who from her height might very well be Sabeela.

The priests received her without a word, for all this drama was enacted in utter silence, and half led, half carried her to the stone post between the fires, where, so far as I could see through the mist—that night I blessed the mist, as we do in church in one of the psalms—no, it is the mist that blesses the Lord, but it does not matter—they bound her to the post. Then, still in utter silence, they turned and marched away down the sloping rock to the mouth of the cave, where they vanished. The canoe also paddled backwards a few yards—not far, I judged from the number of strokes taken—and there floated quietly.

So far all had happened as Dramana told us that it must. In a whisper I asked her if the priests would return. She answered no; no one would come on to the rock till sunrise, when Heu-Heu, accompanied by women, would issue from the cave to take his bride. She swore that this was true, since it was the greatest of crimes for any one to look upon the Holy Bride between the time that she was bound to the rock and the appearance of the sun above the horizon.

"Then the sooner we get to business the better," I said, setting my teeth, and without stopping to ask her what she meant by saying that Heu-Heu would come with the women, when, as we knew well, there was no such person.

"Come on, Hans, while the mist still lies thick; it may lift at any moment," I added.

Swiftly, desperately, we clambered on to the rock, dragging the dead woman after us. Staggering round the nearer fire with our awful burden, we arrived with it behind the post—it seemed to take an age. Here by the mercy of Providence the smoky reek from the fire propelled by a slight breath of air, combined with the hanging fog to make us almost invisible. On the farther side of the post stood Sabeela, bound, her head dropping forward as though she were fainting. Hans swore that it was Sabeela because he knew her "by her smell," which was just like him, but I could not be sure, being less gifted in that way. However, I risked it and spoke to her, though doubtfully, for I did not like the look of her. To tell the truth, I rather feared lest she should have acted on her threat that as a last resource she would take the poison which she said she carried hidden in her hair.

"Sabeela, do not start or cry out. Sabeela, it is we, the Lord Watcher-by-Night and he who is named Light-in-Darkness, come to save you," I said, and waited anxiously, wondering whether I should ever hear an answer.

Presently I gave a sigh of relief, for she moved her head slightly and murmured:

"I dream! I dream!"

"Nay," I answered, "you do not dream, or if you do, cease from dreaming, lest we should all sleep for ever."

Then I crept round the post and bade her tell me where was the knot by which the rope about her was fastened. She nodded downwards with her head; with her hands she could not point, because they were tied, and muttered in a shaken voice:

"At my feet, Lord."

I knelt down and found the knot, since if I cut the rope we should have nothing with which to tie the body to the post. Fortunately, it was not drawn tight because this was thought unnecessary, as no Holy Bride had ever been known to attempt to escape. Therefore, although my hands were cold, I was able to loose it without much difficulty. A minute later Sabeela was free and I had cut the lashings which bound her arms. Next came a more difficult matter, that of setting the dead woman in her place, for, being dead, all her weight came upon the rope. However, Hans and I managed it somehow, having first thrown Sabeela's cloak and veil over her icy form and face.

"Hope Heu-Heu will think her nice!" whispered Hans as we cast an anxious look at our handiwork.

Then, all being done, we retreated as we had come, bending low to keep our bodies in the layer of the mist which now was thinning and hung only about three feet above the ground like an autumn fog on an England marsh. We reached our hole, Hans bundling Sabeela over its edge unceremoniously, so that she fell on to the back of her sister, Dramana, who crouched in it terrified. Never, I think, did two tragically separated relations have a stranger meeting. I was the last of our party, and as I was sliding into the hollow I took a good look round.

This is what I saw. Out of the mouth of the cave emerged two priests. They ran swiftly up the gentle slope of rock till they reached the two columns of burning natural gas or petroleum or whatever it was, one of them halting by each column. Here they wheeled round and through the holes in their masks or veils stared at the victim bound to the post. Apparently what they saw satisfied them, for after one glance they wheeled about and ran back to the cave as swiftly as they had come, but in a methodical manner which showed no surprise or emotion.

"What does this mean, Dramana?" I exclaimed. "You told me that it was against the law for any one to look upon the Holy Bride until the moment of sunrise."

"I don't know, Lord," she answered. "Certainly it is against the law. I suppose that the diviners must have felt that something was wrong and sent out messengers to report. As I have told you, the priests of Heu-Heu are masters of magic, Lord."

"Then they are bad masters, for they have found out nothing," I remarked indifferently.

But in my heart I was more thankful than words can tell that I had persisted in the idea of lashing the dead woman to the post in place of Sabeela. Whilst we were dragging her from the shed, and again when we were lifting her out of the hole on to the rock, Hans had suggested that this was unnecessary, since Dramana had vowed that no man ever looked upon the Holy Bride between her arrival upon the rock and the moment of sunrise, and that all we needed to do was to loose Sabeela.

Fortunately some providence warned me against giving way. Had I done so all would have been discovered and humanly speaking we must have perished. Probably this would have happened even had I not remembered to run back and pick up the pieces of cord that I had cut from Sabeela's wrists and left lying on the rock, since the messengers might have seen them and guessed a trick. As it was, so far we were safe.

"Now, Hans," I said, "the time has come for you to swim to the canoe, which you must do quickly, for the mist seems to be melting beneath the moon and otherwise you may be seen."

"No, Baas, I shall not be seen, for I shall put that bundle from the Tree of Dreams on my head, which will make me look like floating weeds, Baas. But would not the Baas like, perhaps, to go himself? He swims better than I do and does not mind cold so much; also he is clever and the Walloo fools in the boat will listen to him more than they will to me; and if it comes to shooting, he is a better shot. I think, too, that I can look after the Lady Sabeela and the other lady and know how to fire a slow match as well as he can."

"No," I answered, "it is too late to change our plans, though I wish I were going to get into that boat instead of you, for I should feel happier there."

"Very good, Baas. The Baas knows best," he replied resignedly. Then, quite indifferent to conventions, Hans stripped himself, placing his dirty clothes inside the mat in which was wrapped the bundle of twigs from the Tree of Illusions, because, as he said, it would be nice to have dry things to put on when he reached the boat, or the next world, he did not know which.

These preparations made, having fastened the bundle on to his head by the help of the bonds which we had cut off Sabeela's hands, that I tied for him beneath his armpits, he started, shivering, a hideous, shrivelled, yellow object. First, however, he kissed my hand and asked me whether I had any message for my Reverend Father in the Place of Fires, where, he remarked, it would be, at any rate, warmer than it was here. Also he declared that he thought that the Lady Sabeela was not worth all the trouble we were taking about her, especially as she was going to marry someone else. Lastly he said with emphasis that if ever we got out of this country, he intended to get drunk for two whole days at the first town we came to where gin could be brought—a promise, I remember, that he kept very faithfully. Then he sneaked down the side of the rock and holding his revolver and little buckskin cartridge case above his head, glided into the water as silently as does an otter.

By now, as I have said, the mist was varnishing rapidly, perhaps before a draught of air which drew out of the east, as I have noticed it often does in those parts of Africa between midnight and sunrise, even on still nights. On the face of the water it still hung, however, so that through it I could only discover the faint outline of the canoe about a hundred yards away.

Presently, with a beating heart, I observed that something was happening there, since the canoe seemed to turn round and I thought that I heard astonished voices speaking in it, and saw people standing up. Then there was a splash and once more all became still and silent. Evidently Hans reached the boat safely, though whether he had entered it I could not tell. I could only wonder and hope.

As we could do no good by remaining in our present most dangerous position, I set out to return to the sluice shed where other matters pressed, carrying all our gear as before, but, thank goodness! without the encumbrance of the corpse. Sabeela seemed to be still half dazed, so at present I did not try to question her. Dramana took her left arm and I her right and, supporting her thus, we ran, doubled up, back to the shed and entered it in safety. Leaving the two women here, I went out on to the little pier and crouched at the top of the fishermen's steps, watching and waiting for the coming of Hans with the canoe to take us off, for, as you may remember, the arrangement was that I was not to fire the slow matches until it had arrived.

No canoe appeared. During all the long hours—they seemed an eternity —before the breaking of the dawn did I wait and watch, returning now and again to the shed to make sure that Dramana and Sabeela were safe. On one of these visits I learned that both her father, the Walloo, and Issicore were in the canoe, which made its non-arrival not to be explained, that is, if Hans reached it safely. But if he had not, or perhaps had been killed or met with some other accident in attempting to board it, then the explanation was easy enough, as her crew would not know our plight or that we were waiting to be rescued. Lastly they might have refused to make the attempt—for religious reasons.

The problem was agonizing. Before long there would be light and without doubt we should be discovered and killed, perhaps by torture. On the other hand, if I fired the powder the noise of the explosion would probably be heard, in which case also we should be discovered. Yet there was an argument for doing this, since then, if things went well, the water would rush in and give those priests something to think about that would take their minds off hunting for and capturing us.

I looked about me. The canoe was invisible in the mist. It might be there or it might be gone, only if it were gone and Hans were still alive, I was certain that, as arranged, to advise me he would have fired his pistol, which, to keep the cartridges dry, he had carried above his head in his left hand. Indeed, I thought it probable that, rather than desert me thus, he would have swum back to the island, so that we might see the business through together. The longer I pondered all these and other possibilities, the more confused I grew and the more despairing. Evidently something had happened, but what—what?

The water continued to rise; now all the steps were covered and it was within an inch or two of the surface of the pier on which I must crouch. It was a mighty flood that looked as though presently it would begin to flow over the top of the sea wall, in which case the sluice shed would undoubtedly be inundated and made uninhabitable.

As I think I told you, a few yards to our right, rising above the top of the sea wall to a height of seven or eight feet, was a great rock that had the appearance of a boulder ejected at some time from the crater of the volcano, which rock would be easy to climb and was large enough to accommodate the three of us. Moreover, no flood could reach its top, since to do so it must cover the land beyond to a depth of many feet. Considering it and everything else, suddenly I came to a conclusion, so suddenly indeed and so fixedly that I felt as though it were inspired by some outside influence.

I would bring the women out and make them lie down upon the top of that boulder, trusting to Dramana's dark cloak to hide them from observation even in that brilliant moonlight. Then I would return to the shed and set light to the match, and, after I had done this, join them upon the rock whence we could see all that happened, and watch for the canoe, though of this I had begun to despair.

Abandoning all doubts and hesitations, I set to work to carry out this scheme with cold yet frantic energy. I fetched the two sisters, who, imagining that relief was in sight, came readily enough, made them clamber up the rock and lie down there on their faces, throwing Dramana's large dark cloak over both of them and our belongings. Then I went back to the shed, struck a light, and applied it to the ends of the slow matches, that began to smoulder well and clearly. Rushing from the shed, I locked the heavy door and sped back to the rock, which I climbed.

Five minutes passed, and just as I was beginning to think that the matches had failed in some way, I heard a heavy thud. It was not very loud; indeed, at a distance of even fifty yards I doubted whether any one would have noticed it unless his attention were on the strain. That shed was well built and roofed and smothered sounds. Also this one had nothing of the crack of a rifle about it, but rather resembled that which is caused by something heavy falling to the ground.

After this for a while nothing particular happened. Presently, however, looking down from my rock I saw that the water in the sluice, which, being retained by the stone door in the shed, hitherto had been still, was now running like a mill race, and with a thrill of triumph learned that I had succeeded.

The sluice was down and the flood was rushing over it!

Watching intently, a minute or so later I observed a stone fall from the coping of the channel, for it was full to the brim, then another, and another, till presently the whole work seemed to melt away. Where it had been was now a great and ever-growing gap in the sea wall through which the swollen waters of the lake poured ceaselessly and increasingly. Next instant the shed vanished like a card house, its foundations being washed out, and I perceived that over its site, and beyond it, a veritable river, on the face of which floated portions of its roof, was fast inundating the low-lying lands behind that had been protected by the wall.

I looked at the east; it was lightening, for now the blackness of the sky where it seemed to meet the great lake, had turned to grey. The dawn was at hand.

With a steady roar, through the gap in the sea wall which grew wider every moment, the waters rushed in, remorseless, inexhaustible; the aspect of them was terrifying. Now our rock was a little island surrounded by a sea, and now in the east appeared the first ray from the unrisen sun stabbing the rain-washed sky like a giant spear. It was a wondrous spectacle and, thinking that probably it was the last I should ever witness upon earth, I observed it with great interest.

By this time the women at my side were sobbing with terror, believing that they were going to be drowned. As I was of the same opinion, for I felt our rock trembling beneath us as though it were about to turn over or, washed from its foundations, to sink into some bottomless gulf, and could do nothing to help them, I pretended to take no notice of their terror, but only stared towards the east.

It was just then that, emerging out of the mist on the face of the waters within a few yards of us, I saw the canoe. Hear the sound of the paddles I could not, because of the roar of the rushing water. In it at the stern, with his pistol held to the head of the steersman, stood Hans.

I rose up, and he saw me. Then I made signs to him which way he should come, keeping the canoe straight over the crest of the broken wall where the water was shallow. It was a dangerous business, for every moment I thought it would overset or be sucked into the torrent beyond, where the sluice channel had been; but those Walloos were clever with their paddles, and Hans's pistol gave them much encouragement.

Now the prow of the canoe grated against the rock, and Hans, who had scrambled forward, threw me a rope. I held it with one hand and with the other thrust down the shrinking women. He seized them and bundled them into the canoe like sacks of corn. Next I threw in our gear and then sprang wildly myself, for I felt our stone turning. I half fell into the water, but Hans and someone else gripped me and I was dragged in over the gunwale. Another instant and the rock had vanished beneath the yellow, yeasty flood!

The canoe oscillated and began to spin round; happily it was large and strong, with at least a score of rowers, being hollowed from a single, huge tree. Hans shrieked directions and the paddlers paddled as never they had done before. For quite a minute our fate hung doubtful, for the torrent was sucking at us and we did not seem to gain an inch. At last, however, we moved forward a little, towards the Rock of Sacrifice this time, and with sixty seconds were safe and out of the reach of the landward rush of the water.

"Why did you not come before, Hans?" I asked.

"Oh, Baas, because these fools would not move until they saw the first light, and when the Walloo and Issicore wanted to, told them that they would kill them. They said it was against their law, Baas."

"Curse them all for ten generations!" I exclaimed, then was silent, for what was the use of arguing with such a superstition-ridden set?

Superstition is still king of most of the world, though often it calls itself Religion. These Walloos thought themselves very religious indeed.

Thus ended that terrible night.

CHAPTER XIV

THE END OF HEU-HEU

Opposite to the Rock of Offering the canoe came to a standstill quite close to the edge of the rock. I inquired why, and the old Walloo, who sat in the middle of the boat draped in wondrous and imperial garments and a headdress, that, having worked itself to one side in the course of our struggles, made him look as though he were drunk, answered feebly:

"Because it is our law, Lord. Our law bids us wait till the sun appears and the glory of Heu-Heu comes forth to take the Holy Bride."

"Well," I answered, "as the Holy Bride is sitting in this boat with her head upon my knee" (this was true, because Sabeela had insisted upon sticking to me as the only person upon whom she could rely, and so, for the matter of that, had Dramana, for *her* head was on my other knee), "I should recommend the glory of Heu-Heu, whatever that may be, not to come here to look for her. Unless, indeed, it wants a hole as big as my fist blown through it," I added with emphasis, tapping my double-barrelled Express which was by my side, safe in its waterproof case.

"Yet we must wait, Lord," answered the Walloo humbly, "for I see that there is still a Holy Bride tied to the post, and until she is loosed our law says that we may not go away."

"Yes," I exclaimed, "the holiest of all brides, for she is stone dead and all the dead are holy. Well, wait if you like, for I want to see what happens, and I think they can't get at us here."

So we hung upon our oars, or rather paddles, and waited, till presently the rim of the red sun appeared and revealed the strangest of scenes. The water of the lake, swollen by weeks of continuous rain and the recent tempest, flowing in with a steady rush that somehow reminded me of the ordered advance of an infinite army, through the great gap in the lake wall that was broadening minute by minute beneath its devouring bite—is there anything so mighty as water in the world, I wonder—had now flooded most of the cultivated land to a depth of several feet.

As yet, however, it had not reached the houses built against the mountain, in one of which we had been lodged. Nor had it overflowed the great Rock of Offering, which, you will remember, stood about the height of a man above the level of the plain, being in fact a large slab of consolidated lava that once had flowed from the crater into the lake in a glacier-like stream of limited breadth. It is true that the circumstance that the rock sloped downwards to the cave mouth seemed to contradict that theory, but this I attribute to some subsequent subsidence at its base, such as often happens in volcanic areas where hidden forces are at work beneath the surface of the earth.

Well, I repeat, the rock was not yet flooded, and so it came about that, at the proper moment, as had happened on this day, perhaps for hundreds of years, Heu-Heu emerged from the cave "to claim his Holy Bride."

"How could he do that?" asked Good triumphantly, thinking, I suppose that he had caught Allan tripping. "You said that Heu-Heu was a statue, so how could he come out of the cave?"

"Does not it occur to you, Good," asked Allan, "that a statue is sometimes carried? However, in this case it was not so, for Heu-Heu himself walked out of that cave, followed by a number of women, with some of the Hairy Folk behind them, and looking at him as he stalked along, hideous and gigantic, I understood two things. The first of these was, how it came about that Sabeela had vowed to me that many had seen Heu-Heu with their eyes, as Issicore also declared he had done himself, 'walking stiffly.' The second, why it was a law that the canoe which brought the Holy Bride should wait until she was removed at dawn; namely in order that those in it might behold Heu-Heu and go back to their land to testify to his bodily existence, even if they were not allowed to give details as to his appearance, because to speak of this would, they believed, bring a 'curse' upon them."

"But there wasn't a Heu-Heu," objected Good again.

"Good," said Allan, "really you are what Hans called me—quite clever. With extraordinary acumen you have arrived at the truth. There wasn't a Heu-Heu. But, Good, if you live long enough," he went on with a gentle sarcasm which showed that he was annoyed, "yes, if you live long enough, you will learn that this world is full of deceptions, and that the Tree of Illusions does not, or rather did not, grow only in Heu-Heu's Garden. As you say, no Heu-Heu existed, but there did exist an excellent copy of him made up with a skill worthy of a high-class pantomime artist; so excellent indeed that from fifty yards or so away, it was impossible to tell the difference between it and the great original as depicted in the cave."

There in all his hairy, grinning horror, "walking stiffly," marched Heu-Heu, eleven or twelve feet high. Or to come to the facts, there marched Dacha on stilts, artistically draped in dyed skins and wearing on the top of or over his head a wickerwork and canvas or cloth mask beautifully painted to resemble the features of his amiable god.

The pious crew of our boat saw him, and bowed their classic heads in reverence to the divinity. Even Issicore bowed, a performance that I observed caused Dramana, yes, and the loving Sabeela herself, to favour him with glances of indignation, not unmixed with contempt. At least this was certainly the case with Dramana, who had lived behind the scenes, but Sabeela may have been moved by other reflections. Perhaps *she* still believed that there was a Heu-Heu, and that Issicore would have done better to show himself less devoted to these religious observances and less willing to surrender her to the god's divine attentions. You may all have noticed that however piously disposed, there is a point at which the majority of women become very practical indeed.

Meanwhile Heu-Heu stalked forward with a gait that might very literally be called stilted, and the bevy of white-robed ladies followed after him apparently singing a bridal song, while behind these, "moping and mowing," came their hairy attendants. By the aid of my glasses, however, I could see that these ladies, at any rate, were not enjoying the entertainment, whatever may have been the case with Dacha inside his paste boards. They stared at the rising water and one of them turned to run but was dragged back into place by her companions, for probably on this solemn occasion flight was a capital offence. So on they came till they reached the post to which we had tied the dead woman, whereon according to custom, the bridesmaids skipped up to release her, while the Hairy Folk ranged themselves behind.

Next moment I saw the first of these bridesmaids suddenly stand still and stare; then she emitted a yell so terrific that it echoed all over the lake like the blast of a train. The others stared also and in their turn began to yell. Then Heu-Heu himself ambled round and apparently had a look, a good look, for by now someone had torn away the veil which I had thrown over the corpse's head. He did not look long, for next moment he was legging, or rather stilting, back to the cave as fast as he could go.

This was too much for me. By my side was my double-barrelled Express rifle loaded with expanding bullets. I drew it from its case, lifted it, and got a bead on to Heu-Heu just above where I guessed the head of the man within to be, for I did not want to kill the brute but only to frighten him. By now the light was good and so was my aim, for a moment later the expanding bullet hit in the appointed spot and cleared away all that top hamper of wicker and baboon skins, or whatever it may have been. Never before was there such a sudden disrobement of an ecclesiastical dignitary draped in all his trappings.

Everything seemed to come off at once, as did Dacha from his stilts, for he went a most imperial crowner that must have flattened his hooked nose upon that lava rock. There he lay a moment, then, leaving his stilts behind him, he rose and fled after the screaming women and their ape-like attendants back into the cave.

"Now," I remarked oracularly to the old Walloo and the others who were terrified at the report of the rifle, "now, my friends, you see what your god is made of."

The Walloo attempted no reply, apparently he was too astonished—disillusionment is often painful, you know—but one of his company who seemed to be a kind of official timekeeper, said that the sun being up and the Holy Bridal being accomplished, though strangely, it was lawful for them to return home.

"No, you don't," I answered. "I have waited here a long time for you and now you shall wait a little while for me, as I want to see what happens."

The timekeeper, however, a man of routine, if one devoid of curiosity, dipped his paddle into the water as a signal to the other rowers to do likewise, whereon Hans hit him hard over the fingers with the butt of his revolver, and then held its barrel to his head.

This argument convinced him that obedience was best, and he drew in the paddle, as did the others, making polite apologies to Hans.

So we remained where we were and watched.

There was lots to see, for by now the water was beginning to run over the rock. It reached the eternal fires with the result that they ceased to be eternal, for they went out in clouds of smoke and steam. Three minutes later it was pouring in a cataract down the slope into the mouth of the cave. Before I could count a hundred, people began to come out of that cave in the greatest of hurries, as wasps do if you stir up their nest with a stick. Among them I recognised Dacha, who had a very good idea of looking after himself.

He and the first of those who followed, wading through the water, got clear and began to scramble up the mountainside behind. But the rest were not so fortunate, for by now the stream was several feet deep and they could not fight it. For a moment they appeared struggling amid the foam and bubbles. Then they were swept back into the mouth of the cave and gathered to the breast of Heu-Heu for the last time. Next, as though at a signal, all the houses, including that in which we had been lodged, crumbled away together. They just collapsed and vanished.

Everything seemed finished and I wondered whether I would put a bullet into Dacha, who now was standing on a ridge of rock and wringing his hands as he watched the destruction of his temple, his god, his town, his women, and his servants. Concluding that I would not, for something seemed to tell me to leave this wicked rascal to destiny, I was about to give the order to paddle away when Hans called to me to look at the mountain top.

I did so, and observed that from it was rushing a great cloud of steam, such as comes from a railway engine when it is standing still with too much heat in its boiler, but multiplied a millionfold. Moreover, as the engine screams in such circumstances, so did the mountain scream, or rather roar, emitting a volume of sound that was awful to hear.

"What's up now, Hans?" I shouted.

"Don't know, Baas. Think that water and fire are having a talk together inside that mountain, Baas, and saying they hate each other, just like badly married man and woman who quarrel in a small hut, Baas, and can't get out. Hiss, spit, go woman; pop, bang, go man——" Here he paused from his nonsense, staring at the mountain top with all his eyes, then repeated in a slow voice, "Yes, pop, bang, go man! Just *look* at him, Baas!"

At this moment, with an amazing noise like to that of a magnified thunderclap, the volcano seemed to split in two and the crest of it to fly off into space.

"Baas," said Hans, "I am called Lord-of-the-Fire, am I not? Well, I am not Lord of that fire and I think that the farther off we get from it, the safer we shall be. *Allemagter!* Look there," and he pointed to a huge mass of flaming lava which appeared to descend from the clouds and plunge into the lake about a couple of hundred yards away, sending up a fountain of steam and foam, like a torpedo when it bursts.

"Paddle for your lives!" I shouted to the Walloos, who began to get the canoe about in a very great hurry.

As she came round—it seemed to take an age—I saw a strange and in a way a terrible sight. Dacha had left his ledge and was running down into the lake, followed by a stream of molten lava, dancing while he ran, as though with pain, probably because the stream had scorched him. He plunged into the water, and just then a great wave formed, driven outwards doubtless by some subterranean explosion. It rushed towards us, and on its very crest was Dacha.

"I think that priest wants us to give him a row, Baas," said Hans. "He has had enough of his happy island home, and wishes to live on the mainland."

"Does he?" I replied. "Well, there is no room in the canoe," and I drew my pistol.

The wave bore Dacha quite close to us. He reared himself in the water, or more probably was lifted up by the pressure underneath, so that almost he appeared to be standing on the crest of the wave. He saw us, he shouted curses upon us and shook his fists, apparently at Sabeela and Issicore. It was a horrible sight.

Hans, however, was not affected, for by way of reply he pointed first to me, then to Sabeela and lastly to himself, after which, such was his unconquerable vulgarity, he put his thumb to his nose and as schoolboys say "cocked a snook" at the struggling high priest.

The wave became a hollow and Dacha disappeared "to look for Heu-Heu," as Hans remarked. That was the end of this cruel but able man.

"I am glad," said Hans after reflection, "that the Predikant Dacha should have learned who sent him down to Heu-Heu before he went there, which he knew well enough or he would not have been so cross, Baas. Has it occurred to the Baas what clever people we are, all of whose plans have succeeded so nicely? At one time I thought that things were going wrong. It was after I scrambled into this canoe and those fools would not move to fetch you and the women, because they said it was against their law. While I was putting on my clothes, which got here quite dry because I was so careful, Baas, for I had asked them to paddle to fetch you while I was still naked and been told that they would not, I wondered whether I should try to make them do so by shooting one of them. Only I thought that I had better wait a while, Baas, and see what happened, because if I shot one, the others might have become more stupid and obstinate than before, and perhaps have paddled away after they had killed me. So I waited, which the Baas will admit was the best thing to do, and everything came right in the end, having doubtless been arranged by your Reverend Father, watching us in the sky."

"Yes, Hans, but if you had made up your mind otherwise, whom would you have shot?" I asked. "The Walloo?"

"No, Baas, because he is old and stupid as a dead owl. I should have shot Issicore because he tires me so much and I should like to save the Lady Sabeela from being made weary for many years. What is the good of a man, Baas, who, when he thinks his girl is being given over to a devil, sits in a boat and groans and says that ancient laws must not be broken lest a curse should follow? He did that, Baas, when I asked him to order the men to row to the steps."

"I don't know, Hans. It is a matter for them to settle between them, isn't it?"

"Yes, Baas, and when the lady has got her mind again and at last that hour comes, as it always does when there is something to pay, Baas, I shall be sorry for Issicore, for I don't think he will look so pretty when she has done with him. No, I think that when he says 'Kiss! Kiss!' she will answer, 'Smack! Smack!' on both sides of his head, Baas. Look, she has turned her back on him already. Well, Baas, it doesn't matter to me, or to you either, who have the Lady Dramana there to deal with. She isn't turning her back, Baas, she is eating you up with her eyes and saying in her heart that at last she has found a Heu-Heu worth something, even though he be small and withered and ugly, with hair that sticks up. It is what is in a man that matters, Baas, not what he looks like outside, as women often used to say to me when I was young, Baas."

Here with an exclamation that I need not repeat, for none of us really like to have our personal appearance reflected upon by a candid friend, however faithful, I lifted the butt of my rifle, purposing to drop it gently on Hans's toes. At that point, however, my attention was diverted from this rubbish, which was Hans's way of showing his joy at our escape, by another blazing boulder which fell quite near to the canoe, and immediately afterwards by the terrific spectacle of the final dissolution of the volcano.

I don't know exactly what happened, but sheets of wavering flame and clouds of steam ascended high into the heavens. These were accompanied by earth-shaking rumblings and awful explosions that resounded like the loudest thunder, each of them followed by the ejection of showers of blazing stones and the rushing out of torrents of molten lava which ran into the lake, making it hiss and boil. After this came tidal waves that caused our canoe to rock perilously, dense clouds of ashes and a kind of hot rain which darkened the air so much that for a while we could see nothing, no, not for a yard before our noses. Altogether, it was a most terrifying exhibition of the forces of nature which, by some connection of ideas, made me think of the Day of Judgment.

"Heu-Heu avenges himself upon us!" wailed the old Walloo, "because we have robbed him of his Holy Bride."

Here his speech came to an end, for a good reason, since a large hot stone fell upon his head, and, as Hans who was next to him explained through the fog, "squashed him like a beetle."

When from the outcry of his followers Sabeela realized that her father was dead, for he never moved or spoke again, she seemed to wake up in good earnest, just as though she felt that the mantle of authority had fallen upon her.

"Throw that hot coal out of the boat," she said, "lest it burn through the bottom and we sink."

With the help of a paddle Issicore obeyed her, and, the body of the Walloo having been covered up with a cloak, we rowed on desperately. By good fortune about this time a strong wind began to blow from the shore towards the island which kept back or drove away the hot rain and pumice dust, so that we could once more see about us. Now our only danger was from the rocks, such as that which had killed the Walloo, that fell into the water all around, sending up spouts of foam. It was just as though we were under heavy bombardment, but happily no more of them hit the canoe, and as we got farther off the island the risk became less. As we found afterwards, however, some of them were thrown as far as the mainland.

Still, there was one more peril to be passed, for suddenly we ran into a whole fleet of rude canoes, or rather bundles of reed and brushwood, or sometimes logs sharpened at both ends by fire, on each of which one of the Hairy savages sat astride directing it with a double-bladed paddle.

I presume that these people must have been a contingent of the aboriginal Wood-folk who had started for the island in obedience to the summons of Heu-Heu, where, as I have told, a great number of them were already gathered preparatory to attacking the town of Walloo. Or they may have been escaping from the island; really I do not know. One thing was clear; however low they may have been in the scale of humanity, they were sharp enough to connect us with the awful, natural catastrophe that was happening, for squeaking and jabbering like so many great apes, they pointed to that vision of hell, the flaming volcano now sinking to dissolution, and to us.

Then with their horrible yells of *Heu-Heu! Heu-Heu!* they set to work to attack us.

There was only one thing to be done—open fire on them, which Hans and I did with effect, and meanwhile try to escape by our superior speed. I am bound to say that those hideous and miserable creatures showed the greatest courage, for undeterred by the sight of the death of their companions whom our bullets struck, they tried to close upon us with the object, no doubt, of oversetting the canoe and drowning us all.

Hans and I fired as rapidly as possible, but we could deal with only a tithe of them, so that speed and manoeuvring were our principal hope. Sabeela stood up in the boat and cried directions to the paddlers, while Hans and I shot, first with the rifles and then with our revolvers.

Still, one huge gorilla-like fellow, whose hair grew down to his beetling eyebrows, got hold of the gunwale and began to pull the canoe over. We could not shoot him because both rifles and revolvers were empty; nor did our blows make him loosen his grip. The canoe rocked from side to side increasingly, and began to take in water.

Just as I feared that the end had come, for more hairy men were almost on to us, Sabeela saved the situation in a bold and desperate fashion. By her side lay the broad spear of that priest whom Hans had killed in the sluice shed, knocking him backwards into the water pit. She seized it and with amazing strength stabbed the great beast-like creature who had hold of the canoe and was putting all his weight on it to force the gunwale under water. He let go and sank. By skilful steering we avoided the others, and in three minutes were clear of them, since they could not keep pace with us on their rude craft.

"Plenty to do to-night, Baas!" soliloquized Hans, wiping his brow. "Perhaps if a crocodile does not swallow us between here and the shore, or these fools do not sacrifice us to the ghost of Heu-Heu, or we are not killed by lightning, the Baas will let me drink some of that native beer when we get back to the town. All this fire about has made me very thirsty."

Well, we arrived there at last—a generation seemed to have passed since I left that quay, which we found crowded with the entire terror-stricken population of the place. They received the body of the Walloo in respectful silence, but it seemed to me without any particular grief.

Indeed, these people appeared to have outworn the acuter human emotions. All such extremes, I suppose, had been smoothed away from their characters by time, and by the degrading action of the vile fetishism under which they lived. In short, they had become mere handsome, human automata who walked about with their ears cocked listening for the voice of the god and catching it in every natural sound. To tell the truth, however interesting may have been their origin, in their decadence they filled me with contempt.

The reappearance of Sabeela astonished them very much but seemed to cause no delight.

"She is the god's wife," I heard one of them say. "It is because she has run away from the god that all these misfortunes have happened." She heard it also and rounded on them with spirit, having by now quite recovered her nerve, or so it seemed, which is more than could be said of Issicore, who, although he should have been wild with joy, remained depressed and almost silent.

"What misfortunes?" she asked. "My father is dead, it is true, killed by a hot stone that fell upon him and I weep for him. Still, he was a very old man who must soon have passed away. For the rest, is it a misfortune that through the courage and power of these strangers I, his daughter and heiress, have been freed from the clutches of Dacha? I tell you that Dacha was the god; Heu-Heu whom you worship was but a painted idol. If you do not believe it, ask the White Lord here, and ask my sister Dramana whom you seem to have forgotten, who in past years was given to him as a Holy Bride. Is it a misfortune that Dacha and his priests have been destroyed, and with him the most of the savage hairy Wood-folk, our enemies? Is it a misfortune that the hateful smoking mountain should have melted away in fire, as it is doing now, and with it the cave of mysteries, out of which came so many oracles of terror, thus fulfilling the prophecy that we should be delivered from our burdens by a white lord from the south?"

At these vigorous words the frightened crowd grew silent and hung their heads. Sabeela looked about her for a little while, then went on:

"Issicore, my betrothed, come forward and tell the people you rejoice that these things have happened. To save me from Heu-Heu, at my prayer you travelled far to ask succour of the great Magician of the South. He has sent the succour and I have been saved. Yet you helped to row the boat which took me to the sacrifice. For that I do not blame you, because you must do so, being of the rank you are, or be cursed under the ancient law. Now I have been saved, though not by you, who, thinking the White Lord dead upon the Holy Isle, consented to my surrender to the god, and the law is at an end with the destruction of Heu-Heu and his priests, slain by the wisdom and might of that White Lord and his companion. Tell them, therefore, how greatly you rejoice that you have not journeyed in vain, and they did not listen in vain to your petition for help; that I stand before them here also free and undefiled, and that henceforth the land is rid of the curse of Heu-Heu. Yes, tell the people these things and give thanks to the noble-hearted strangers who brought them to pass and saved me with Dramana my sister."

Now, tired out as I was, I watched Issicore not without excitement, for I was curious to hear what he had to say. Well, after a pause, he came forward and answered in a hesitating voice:

"I do rejoice, Beloved, that you have returned safe, though I hoped when I led the White Lord from the South, that he would have saved you in some fashion other than by working sacrilege and killing the priests of the god with fire and water, men who from the beginning have been known to be divine. You, the Lady Sabeela, declare that Heu-Heu is dead, but how know we that he is dead? He is a spirit, and can a spirit die? Was it a dead god who threw the stone that killed the Walloo, and will he not perhaps throw other stones that will kill us, and especially you, Lady, who have stood upon the Rock of Offerings, wearing the robe of the Holy Bride?"

"Baas," inquired Hans reflectively, in the silence which followed these timorous queries, "do you think that Issicore is really a man, or is he in truth but made of wood and painted to look like one, as Dacha was painted to look like Heu-Heu?"

"I thought that he was a man yonder in the Black Kloof, Hans," I answered, "but then he was long way off Heu-Heu. Now I am not so sure. But perhaps he is only very frightened and will come to himself by and by."

Meanwhile Sabeela was looking her extremely handsome lover up and down; up and down she looked him, and never a word did she say—at least, to him. Presently, however, she spoke to the crowd in a commanding voice, thus:

"Take notice that my father being dead, I am now the Walloo, and one to be obeyed. Go about your tasks fearing nothing, since Heu-Heu is no more and the most of the Hairy Folk are slain. I depart to rest, taking with me these, my guests and deliverers," and she pointed to me and Hans. "Afterwards I will talk with you, and with you also, my lord

Issicore. Bear the late Walloo, my father, to the burial place of the Walloos."

Then she turned and, followed by us and the members of her household, went to her home.

Here she bade us farewell for a while, since we were all half dead with fatigue and sorely needed rest. As we parted, she took my hand and kissed it, thanking me with tears welling from her beautiful eyes for all that I had done, and Dramana did likewise.

"How comes it, Baas," said Hans as we ate food and drank of the native beer before we lay down to sleep, "that those ladies did not kiss my hand, seeing that I too have done something to help them?"

"Because they were too tired, Hans," I answered, "and made one kiss serve for both of us."

"I see, Baas, but I expect that to-morrow they will still be too tired to kiss poor old Hans."

Then he filled the cup out of which he had been drinking with the last of the liquor from the jar and emptied it at a swallow. "There, Baas," he said; "that's only right; you may take all the kisses, so long as I get the beer."

Exhausted as I was I could not help laughing, although to tell the truth, I should have liked another glass myself. Then I tumbled on to the couch and instantly went to sleep.

It is a fact that we slept all the rest of that day and all the following night, waking only when the first rays of the sun shone into our room through the window place. At least, I did, for when I opened my eyes, feeling a different creature and blessing Heaven for its gift of sleep to man, Hans was already up and engaged in cleaning the rifles and revolvers.

I looked at the ugly little Hottentot, reflecting how wonderful it was that so much courage, cunning, and fidelity should be packed away within his yellow skin and projecting skull. Had it not been for Hans, without a doubt I should now be dead, and the women also. It was he who had conceived the idea of letting down the sluice gate by exploding gunpowder beneath the pin of the lever. I had racked my brain for expedients, but this, the only one possible, escaped me. How tremendous had been the results of that inspiration—all of them due to Hans.

Although certain ideas had occurred to me, the most that I had hoped to do was to flood the low-lying lands, and perhaps the cave, in order to divert the attention of the priests while we were attempting escape. As it was we had loosed the forces of nature with the most fearful results. The water had run down the vent-holes of the eternal fires and into the bowels of the volcano, there to generate steam in enormous volumes, of which the imprisoned strength had been so great that it had rent the mountain like a rotten rag and destroyed the home of Heu-Heu for ever, and with it all his votaries.

It was a fearful event in which I thought I saw the mind of Providence acting through Hans. Yes, the cunning of the Hottentot had been used by the Powers above to sweep from the earth a vile tyranny and to destroy a blood-soaked idol and its worshippers.

Without a doubt—or so I believe in my simple faith—this had been designed from the beginning. When some escaped follower of Heu-Heu painted the picture in the Bushmen's cave, probably hundreds of years ago, it was already designed. So was Zikali's desire for a certain medicine, or his insatiable thirst for knowledge, or whatever it was that caused him to persuade me to undertake this mission, and so was all the rest of the story.

Again, with what wonderful judgment Hans had acted after his brave swim to the canoe!

Had he tried to force those fetish-ridden cravens to come to our rescue at once, as I directed him to do, the probability was that, fearing to break their silly law, they would have resisted, or perhaps have rowed right away, leaving us to our fate, after knocking him on the head with a paddle. But he had the patience to wait, although, as he told me afterwards, his heart was torn in two with anxiety for my sake. Balancing everything in his artful and experienced mind he had found patience to wait until the conditions of their "law" were fulfilled, when they came willingly enough.

From Hans my thoughts turned to Issicore. How was it that this man's character had changed so completely since he arrived in his native country? His journey to seek aid made alone over hundreds of miles, was a really remarkable performance, showing great courage and determination. Also as a guide, although silent and abstracted, he had never lacked for resource or energy. But from the day that he arrived home, morally he had gone to pieces. It was with the greatest difficulty that he could be persuaded to row us to the island, where at the first sign of danger he had left us to our fate and fled away.

Again, he had meekly helped to conduct Sabeela, whom, when he was at the Black Kloof evidently he loved to desperation, to her doom without lifting a finger to save her from a hideous destiny. Lastly, only a few hours ago, he had made a pusillanimous and contemptible speech, which I could see shocked and disgusted his betrothed, who, for her part, after her rescue and the death of her father, seemed to have gained the courage that he had lost, and more.

It was inexplicable, at any rate to me, and in my bewilderment I referred the problem to Hans.

He listened while I set out the case as it appeared to me, then answered:

"The Baas does not keep his eyes open—at any rate, in the daytime, when he thinks everything is safe. If he did, he would understand why Issicore has become soft as a heated bar of iron. What makes men soft, Baas?"

"Love," I suggested.

"Yes. At times love makes some men soft—I mean men like the Baas. And what else, Baas?"

"Drink," I answered savagely, getting it back on Hans.

"Yes, at times drink makes some men soft. Men like me, Baas, who know that now and again it is wise to cease from being wise, lest Heaven should grow jealous of our wisdom and want to share it. But what makes all men soft?"

"I don't know."

"Then once more I must teach the Baas, as his Reverend Father, the Predikant, told me to do when I saw that the Baas had used up all his wits, saying to me before he died, 'Hans, whenever you perceive that my son Allan, who does not always look where he is going, walks into water and gets out of his depth, swim in and pull him out, Hans.'"

"You little liar!" I ejaculated, but taking no notice, Hans went on:

"Baas, it is *fear* that makes all men soft. Issicore is bending about like a heated ramrod because within him burns the fire of fear."

"Fear of what, Hans?"

"As I have said, if the Baas had kept his eyes open, he would know. Did not the Baas notice a tall, dark-faced priest before whom the crowd parted, who came up to Issicore when first we landed on the quay here?"

"Yes, I saw such a man. He bowed politely and I thought was greeting Issicore and making him some present."

"And did the Baas see what kind of a present he made him and hear his words of wisdom? The Baas shakes his head. Well, I did. The present he gave to Issicore was a little skull carved out of black ivory or shell, or it may have been of polished lava rock. And the words of welcome were, 'The gift of Heu-Heu to the lord Issicore, that gift which

Heu-Heu sends to all who break the law and dare to leave the Land of the Walloos.' Those were the words, for standing near by, I heard them, though I kept them from the Baas, waiting to see what would happen afterwards.

"Then the priest went away, and what Issicore did with the little black skull I do not know. Perhaps he wears it round his neck, as he hasn't got a watch chain, just as the Baas used to wear things that ladies had given him, or their pictures in a little silver brandy flask."

"Well, and what about this skull, Hans? What does it mean?"

"Baas, I made inquiries of an old man in that canoe, to pass the time away, Baas, as Issicore was at the other end and could not hear me. It means *death*, Baas. Does not the Baas remember how we were told at the Black Kloof that those who dared to leave the Land of Heu-Heu were always smitten with some sickness and died? Well, Baas, Issicore got out all right and left the sickness behind him, I expect because the priests did not know that he was going. But he made a mistake, Baas, that of coming back again, being drawn by his love of Sabeela, just as a fish is drawn by the bait on the hook, Baas. And now the hook is fast in his mouth, for the priests knew of his return well enough, Baas, and of course were waiting for him."

"What do you mean, Hans? How can the priests hurt Issicore, especially when they are all dead?"

"Yes, Baas, they are all dead and can harm no one, but Issicore is right when he says that Heu-Heu is not dead, because the devil never dies, Baas. His priests are dead, but Heu-Heu could kill the old Walloo, and so he can kill Issicore. There is a great deal in this fetish business, Baas, that good Christians like you and I do not understand. It won't work on Christians, Baas, which is why Heu-Heu can't kill us, but those who worship the Black One, at last the Black One takes by the throat."

I thought to myself that here Hans, although he did not know it, was enunciating one of the profoundest and most fundamental of truths, since those who bow the knee to Baal are Baal's servants and live under his law, even to the death, and what is Baal but Heu-Heu, or Satan? The fruit is always the same, by whatever name the tree may be called. However, I did not enter upon this argument with Hans, whom it would have bewildered, but only asked him what he meant and what he imagined was going to happen to Issicore. He answered:

"I mean just what I have said, Baas; I mean that Issicore is going to die. That old man told me that those who 'receive the Black Skull,' always die within the month, and often more quickly. From the look of him, I should think that Issicore will not last more than a week. Although so handsome, he is really very dull, Baas, so it does not much matter, especially as the Lady Sabeela will get over it quite soon. That is why Issicore has changed, Baas. It is because the fear of death is upon him. In the same way Sabeela has changed because the fear of death and what to her, perhaps, is worse, has passed away."

"Bosh!" I exclaimed, but internally I had my doubts. I knew something of this fetish business, although I believed it to be the greatest of rubbish, I was sure that it is extremely dangerous rubbish. The secret soul of man, especially of savage, or primitive and untaught man, or the sub-conscious self, or whatever you choose to call it, is a terrible entity when brought into action by the hereditary superstitions that are born in his blood. In nine cases out of ten, if the victim of those superstitions is told with the accustomed ceremonies by the oracle of the god or devil from which they flow, that he will die, he does die. Nothing kills him, but he commits a kind of moral suicide. As Hans had said— Fear makes him soft. Then some kind of nervous disease penetrates his system and at the appointed hour withers up his physical life and causes him to pass away.

Such, as it proved, was to be the fate of that Apollo-like person, the unhappy Issicore.

CHAPTER XV

SABEELA'S FAREWELL

Now of this story there is little left to tell, and as it is very late and I see that you are all yawning, my friends [this was not true, for we were deeply interested, especially over the moral or spiritual problem of Issicore], I will cut that little as short as I can. It shall be a mere footnote.

After we had eaten that morning, we went to see Sabeela, whom we found very agitated. This was natural enough, considering all she had gone through, as after mental strain and the passing of great perils, a nervous reaction invariably follows. Also, in a sudden and terrible fashion, she had lost her father, to whom she was attached. But the real cause of her distress was different.

Issicore, it seemed, had been taken very ill. Nobody knew what was the matter with him, but Sabeela was persuaded that he had been poisoned. She begged me to visit him at once and cure him—a request that made me indignant. I explained to her that I was no authority on their native poisons, if he suffered from anything of the sort, and had few medicines with me, the only one of which that dealt with poisons was an antidote to snake bites. However, as she was very insistent, I said that I would go and see what I could do, which would probably be nothing.

So, together with Hans, I was conducted by some of the old headmen, or councillors of the Walloo, such people as in Zululand we should call *Indunas*, to the house of Issicore, a rather fine building of its sort at the other end of the town. We walked by the road that ran along the edge of the lake, which gave us an opportunity to observe the island, or rather what had been the island.

Now it was nothing but a low, dark mass, over which hung dense clouds of steam. When the winds stirred these clouds, I saw that beneath them were red streams of lava that ran into the lake. There were no more eruptions and the volcano appeared to have vanished away. Much dust was still falling. It lay thick upon the roadway and all the trees and other vegetation were covered with it, turning the landscape to a hue of ashen grey. Otherwise no damage had been done on the mainland, except that here and there boulders had fallen and some of the lower-lying fields were inundated by the great flood, which was now abating, although the river still overflowed its banks.

We reached the house of Issicore and were shown into his chamber, where he lay upon a couch of skins, attended by some women who, I understood, were his relatives. When Hans and I entered, these women bowed and went out, leaving us alone with the patient. A glance told me that he was a dying man. His fine eyes were fixed on vacancy; he breathed in gasps; his fingers clasped and unclasped themselves automatically, and from time to time he was taken with violent shiverings. These I thought must be due to some form of fever until I had tested his temperature with the thermometer I had in my little medicine case and found that it was two degrees below normal. On being questioned, he said that he had no pain and suffered only from great weakness and from a whirling of the head, by which I suppose meant giddiness.

I asked him to what he attributed his condition. He answered:

"To the curse of Heu-Heu, Lord Macumazahn. Heu-Heu is killing me."

I inquired why, for to argue about the folly of the business was futile, and he replied:

"For two reasons, Lord: first, because I left the land without his leave, and secondly, because I rowed you and the yellow man called Light-in-Darkness to the Holy Isle, to visit which unsummoned is the greatest of crimes. For this cause I must die more quickly than otherwise I should have done, but in any case my doom was certain, because I left the land to seek help for Sabeela. Here is the proof of it," and from somewhere about his person he produced the little black Death's Head which Hans had described to me. Then, without allowing me to touch the horrid thing, he hid it away again.

I tried to laugh him out of this idea, but he only smiled sadly and said:

"I know that you must have thought me a coward, Lord, because of the way I have borne myself since we reached this town of Walloo, but it was the curse of Heu-Heu working within me that changed my spirit. I pray you to explain this to Sabeela, whom I love, but who I think also believes me a coward, for yesterday I read it in her eyes. Now while I have still strength I would speak to you. First, I thank you and the yellow man, Light-in-Darkness, who by courage or by magic—I know not which—have saved Sabeela from Heu-Heu, and have destroyed his House and his priests and, I am told, his image. Heu-Heu, it is true, lives on since he cannot die, but henceforward here he is without a home or a shape or a worshipper, and therefore his power over the souls and bodies of men is gone, and among the Walloos, in time his worship will die out. Perhaps no more of my people will perish by the curse of Heu-Heu, Lord."

"But why should you die, Issicore?"

"Because the curse fell on me first, Lord, while Heu-Heu reigned over the Walloos, as he has done from the beginning, he who was once their earthly king."

I began to combat this nonsense, but he waved his hand in protest, and went on:

"Lord, my time is short and I would say something to you. Soon I shall be no more and forgotten, even by Sabeela, whose husband I had hoped to become. I pray, therefore, that you will marry Sabeela."

Here I gasped, but held my peace till he had finished.

"Already I have caused her to be informed that such is my last wish. Also I have caused all the elders of the Walloos to be informed, and at a meeting held this morning they decided that this marriage would be right and wise, and have sent a messenger to tell me to die as quickly as I can, in order that it may be arranged at once."

"Great Heavens!" I exclaimed, but again he motioned to me to be silent, and went on:

"Lord, although she is not of your race, Sabeela is very beautiful, very wise also, and with you for her husband she may be able once more to build up the Walloos into a great people, as tradition says they were in the old days before there fell upon them the curse of Heu-Heu, which is now broken. For you, too, are wise and bold, and know many things which we do not know, and the people will serve you as a god and perhaps come to worship you in place of Heu-Heu, so that you found a mighty dynasty. At first this thought may seem strange to you, but soon you will come to see that it is great and good. Moreover, even if you were unwilling, things must come about as I have said."

"Why?" I asked, unable to contain myself any longer.

"Because, Lord, here in this land you must spend the rest of your life, for in it now you are a prisoner, nor with all your courage can you escape, since none will row you down the river, nor can you force a way, for it will be watched. Moreover, when you return to the house of the Walloo you will find that your cartridges have been taken, so that except for a few that you have about you, you are weaponless. Therefore, as here you must live, it is better that you should do so with Sabeela rather than with any other woman, since she is the fairest and the cleverest of them all. Also by right of blood she is the ruler, and through her you will become Walloo, as I should have done according to our custom."

At this point he closed his eyes and for a while appeared to become senseless. Presently he opened them again and, staring at me, lifted his feeble hands and cried:

"Greeting to the Walloo! Long life and glory to the Walloo!"

Nor was this all, for, to my horror, from the other side of the partition that divided the house I heard the women whom I have mentioned echo the salutation:

"Greeting to the Walloo! Long life and glory to the Walloo!"

Then again Issicore became senseless; at least, nothing I said seemed to reached his understanding. So after waiting for a time Hans and I went away, thinking that all was over. This, however, was not so, since he lived till nightfall and, I was told, recovered his senses for some hours before the end, during which time Sabeela visited him, accompanied by certain of the notables or elders. It was then, as I suppose, that this ill-fated but most unselfish Issicore, the handsomest man whom ever I beheld, to his own satisfaction, if not to mine, settled everything for what he conceived to be the welfare of his country and his ladylove.

"Well, Baas," said Hans when we were outside the house, "I suppose we had better go home. It is *your* home now, isn't it, Baas? No, Baas, it is no use looking at that river, for you see these Walloos are so kind that they have already provided you with a chief's escort."

I looked. It was true enough. In place of the one man who had guided us to the house there were now twenty great fellows armed with spears who saluted me in a most reverential manner and insisted upon sticking close to my heels, I presume in case I should try to take to them. So back we went, the guard of twenty marching in a soldierlike fashion immediately behind, while Hans declaimed at me:

"It is just what I expected, Baas, for of course if a man is very fond of women, in his inside, Baas, they know it and like him—no need to tell them in so many words, Baas—and being kind-hearted, are quite ready to be fond of him. That is what has happened here, Baas. From the moment that the lady Sabeela saw you, she didn't care a pinch of snuff for Issicore, although he was so good-looking and had walked such a long way to help her. No, Baas, she perceived something in you which she couldn't find in two yards and a bit of Issicore, who after all was an empty kind of drum, Baas, and only made a noise when you hit him—a little noise for a small tap, Baas, and a big noise for a bang. Moreover, whatever he was, he is done now, so it is no use wasting time talking about him.

"Well, this won't be such a bad country to live in now that the most of those Heuheua are dead—look! there are some of their bodies lying on the shore—and no doubt the beer can be brewed stronger, and there is tobacco. So it will be all right till we get tired of it, Baas, after which, perhaps, we shall be able to run away. Still, I am glad none of them wish to marry me, Baas, and make me work like a whole team of oxen to drag them out of their mudholes."

Thus he went on pouring out his bosh by the yard, and literally I was so crushed that I couldn't find a word in answer. Truly, it is the unexpected that always happens. During the last few days I had foreseen many dangers and dealt with some. But this was one of which I had never dreamed. What a fate! To be kept a prisoner in a kind of gilded cage and made to labour for my living too, like a performing monkey. Well, I would find a way between the bars or my name wasn't Allan Quatermain. Only what way? At the time I could see none, for those bars seemed to be thick and strong. Moreover, there were those gentlemen with the spears behind.

In due course we arrived at the Walloo's house without incident and went straight to our room where, after investigation in a corner, Hans called out:

"Issicore was quite right, Baas. All the cartridges have gone and the rifles also. Now we have only got our pistols and twenty-four rounds of ammunition between us."

I looked. It was so! Then I stared out of the window-place, and behold! there in the garden were the twenty men already engaged in marking out ground for the erection of a guard-hut.

"They mean to settle there, so as to be nice and handy in case the Baas wants them—or they want the Baas," said Hans significantly, adding, "I believe that wherever he goes the Walloo always has an escort of twenty men!"

Now for the next few days I saw nothing of Sabeela, or of Dramana either, since they were engaged in the ceremonious obsequies, first of the Walloo and next of the unlucky Issicore, to which for some religious reason or other, I was not invited.

Certain headmen or Indunas, however, were always waiting to pounce on me. Whenever I put my nose out-of-doors they appeared, bowing humbly, and proceeded to take the occasion to instruct me in the history and customs of the Walloo people, till I thought that my boyhood had returned and I was once more reading "Sandford and Merton" and acquiring knowledge through the art of conversation. Those old gentlemen bored me stiff. I tried to get rid of them by taking long walks at a great pace, but they responded nobly, being ready to trot by my side till they dropped, talking, talking, talking. Moreover, if I could outwalk those ancient councillors, the guard of twenty who formed a kind of chorus on these expeditions, were excellent hands with their legs, as an Irishman might say, and never turned a hair. Sometimes they turned me, however, if they thought I was going where I should not, since then half of them would dart ahead and politely bar the way.

At length, on the third or fourth day, all the ceremonies were finished and I was summoned into Sabeela's presence.

As Hans said afterwards, it was all very fine. Indeed, I thought it pathetic with its somewhat tawdry conditions of ancient, almost forgotten ceremonial inherited from a highly civilized race that was now sinking into barbarism. There was the Lady Sabeela, very beautiful to see, for she was a lovely woman and grandly dressed in a half-wild fashion, who played the part of a queen and not without dignity, as perhaps her ancestresses had done thousands of years before on some greater stage. Here too were her white-haired attendants or Indunas, the same who bored me out walking, representing the councillors and high officials of forgotten ages.

Yet the Queen was no longer a queen; she was merging into the savage chieftainess, as the councillors were into the chattering mob that surrounds such a person in a thousand kraals or towns of Africa. The proceedings, too, were very long, for each of these councillors or elders made a speech in which he repeated all that the others had said before, narrating with variations everything that happened in the land since I had set foot within it, together with fancy accounts of what Hans and I had done upon the island.

From these speeches, however, I learned one thing, namely, that most of the wild Hairy Folk, who were named Heuheua, had perished in the great catastrophe of the blowing up of the mountain, only a few, together with the old men, the children and the females, being left to carry on the race. Therefore, they said, the Walloos were safe from attack, at any rate, for a couple of generations to come, as might be learned from the wailings which arose in the forest at night—that, as a matter of fact, I had heard myself—pathetic and horrible sounds of almost animal grief. This, said these merciless sages, gave the Walloos a great opportunity, for now was the time to hunt down and kill the Wood-folk to the last woman and child—a task which they considered I was eminently fitted to carry out!

When they had all spoken, Sabeela's turn came. She rose from her throne-like chair and addressed us with real eloquence. First of all she pointed out that she was a woman suffering from a double grief—the death of her father and that of the man to whom she had been affianced, losses that made her heart heavy. Then, very touchingly, she thanked Hans and myself for all we had done to save her. But for us, she said, either she would now have been dead or nothing but a degraded slave in the house of Heu-Heu, which we had destroyed together with Heu-Heu himself, with the result that she and the land were free once more. Next she announced in words which evidently had been prepared, that this was no time for her to think of past sorrows or love, who now must look to the future. For a man like myself there was but one fitting reward, and that was the rule over the Walloo people, and with it the gift of her own person.

Therefore, by the wish of her Councillors, she had decreed that we were to be wed on the fourth morning from that of the present day, after which, by right of marriage, I was publicly to be declared the Walloo. Meanwhile, she summoned me to her side (where an empty chair had been set in preparation for this event) that we might exchange the kiss of betrothal.

Now, as may be imagined, I hung back; indeed, never have I felt more firmly fixed to a seat than at that fearsome moment. I did not know what to say, and my tongue seemed glued to the roof of my mouth. So I just sat still with all those old donkeys staring at me, Sabeela watching me out of the corners of her eyes and waiting. The silence grew painful, and in its midst Hans coughed in his husky fashion, then delivered himself thus.

"Get up, Baas," he whispered, "and go through with it. It isn't half as bad as it looks, and indeed, some people would like it very much. It is better to kiss a pretty lady than to have your throat cut, Baas, for that is what I think will happen if you don't, because a woman whom you don't kiss, after she has asked you in public, *always* turns nasty, Baas."

I felt that there was force in this argument, and, to cut a long story short, I went up into that chair and did—well—all that was required. Lord! what a fool I felt while those idiots cheered and Hans below grinned at me like a whole cageful of baboons. However, it was but ceremonial, a mere formality, just touching the brow of the fair Sabeela with my lips and receiving an acknowledgment in kind.

After this we sat a while side by side listening to those old Walloo Councillors chanting a ridiculous song, something about the marriage of a hero to a goddess, which I presume they must have composed for the occasion. Under cover of the noise, which was great, for they had excellent lungs, Sabeela spoke to me in a low voice and without turning her face or looking at me.

"Lord," she said, "try to look less unhappy, lest these people should suspect something and listen to what we are saying. The law is that we should meet no more till the marriage day, but I must see you alone to-night. Have no fear," she added with a rather sarcastic smile, "for, although I must be alone, you can bring your companion with you, since what I have to say concerns you both. Meet me in the passage that runs from this chamber to your own, at midnight when all sleep. It has no window places and its walls are thick, so that there we can be neither seen nor heard. Be careful to bolt the door behind you, as I will that of this chamber. Do you understand?"

Clapping my hands hilariously to show my delight in the musical performance, I whispered back that I did.

"Good. When the singing comes to an end, announce that you have a request to make of me. Ask that to-morrow you may be given a canoe and paddlers to row to the island to learn what has happened there and to discover whether any of the Wood-folk are still alive upon its shores. Say that if so measures must be taken to make an end of them, lest they should escape. Now speak no more."

At length the song was finished, and with it the ceremony. To show that this was over, Sabeela rose from her chair and curtseyed to me, whereon I also rose and returned the compliment with my best bow. Thus, then, we bade a public farewell of each other until the happy marriage morn. Before we parted, however, I asked as a favour in a loud voice that I might be permitted to visit the island, or, at any rate, to row round it, giving the reasons she had suggested. To this she answered, "Let it be as my Lord wishes," and before any one could raise objections, withdrew herself, followed by some serving woman and by Dramana, who I thought did not seem too pleased at the turn events had taken.

I pass on to that midnight interview. At the appointed time, or rather a little before it, I went into the passage accompanied by Hans, who was most unwilling to come for reasons which he gave in a Dutch proverb to the effect of our own; that two's company and three's none. Here we stood in the dark and waited. A few minutes later the door at the far end of it opened—it was a very long passage—and walking down it appeared Sabeela, clad in white and bearing in her hand a naked lamp. Somehow in this garb and in these surroundings, thus illumined, she looked more beautiful than I had ever seen her, almost spirit-like indeed. We met, and without any greeting she said to me:

"Lord Watcher-by-Night, I find you watching by night according to my prayer. It may have seemed a strange prayer to you, but hearken to its reason. I cannot think that you believe me to desire this marriage, which I know to be hateful to you, seeing that I am of another race to yourself and that you only look upon me as a half-savage woman whom it has been your fortune to save from shame or death. Nay, contradict me not, I beseech you, since at times the truth is good. Because it is so good I will add to it, telling you the reason why I also do not desire this marriage, or rather the greatest reason; namely, that I loved Issicore, who from childhood had been my playmate until he became more than playmate."

"Yes," I interrupted, "and I know that he loved you. Only then why was it that on his deathbed he himself urged on this matter?"

"Because, Lord, Issicore had a noble heart. He thought you the greatest man whom he had ever known, half a god indeed, for he told me so. He held also that you would make me happy and rule this country well, lifting it up again out of its long sleep. Lastly, he knew that if you did not marry me, you and your companion would be murdered. If he judged wrongly in these matters, it must be remembered, moreover, that his mind was blotted with the poison that had been given to him, for myself I am sure that he did not die of fear alone."

"I understand. All honour be to him," I said.

"I thank you. Now, Lord, know that, although I am ignorant I believe that we live again beyond the gate of Death. Perhaps that faith has come down to me from my forefathers when they worshipped other gods besides the devil Heu-Heu; at least, it is mine. My hope is, therefore, that when I have passed that gate, which perhaps will be before so very long, on its farther side I shall once more find Issicore—Issicore as he was before the curse of Heu-Heu fell upon him and he drank the poison of the priests—and for this reason I desire to wed no other man."

"All honour be to you also," I murmured.

"Again, I thank you, Lord. Now let us turn to other matters. To-morrow after midday a canoe will be ready, and in it you will find your weapons that have been stolen and all that is yours. It will be manned by four rowers; men known to be spies of the priests of Heu-Heu, stationed here upon the mainland to watch the Walloos, who in time would themselves have become priests. Therefore, now that Heu-Heu has fallen they are doomed to die, not at once but after a while, perhaps, as it will seem, by sickness or accident, because if they live, the Walloo Councillors fear lest they should re-establish the rule of Heu-Heu. They know this well, and therefore they desire above all things to escape the land while their life is yet in them."

"Have you seen these men, Sabeela?"

"Nay, but Dramana has seen them. Now, Lord, I will tell you something, if you have not guessed it for yourself, though I do this not without shame. Dramana does not desire our marriage, Lord. You saved Dramana as well as myself, and Dramana, like Issicore, has come to look on you as half a god. Need I say more, save that, of course, for this reason she does desire your escape, since she would rather that you went free and were lost to both of us than that you should bide here and marry me. Have I said enough?"

"Plenty," I answered, knowing that she spoke truth.

"Then what is there to add, save that I trust all will go well, and that by the dawn of the day that follows this, you and the yellow man, your servant, will be safely out of this accursed land. If that comes about, as I believe it will, for after the dusk has fallen and before the moon rises those who guide the canoe will bring it, not to the quay, but into the mouth of the river down which you must paddle by the moonlight; then I pray of you at times in your own country to think of Sabeela, the broken-hearted chieftainess of a doomed people, as day by day, when she rises and lays herself down to sleep, she will think of you who saved her and all of us from ruin. My Lord, farewell, and to you, Light-in-Darkness, also farewell."

Then she took my hand, kissed it, and, without another word, glided away as she had come.

This was the last that ever I saw or heard of Sabeela the Beautiful. I wonder whether she lived long. Somehow I do not think so; that night I seemed to see death in her eyes.

CHAPTER XVI

THE RACE FOR LIFE

Now, like a Scotch parson, I have come to "lastly"—that inspiring word at which the sleepiest congregation awakes. The morning following this strange midnight meeting, Hans and I spent in our room, for it appeared to be the ancient Walloo etiquette that, save by special permission, the prospective bridegroom should not go out for several days before the marriage, I suppose because of some primitive idea that his affections might be diverted by the sight of alien beauty.

At midday we ate, or, so far as I was concerned, pretended to eat, for anxiety took away my appetite. A little while afterwards, to my intense relief, the captain of our prison-warders, for that is what they were, appeared and said that he was commanded to conduct us to the canoe which was to paddle us to inspect what remained of the island. I replied that we would graciously consent to go. So taking all our small possessions with us, including a bundle containing our spare clothes and the twigs from the Tree of Illusions, we departed and were escorted to the quay by our guards, of whose faces I was heartily tired. Here we found a small canoe awaiting us, manned by four secret-faced men, strong fellows all of them, who raised their paddles in salute. Apparently the place had been cleared of loiterers, since there was only one other person present, a woman wrapped in a long cloak that hid her face.

As we were about to enter the canoe this woman approached us and lifted her head. She was Dramana.

"Lord," she said, "I have been sent by my sister, the new Walloo, to tell you that you will find the iron tubes which spit out fire and all that belongs to them under a mat in the prow of the canoe. Also she bids me wish you a prosperous journey to the island that aforetime was named Holy, which island she wishes never to see again."

I thanked her and bade her convey my greeting to the Walloo, my bride to be, adding in a loud voice, that I hoped ere long to be able to do this in person when her "veil fell down."

Then I turned to enter the canoe.

"Lord," said Dramana with a convulsive movement of her hands, "I make a prayer to you. It is that you will take me with you to look my last upon that isle where I dwelt so long a slave, which I desire to see once more—now that I am free."

Instinctively I felt that a crisis had arisen which demanded firm and even brutal treatment.

"Nay, Dramana," I answered, "it is always unlucky for an escaped slave to revisit his prison, lest once more its bars should close about that slave."

"Lord," she said, "the loosed prisoner is sometimes dazed by freedom, so that the heart cries again for its captivity. Lord, I am a good slave and a loving. Will you not take me with you?"

"Nay, Dramana," I answered as I sprang into the canoe. "This boat is fully loaded. It would not be for your welfare or for mine. Farewell!"

She gazed at me earnestly with a pitiful countenance that grew wrathful by degrees, as might well happen in the case of a woman scorned: then, muttering something about being "cast off," burst into angry tears and turned away. For my part I motioned to the oarsmen to loose the craft and departed, feeling like a thief and traitor. Yet I was not to blame, for what else could I do? Dramana, it is true, had been a good friend to us, and I liked her. But we had repaid her help by saving her from Heu-Heu, and for the rest, one must draw the line somewhere. If once she had entered that canoe, metaphorically speaking, she would never have got out of it again.

Presently we were out on the open lake where the wavelets danced and the sun shone brightly, and glad I was to be clear of all those painful complications and once more in the company of pure and natural things. We paddled away to the island and made the land, or rather drew near to it, at the spot where the ancient city had stood in which we had found the petrified men and animals. But we did not set foot on it, for everywhere little streams of glowing lava trickled down into the lake and the ruins had vanished beneath a sea of ashes. I do not think that any one will ever again behold those strange relics of a past I know not how remote.

Turning, we paddled on slowly round the island till we came to the place where the Rock of Offering had been, upon which I had experienced so terrible an adventure. It had vanished, and with it the cave mouth, the garden of Heu-Heu, its Tree of Illusions, and all the rich cultivated land. The waters of the lake, turbid and steaming, now beat against the face of a stony hillock which was all that remained of the

Holy Isle. The catastrophe was complete; the volcano was but a lump of lava from the dying heart of which its life-blood of flame still palpitated in red and ebbing streams. I wonder whether its smothered fires will ever break out again elsewhere. For aught I know they may have done so already somewhere on the mainland.

By the time that we had completed our journey round the place on which no living creature now was left, though once or twice we saw the bloated body of a Heuheua savage bobbing about in the water, the sun was setting, and it was dark before we were again off the town of the Walloos. While any light remained by which we could be seen, we headed straight for the landing place, that which we had left when we started for the island.

The moment that its last rays faded, however, there was a whispered conference between our four paddlemen, the ex-neophytes of Heu-Heu. Then the direction of the canoe was altered, and instead of making for the main land, we rowed on parallel with it till we came to the mouth of the Black River. It was so dark that I could not discern the exact time at which we left the lake and entered the stream; indeed, I did not know that we were in it until the increased current told me so. This current was now running very strongly after the great flood and bore us along at a good pace. My fear was lest in the gloom we should be dashed against rocks on the banks, or caught by the overhanging branches of trees or strike a snag, but those four men seemed to know every yard of the river and managed to keep us in its centre, probably by following the current where it ran most swiftly.

So we went on, not paddling very fast for fear of accidents, until the moon rose, which, as she was only a few days past her full, gave us considerable light even in that dark place. So soon as her rays reached us our paddlers gave way with a will, and we shot down the flooded stream as a great speed.

"I think we are all right now, Baas," said Hans, "for with so good a start those Walloos could scarcely catch us, even if they try. We are lucky, too, for you have left behind you two ladies who between them would have torn you into pieces, and I have left a place where the fools who live in it wearied me so much that I should soon have died."

He paused for a moment, then added in a horrified voice:

"*Allemagter!* we are not so lucky after all; we have forgotten something."

"What?" I asked anxiously.

"Why, Baas, those red and white stones we came to fetch, of which, before Heu-Heu dropped a red-hot rock upon his head, that old *kraansick*." (that is, mad) "Walloo, promised us as many as we wished. Sabeela would have filled the boat with them if we had only asked her, and we should never have had to work any more, but could have sat in fine houses and drunk the best gin from morning to night."

At these words I felt positively sick. It was too true. Amongst other pressing matters, concerning life, death, marriage, and liberty, I had forgotten utterly all about the diamonds and gold. Still when I came to think of it, although perhaps Hans might have done so, in view of the manner of our parting, I did not quite see how I could have asked Sabeela for them. It would have been an anticlimax and might have left a nasty taste in her mouth. How could she continue to look upon a man as—well, something quite out of the ordinary, who called her back to remind her that there was a little pecuniary matter to be settled and a fee to be paid for services rendered? Further, the sight of us bearing sacks of treasure might have excited suspicion; unless, indeed, Sabeela had caused them to be placed in the boat as she did in the case of the guns. Also they would have been heavy and inconvenient to carry, as I explained to Hans. Yet I did feel sick, for once more my hopes of wealth, or, at any rate, of a solid competence for the rest of my days, had vanished into thin air.

"Life is more than gold," I said sententiously to Hans, "and great honour is better than both."

It sounded like something out of the Book of Proverbs, but somehow I had not got it quite right though I reflected that fortunately Hans would not know the difference. However, he knew more than I thought, for he answered:

"Yes, Baas, your Reverend Father used to talk like that. Also he said that it was better to live on watercresses with an easy mind, however angry they might make your stomach, than to dwell in a big hut with a couple of cross women, which is what would have happened to you, Baas, if you had stopped at Walloo. Besides, we are quite safe now, even if we haven't got the gold and diamonds, which, as you say, are heavy things, so safe that I think I shall go to sleep, Baas. *Allemagter!* Baas, *what's that?*"

"Only those poor hairy women howling over their dead in the forest," I answered rather carelessly, for their cries, which were very distressing in the silence of the river, still echoed in my ears. Also I was still thinking of the lost diamonds.

"I wish it were, Baas. They might howl till their heads fell off for all I care. But it isn't. It's paddles. *The Walloos are hunting us, Baas.* Listen!"

I did listen, and to my horror heard the regular stroke of paddles striking the water at a distance behind us, a great number of them, fifty I should say. One of the big canoes must be on our track.

"Oh, Baas!" said Hans, "it is your fault again. Without doubt that lady Dramana loves you so much that she can't make up her mind to part with you and has ordered out a big canoe to fetch you back. Unless, indeed," he added with an access of hopefulness, "it is the Lady Sabeela sending a farewell gift of jewels after us, having remembered that we should like some to make us think of her afterwards."

"It is those confounded Walloos sending a gift of spears," I answered gloomily, adding, "Get the rifles ready, Hans, for I'm not going to be taken alive."

Whatever the cause, it was clear that we were being pursued, and in my heart I did wonder whether Dramana had anything to do with it. No doubt I had treated her rudely because I could not help it, also Dramana had been badly trained among those rascally priests. But I hoped, and still hope, that she was innocent of this treachery. The truth of the matter I never learned.

Our crew of escaping priestly spies had also heard the paddles, for I saw the frightened look they gave to each other and the fierce energy with which they bent themselves to their work. Good heavens! how they paddled, who knew that their lives hung upon the issue. For hour after hour away we flew down that flooded, rushing river, while behind us, drawing nearer minute by minute, sounded the beat of those insistent paddles. Our canoe was swift, but how could we hope to escape from one driven by fifty men when we had but four?

It was just as we passed the place where we had slept on our inward journey—for now we had left the forest behind and were between the cliffs, travelling quite twice as fast as we had done up stream—that I caught sight of the pursuing boat, perhaps half a mile behind us, and saw that it was one of the largest of the Walloo fleet. After this, owing to the position of the moon, that in this narrow place left the surface of the water quite dark, I saw it no more for several hours. But I heard it drawing nearer, ever nearer, like some sure and deadly bloodhound following on the spoor of a fleeing slave.

Our men began to tire. Hans and I took the paddles of two of them to give the pair a rest and time to eat; then for a spell the paddles of the other two, while they did likewise. This, however, caused us to lose way, since we were not experts at the game, though here after the flood the river rushed so fast that our lack of skill made little difference.

At length the daylight came and gathered till at last the glimmer of it reached us in our cleft, and by that faint, uncertain light I saw the pursuing canoe not a hundred yards behind. In its way it was a very weird and impressive spectacle. There were the precipitous, towering cliffs, between or rather above which appeared a line of blue sky. There was the darksome, flood-filled, foaming river, and there on its surface was our tiny boat propelled by four weary and perspiring men, while behind came the great war canoe whose presence could just be detected in a dim outline and by the white of the water where its oarsmen smote it into froth.

"They are coming up fast, Baas, and we still have a long way to go. Soon they will catch us, Baas," said Hans.

"Then we must try to stop them for a while," I answered grimly. "Give me the Express rifle, Hans, and do you take the Winchester."

Then, lying down in the canoe and resting the rifles on its stern, we waited our opportunity. Presently we came to a place where at some time there had been a cliff-slide, for here the debris of it narrowed the river, turning it, now that it was so full, into something like a torrent. At this spot, also, because of the enlargement of the cleft, more light reached us, so that we could see our pursuers, who were about fifty yards away, not clearly indeed, but well enough for our purpose.

"Aim low and pump it into them, Hans," I said, and next instant discharged both barrels of the Express at the foremost rowers.

Hans followed suit, but, as the Winchester held five cartridges, went on firing after I had ceased.

The result was instantaneous. Some men sank down, some paddles fell into the water—I could not tell how many—and a great cry arose from the smitten or their companions. He who steered or captained the canoe from the prow apparently was among the hit. She veered round and for a while was broadside on to the current, exposing her bottom and threatening to turn over. Into this, having loaded, I sent two expanding bullets, hoping to spring a leak in her, though I was not certain if I should succeed, as the wood of these canoes is thick. I think I did, however, since even when she had got on her course again she came more slowly, and I thought that once I saw a man bailing.

On we went, making the most of the advantage that this check gave to us. But by now our men were very tired and their hands were raw from blisters, so that only the terror of death forced them to continue paddling. Indeed, at the last our progress grew very slow, and in fact was due more to the current than to our own efforts. Therefore the following canoe, which as was customary in Walloo boats of that size, probably carried spare paddle men, once more gained upon us.

Hereabouts the river wound between its cliffs so that we only got sight of it from time to time. Whenever we did so I took the Winchester and fired, no doubt inflicting some damage and checking its advance.

At length the winding ceased and we reached the last stretch, a clear run of a mile or so before the river ended in the swamp that I have described.

By this time pursuers and pursued, both of us, were going but slowly, drifting rather than paddling, since all were exhausted. Whenever I could get a sight I fired away, but still with a sullen determination and in utter silence our assailants came up, till now they were scarcely twenty paces from us, and some of them threw spears, one of which stuck in the bottom of our canoe, just missing my foot. At this spot the cliffs drew so near together at the top that I ceased shooting, as I could not see to aim, and, having no cartridges to waste, decided to keep those that remained for the emergency of the last attack.

Now we were in the ultimate reach of the river, and now at last we grounded upon the first mudbank of the swamp. Those who remained unhurt of the following Walloos made a final effort to overtake us; by the strong light that flowed from the open land beyond us I could see their glaring eyeballs and their tongues hanging from their jaws with exhaustion. I yelled an order.

"Seize everything we have and run for it!" I cried, grabbing at my rifle and such other articles as were within reach, including the remaining cartridges.

The others did likewise—I do not think that anything was left in that canoe except the paddles. Then I leapt on to the shore and ran to the right, following the edge of the swamp, the rest coming after me. Fifty yards or more away I sank down upon a little ridge from sheer exhaustion and because my cramped legs would no longer carry me, and watched to see what would happen. Indeed, I was so worn out that I felt I would rather die where I was than try to flee farther.

We grouped ourselves together, awaiting the crisis, for I thought that surely we should be attacked. But we were not. At the mudbank the pursuing Walloos ceased from their efforts. For a little while they sat dejectedly in their craft till they had recovered breath.

Then for the first time those mute hunting-hounds gave tongue, for they shouted maledictions on us, and especially on our four paddlers, the neophytes of Heu-Heu, telling these that although to follow them farther was not lawful, they would die, as Issicore died who left the land. One of our men, stung into repartee, retaliated in words to the effect that some of them had died in attempting to keep us in the land, as they would find if they counted their oarsmen.

To this obvious truth the pursuers made no answer, nor did they inform us who sent them on the chase. Securing our small canoe, they laid in it certain dead men who had fallen beneath the bullets of Hans and myself, and departed slowly up stream, towing it after them. This was the last that I saw of their handsome, fanatical faces and of their confounded country in which I went so near to death, or to becoming a prisoner for life, that might have been worse.

"Baas," said Hans, lighting his pipe, "that was a great journey and one which it will be nice to think about, now that it is over, though I wish that we had killed more of those Walloo men-stealers."

"I don't, Hans; I hated being obliged to shoot them," I answered; "nor do I wish to think any more of that race for our lives, unless it comes back in a nightmare when I can't help doing so."

"Don't you, Baas? I find such thoughts pleasant when the danger is past and we who might have been dead are alive, and the others who were alive are dead and telling the tale to Heu-Heu."

"Each to his taste; yours isn't mine," I muttered.

Hans puffed at his pipe for a while, and went on:

"It's funny, Baas, that those *carles* did not get out of their canoe and come to kill us with their spears. I suppose they were afraid of the rifles."

"No, Hans," I answered, "they are brave men who would not have stopped because of the bullets. They were afraid of more than these: they feared the Curse which says that those who leave their land will die and go to hell. Heu-Heu has done us a good turn there, Hans."

"Yes, Baas, no doubt he has become a Christian in the Place of Fires and is repaying good for evil, turning the other cheek, Baas. I felt like that myself when I thought those Walloos were going to catch us, but now I feel quite different. Baas, you remember how your Reverend Father used to say that if you love Heaven, Heaven looks after you and pulls you out of every kind of mudhole. That's why I'm sitting here smoking, Baas, instead of making meat for crocodiles. If it wasn't for our forgetting about those jewels, it has looked after us very well, but there are so many up there that perhaps Heaven forgot them also."

"No, Hans," I said, "Heaven remembered that if we had tried to carry bags of stones out of that boat, as well as Zikali's medicine and the rest, the Walloos would have caught us before we got away. They were quite close, Hans."

"Yes, Baas, I see, and that was very nice of Heaven. And now, Baas, I think we had better be moving. Those Walloos might forget about the curse for a little while and come back to look for us. Heaven is a queer thing, Baas. Sometimes it changes its face all of a sudden and grows angry—just like the lady Dramana did when you said that you wouldn't take her with you in the canoe yesterday."

Allan paused to help himself to a little weak whisky and water, then said in his jerky fashion:

"Well, that's the end of the story, of which I am glad, whatever you may be, for my throat is dry with talking. We got back to the wagon all right after sundry difficulties and a tiring march across the desert, and it was time we did so, for when we arrived we had only three rifle cartridges left between us. You see we were obliged to fire such a lot at the Heuheua, when they attacked us on the lake, and afterwards at those Walloos to prevent them from catching us that night. However, there were more in the wagon, and I shot four elephants with them going home. They had very large tusks, which afterwards I sold for about enough to cover the expenses of the journey."

"Did old Zikali make you pay for those oxen?" I asked.

"No, he did not, because I told him that if he tried it on I would not give him his bundle of *mouti* that we cut from the Tree of Illusions and carried safely all that way. So as he was very keen on the medicine, he made me a present of the oxen. Also I found my own there grown fat and strong again. It was a curious thing, but the old scoundrel seemed to know most of what had happened to us before ever I told him a word. Perhaps he learned it all from one of those acolytes of Heu-Heu who fled with us because they feared that they would be murdered if they stayed in their own land. I forgot to tell you that these men—most uncommunicative persons—melted away upon our homeward journey. Suddenly they were missing. I presume that they departed to set up as witch doctors on their own account. If so, very possibly one or more of them may have come into touch with Zikali, the head of the craft in that part of Africa, and before I reached the Black Kloof.

"The first thing he asked me was: 'Why did you not bring any gold and diamonds away with you? Had you done so, you might have become rich who now remain poor, Macumazahn.'

"'Because I forgot to ask for them,' I said.

"'Yes, I know you forgot to ask for them. You were thinking so much of the pain of saying goodbye to that beautiful lady whose name I have not learned that you forgot to ask for them. It is just like you, Macumazahn. *Oho! Oho!* it is just like you.'

"Then he stared at his fire for a while, in front, of which, as usual, he was sitting, and added: 'Yet somehow I think that diamonds will make you rich one day, when there is no woman left to say good-bye to, Macumazahn.'

"It was a good shot of his, for, as you fellows know, that came about at King Solomon's mines, didn't it? when there was 'no woman left to say good-bye to.'"

Here Good turned his head away, and Allen went on hurriedly, I think because he remembered Foulata, and saw that his thoughtless remark had given pain.

"Zikali was very interested in all our story and made me stop at the Black Kloof for some days to tell him every detail.

"'*I* knew that Heu-Heu was an idol,' he said, 'though I wanted you to find it out for yourself, and therefore told you nothing about it, just as I knew that handsome man, Issicore, would die. But I didn't tell him anything about that either, because, if I had, you see he might have died before he had shown you the way to his country, and then I shouldn't have got my *mouti*, which is necessary to me, for without it how should I paint more pictures on my fire? Well, you brought me a good bundle of leaves which will last my time, and as the Tree of Illusions is burned and there is no other left in the world, there will be no more of it. I am glad that it is burned, for I do not wish that any wizard should arise in the land who will be as great as was Zikali, Opener-of-Roads. While that tree grew the high priest of Heu-Heu was almost as great, but now he is dead and his tree is burned, and I, Zikali, reign alone. That is what I desired, Macumazahn, and that is why I sent you to Heuheua Land.'

"'You cunning old villain!' I exclaimed.

"'Yes, Macumazahn, I am cunning just as you are simple, and my heart is black like my skin, just as yours is white like your skin. That is why I am great, Macumazahn, and wield power over thousands and accomplish my desires, whereas you are small and have no power and will die with all your desires unaccomplished. Yet, in the end, who knows, who knows? Perhaps in the land beyond it may be otherwise. Heu-Heu was great also and where is Heu-Heu to-day?'

"'There never was a Heu-Heu,' I said.

"'No, Macumazahn, there never was a Heu-Heu, but there were priests of Heu-Heu. Is it not so with many of the gods men set up? They are not and never were, but their priests *are* and shake the spear of power and pierce the hearts of men with terrors. What, then, does it matter about the gods whom no man sees, when the priest is there shaking the spear of power and piercing the hearts of their worshippers? The god is the priest or the priest is the god—have it which way you like, Macumazahn.'

"'Not always, Zikali.' Then, as I did not wish to enter into argument with him on such a subject, I asked, 'Who carved the statue of Heu-Heu in the Cave of Illusions? The Walloos did not know.'

"'Nor do I, Macumazahn,' he answered. 'The world is very old and there have been peoples in it of whom we have heard nothing, or so my Spirit tells me. Without doubt one of those peoples carved it thousands of years ago, an invading people, the last of their race, who had been driven out elsewhere and coming south, those who were left of them, hid themselves away from their enemies in this secret place amid a horde of savages so hideous that it was reported to be haunted by demons. There, in a cave in the midst of a lake where they could not be come at, they carved an image of their god, or perhaps of the god of the savages, whom it seems that it resembled.

"'Mayhap the savages took their name from Heu-Heu, or mayhap Heu-Heu took his name from them. Who can tell? At any rate, when men seek a god, Macumazahn, they make one like themselves, only larger, uglier, and more evil, at least in this land, for what they do elsewhere I know not. Also, often they say that this god was once their king, since at the bottom all worship their ancestors who gave them life, if they worship anything at all, and often, too, because they gave them life, they think that they must have been devils. Great ancestors were the first gods, Macumazahn, and if they had not been evil they would never have been great. Look at Chaka, the Lion of the Zulus. He is called great because he was so wicked and cruel, and so it was and is with others if they succeed, though, if they fail, men speak otherwise of them.'

"'That is not a pretty faith, Zikali,' I said.

"'No, Macumazahn, but then little in the world is pretty, except the world itself. The Heuheua are not pretty, or rather were not, for I think that you killed most of them when you blew up the mountain, which is a good thing. Heu-Heu was not pretty, nor were his priests. Only the Walloos, and especially their women, remain pretty because of the old blood that runs in them, the high old blood that Heu-Heu sucked from their veins.'

"'Well, Heu-Heu has gone, Zikali, and now what will become of the Walloos?'

"'I cannot say, Macumazahn, but I expect they will follow Heu-Heu, who has taken hold of their souls and will drag them after him. If so, it does not matter, since they are but the rotting stump of a tree that once was tall and fair. The dust of Time hides many such stumps, Macumazahn. But what of that? Other fine trees are growing which also will become stumps in their season, and so on for ever."

"Thus Zikali held forth, though of what he said I forget much. I daresay that he spoke truth, but I remember that his melancholy and pessimistic talk depressed me, and that I cut it as short as I could. Also it did not really explain anything, since he could not tell me who the Walloos or the Hairy Folk were, or why they worshipped Heu-Heu, or what was their beginning, or what would be their end.

"All these things remained and remain lost in mystery, since I have never heard anything more of them, and if any subsequent travellers have visited the district where they live, which is not probable, they did not succeed in ascending the river, or if they did, they never descended it again. So if you want to know more of the story, you must go and find it out for yourselves. Only, as I think I said, I won't go with you."

"Well," said Captain Good, "it is a wonderful yarn. Hang me, if I could have told it better myself!"

"No, Good," answered Allan, as he lit a hand candle, "I am quite sure that you could not, because, you see, facts are one thing and what you call 'yarns' are another. Good-night to you all, good-night."

Then he went off to bed.

Printed in Great Britain
by Amazon